CW00518696

SHIELD OF WINTER

The Legend of the Gods Book II

AARON HODGES

Edited by Genevieve Lerner
Proofread by Sara Houston
Illustration by Alex Raspad
Map by Michael Hodges

Copyright © June 2018 Aaron Hodges
First Edition. All Rights Reserved.
ISBN: 978-09951114-00

ABOUT THE AUTHOR

Aaron Hodges was born in 1989 in the small town of Whakatane, New Zealand. He studied for five years at the University of Auckland, completing a Bachelors of Science in Biology and Geography, and a Masters of Environmental Engineering. After working as an environmental consultant for two years, he grew tired of office work and decided to quit his job in 2014 and see the world. One year later, he published his first novel - Stormwielder.

FOLLOW AARON HODGES...

And receive TWO FREE novels and a short story!
www.aaronhodges.co.nz/newsletter-signup/

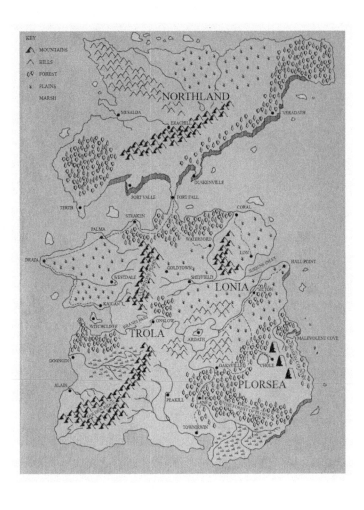

PROLOGUE

Betran coughed as a whiff of smoke drifted towards him from the fireplace. Leaning sideways on his stool, he hacked up a gob of phlegm and spat it on the mudbrick floor, then took another swig of ale to wash away the acrid taste of the coal fumes. The mood in the tavern was sombre, the low curved ceiling seeming to mute what little conversation there was to be had. Not that Betran was in any mood to talk with his fellow Trolans.

Catching the eye of the man behind the counter, he raised a finger and pointed at his empty mug. The bartender narrowed his eyes, but after a moment's hesitation swept up the mug and wandered over to the kegs lining the wall behind the bar.

Golden ale streamed from the keg while Betran allowed his gaze to roam around the room. The hour was growing late, and the few customers in the underground tavern were finally beginning to disperse. The poorly constructed tables were almost empty, leaving only a few men sitting at the bar. Most of them were known to Betran, except for the man seated two stools down from him.

His chest tightened as he stared at the stranger. Even seated, he was the largest man Betran had ever seen. Barrel-chested with arms like tree trunks, he seemed to radiate a power all of his own. He had been sitting in the gloomy tavern for over an hour now, downing tankard after tankard of the innkeeper's finer ale. Betran had caught a glint of gold the last time the man had reached for his belt purse, and had been watching him ever since.

Swallowing, he looked away as the man caught the attention of a barmaid and waved for another drink. She flashed him a smile as he slipped a silver shilling into her palm. It wasn't long before she returned, the tankard almost overflowing.

A few moments later, the bartender finally came back with Betran's own mug. Scowling, he reached out to take it, but the man lifted the drink out of reach.

"Ya got the coin for it, Betran?" he asked, his voice gruff from the days spent in the smoky tavern.

Betran's stomach twisted with anger as he glared at the man. He was well known here—had grown up just down the road in old Kalgan, before the Tsar had burned everything above ground-level to ash. Only a few thousand survivors lived amongst the ruins now, making do with what they could as they slowly rebuilt the former jewel of Trola. Normally, locals were only asked to settle their bill at the end of the night.

But then, Betran shouldn't have been surprised. It had been months now since he and the other labourers had finished restoring the bathhouse, and with no new prospects on the horizon, Betran was quickly growing desperate. Word had obviously gotten around he had little coin left to spare.

Gritting his teeth, Betran reached into his purse and slammed a silver shilling down on the bench. "Good enough for you?" he snapped.

The innkeeper only smiled and swept the coin into his

pocket. "Good for now." He placed the tankard in front of Betran and moved away.

Muttering under his breath, Betran lifted the tankard and gulped down a mouthful of the cool liquid. His eyes flickered back to the stranger. He was already halfway through the new drink, making it his eighth in less than two hours. Betran had known strong men to slide unconscious beneath a table with less, yet the man still seemed alert. Only a slight swaying on his stool suggested the ale was taking effect.

Betran shivered as the man looked around, the amber eyes seeming to stare straight through him. He quickly looked away, fixing his eyes on his tankard of ale. When he finally looked back up, the man had returned to his drink.

Unconsciously, Betran dropped his hand to the knife on his belt. It would take only moments to follow the man into some darkened alleyway and drive the blade through his back. No one would miss the stranger—or the purse on his belt. Even a single gold Libra would be enough to feed Betran's family for a month, and from what he'd glimpsed, the stranger had far more than that.

How did it come to this?

A sick feeling settled in Betran's stomach as he contemplated his victim. Six years ago, he'd been an officer in the Trolan army, marching to glory against the Plorseans, determined to liberate his nation from the tyranny of the Tsar. But within the year, his dreams had turned to ash, scattered to the winds along with the remnants of the Trolan army.

He had only survived because his cohort had been cut off from Kalgan while out on a scouting trip. Harried by marauding bands of Plorsean soldiers, they'd retreated into the mountains and watched from afar as the city fell.

Now, six years later, Trola was a shadow of its former glory. Kalgan was slowly being rebuilt, but elsewhere the fields lay untended, towns and villages empty of life. Even here, much of the city remained underground, its former cellars and basements converted to taverns and homes, as though Kalgan's occupants feared reprisal if they showed their heads above ground. But even the darkness could not hide them from the Tsar's taxes; as things stood, an entire generation was hovering on the brink of starvation.

Thinking of his wife and child back home, Betran sucked in a breath, steeling himself for the task to come. He clenched his fists, seeking to calm the trembling in his hands. Petra and his son, Onur, were relying on him. He had come here to drown his despair in ale, but now that an opportunity had shown itself, he could not allow it to pass him by.

Courage, Betran.

The thought made his heart beat faster. He'd been a brave man once, before the weight of poverty had dragged him down. What his former self would think of him now, he could only guess. Would he understand the desperation, the despair that had driven him to this point? Or would he despise the filthy man who sat silently at a tavern, contemplating theft and murder?

His hands were shaking again. Clenching the hilt of his dagger, he ran his mind over the plan. There was no doubt the stranger was a fighter—and while he didn't seem to be carrying a weapon, Betran had no desire to risk a direct confrontation. No, he would wait for the giant to leave and follow him, then strike when the moment was right.

You are not a murderer, Betran.

The thought came to him unbidden, but he pushed it aside. Thoughts of honour and morality in Trola had died along with its freedom. Few could afford such luxuries now. The city had become a place of corruption, where the strong ruled and the weak were used and discarded at will.

Betran tensed as the stranger pushed back his stool and stood. Slamming a handful of shillings on the bar top, he swayed on his feet, then bid the barmaid goodbye and headed for the door.

For a moment Betran hesitated. Then he stood and started after the man.

As the giant strode towards the worn stone steps leading up to the street, a bang came from the door above. The sound of raised voices echoed down into the tavern. Betran froze as a group of middle-aged men came thumping down the stairwell. They stopped as they reached the bottom and found themselves face-to-face with the giant. A long silence stretched out as the five newcomers stared at the stranger.

"You going to stand there all day, sonny, or are you going to get out of my way?" the stranger asked suddenly.

Betran winced as he heard the man's Plorsean accent. Until now, the stranger had only spoken in hushed tones, his origins disguised by the other noises in the tavern. The faces of the newcomers darkened as the one barring the way dropped a hand to the knife on his belt.

"Plorsean, are ya?" His eyes narrowed. "You look familiar."

The giant stood in silence and returned the man's stare. The other newcomers fanned out as the ringleader continued. "Yes, I do know you. You're the Butcher of Kalgan. I heard you were dead."

"Apparently not." The giant's words were softly spoken, but they reverberated through the tavern.

Betran retreated a step, the ale in his stomach curdling with sudden fear. Even the ringleader swallowed, but a glance at his friends seemed to restore some of his courage. Advancing a step, he forced a grin. "You're a wanted man, butcher," he growled. "Though most in these parts would kill you for free."

"They're welcome to try," the giant replied.

"Might be we will," snapped the man, drawing his dagger.

In that moment, the giant surged forward. One hand

flashed out, blocking the dagger's thrust, the other snapping out to catch the ringleader in the jaw. A sharp *crack* echoed from the low ceiling as the man collapsed. He struck the floor with an audible thud, and did not rise again.

Straightening, the giant swept his gaze over the remaining men. "You know my name. If any of you wish to stop me, you're welcome to try. One way or another, I'll be leaving through that door."

The men around the stranger wavered, their eyes wide, faces pale. Silently, the man started forward. His attackers exchanged glances. The man had almost reached the stairs when Betran saw the change come over them. With the giant's back exposed, one man drew his dagger and leapt. The others followed, weapons in hand.

As the first reached the stranger, he raised his dagger to strike. Before the blow could fall, the giant spun, his fist flashing out to catch his attacker in the face. The Trolan staggered back into two of his fellows, slowing their charge. The final man leapt past them, dagger held low.

Roaring, the giant swung to meet his attacker. His hands swept down and caught the knifeman by the wrist. Before the assailant could tear himself free, he was dragged forward into a crunching headbutt. Betran winced as the man dropped without a sound. His dagger slid across the floor, coming to a rest at Betran's feet.

Beyond, the remaining three had recovered, but the giant was already closing on them. Stepping in close, he caught two by the head and slammed them together with a sickening *thud*. As he released them, their legs crumpled beneath them, and they slid to the ground.

The last man, realising he was alone, tried to flee up the stairs, but the giant caught him by the collar. He cried out as he was hauled back, trying to bring his dagger to bear. The giant punched him square in the forehead, and the weapon slid from his suddenly limp fingers.

Grunting, the stranger released the man, allowing him to tumble to the floor alongside his comrades. Silently his gaze studied the room. Betran shuddered as the amber eyes settled on him.

"What about you?" the giant growled.

His mouth suddenly dry, Betran jerked his head sideways. "No…no I'm good," he stuttered. The giant stared back, seeming to see right through him. Betran glanced at the dagger lying at his feet. He quickly kicked it away, then drew his own blade from his belt and tossed it aside. Raising his hands, he nodded at the discarded weapons. "See?"

To his surprise, the stranger chuckled. Moans came from the fallen men as he walked past them and slapped a hand down on Betran's shoulder. "That's good to hear!" he boomed. "I was meant to be keeping a low profile. The name's Devon."

"I know who you are," Betran said, staring up into the man's grizzled face. "My name is Betran. You killed my brother in the battle for Branei Pass."

For half a second, a look of pain crossed the giant's face. Then it was gone. "I'm sorry to hear that," Devon said, shaking his head. "There's a lot I regret, from my past. But that's life I suppose. Can't change what's been—only what's to come!"

Betran found himself nodding. "I can believe that," he lamented, thinking of their king's foolhardy march into Plorsea. "There's plenty I regret too."

Devon nodded. "The curse of old age," he said with a grin. He studied the fallen men for a moment. "Don't think they'll be going anywhere for a while. Still, it won't take long now for word to spread I'm in town. Don't suppose you know where I can find someone by the name of Godrin."

A lump lodged in Betran's throat at the mention of the name. Godrin was a former soldier turned crime lord, who'd all but taken over the impoverished city. He had built a reputation for himself during the war as a competent General, and been one of the few to survive the city's fall. His cohort had mostly avoided the final battle and subsequent purge of the army, though there were conflicting rumours about how Godrin had accomplished this.

All anyone knew for sure was that, in the aftermath of the war, Godrin had used his cohort to take control of a section of the city. His territory had only expanded since then. Those under his sway were forced to pay for protection, only adding to the burden imposed on the citizens by the Tsar's taxes.

Godrin was not a man Betran wanted to cross. And if the Butcher of Kalgan was looking for him…

"Why would you be looking for a man like Godrin?" he asked softly.

"I was told he might help me solve a problem."

Betran eyed the man. He sensed if he refused, Devon would become angry again. Yet if Betran took him to Godrin, and Devon killed him, Betran's life would no doubt be at risk from Godrin's conspirators. Biting his lip, he opened his mouth, then closed it again, unable to come to a decision.

Grinning, Devon reached into his belt purse. His hand emerged with a Gold Libra, which he flicked into the air. Jumping in shock, Betran caught the coin before he knew what he was doing. Speechless, he looked from Devon to the coin.

"For the bother," the giant said quietly. "There's another in it for you if you take me to Godrin. I swear, I'm not looking for trouble."

Betran hardly heard Devon's words. He stared down at the coin, his eyes misting, and he quickly blinked back the tears. The coin would get his family through the rest of winter. With the coming of spring, the long task of rebuilding the city would resume and he would have work again. Biting back the emotion swelling in his throat, Betran found himself nodding.

"I'll take you," he said quietly.

Pocketing the coin, he waved at the bartender, who glared back at them, clearly upset about the unconscious patrons lying on his floor. Remembering the man's earlier discourtesy, Betran only grinned and turned away.

Stepping over the failed attackers, he walked towards the stairwell, then cursed as the thud of the door above echoed down to them. A slender stranger appeared on the stairs above. He wore tight-fitting black leggings and a sheepskin jerkin, matched with a fine woollen cloak. His cheeks were clean-shaven, and as he reached up and pulled back his hood, Betran saw there was some grey in his short black hair. His hazel eyes studied the tavern, lingering on the unconscious men, before turning on Devon.

"Kellian, about time you showed up!" Devon boomed from behind Betran.

The newcomer shook his head, a weary look passing across his face. "Yes...well, I see you've been making friends as usual."

Chuckling, Devon took Betran by the shoulder and gave him a friendly push towards the stairs. "Had to do something to pass the time. But you're in luck: while you were busy sleeping, I found someone to take us to Godrin."

"Oh, joy," the newcomer muttered, turning to push open the door.

Betran and Devon joined him, and together they walked out into the streets of Kalgan.

A lana lay on the soft feather mattress and stared up at the panelled ceiling of the canopy bed. A mosaic of gold, silver, and precious gems had been set into the mahogany, depicting a creek running through a wooded valley—but in the past few weeks, Alana had spent so much time lying there she hardly noticed it anymore. Her thoughts were far away, lost in another life, in the sporadic images flickering through her mind.

Images of her father and mother, of her brother, of friends and people she'd once known.

Or so she had believed.

She knew now those memories were lies, a fabrication, some foul construction cast over her mind.

A tremor ran through Alana as she choked back a sob. Forcing her eyes closed, she sought the escape of sleep, though she knew it would not come. How long had she lain in this room now, staring into space, sleeping in fits and bursts amidst the silk sheets? A week? Two?

She no longer had the will to care—how could she, when everything she'd ever known was a lie?

Despite her best efforts, a tear streaked across her cheek as she recalled the words of the Tsar.

My daughter, welcome home…

From the start, she had tried to deny it, to fight and rage against the man. Yet even in those first few moments, his words had rung with truth, sending vibrations down to the very core of her being. In that instant, the hazy memories of her past had shattered, revealing the gaping hole where a lifetime of memories should have been. The truth had left her stumbling through the ruins of her mind, struggling to piece the fragments back together, to answer the one, impossible question.

Who am I?

The question had haunted her through the days and nights, stalking her through every waking hour, following her even into the sanctuary of her dreams. Always the answer seemed to shimmer just out of sight. She could not grasp it, could not quite bring it into focus. Finally she had given up, surrendering to the icy grips of despair.

A sob tore from Alana's chest as she felt the familiar pain. She couldn't go on like this, empty and alone. She was a phantom, an illusion, some dream made real by an unknown power.

Silently, she rose from the bed. The massive room stretched out around her, its furnishings of gold and silver speaking of a wealth she could only ever have dreamed of when living on the streets. Except she knew now that wasn't true. This had been her room since birth, her sanctuary, the one place she should have known before any other. Yet even now she felt only a cold indifference for it.

She stared at the painting on the far wall, of the nobles on the hunt, their bows taut, arrows ready to fly. When Alana had first woken after her capture, she had hardly glanced at the artwork, but on returning to the room, she'd found herself drawn to it. Studying it now, her eyes were pulled as always to the woman standing amidst the hunters. Blonde hair fluttered in an imaginary wind as the woman held her sabre high, a cry on her crimson lips. Her stone-grey eyes seemed to stare down at Alana, an accusation in their murky depths, a perfect reflection of her own.

Thief!

Alana's stomach churned and she looked away, unable to gaze on her own likeness a moment longer. Heart pounding, she crossed the soft carpets, brushed aside the drapes, and stepped out onto the marble balcony. She paused as the wind struck her, its icy touch robbing her of breath. Tears cold on her cheeks, she stood there a moment, sucking in great gulps of air, struggling to lift her soul free of the despair that gripped it.

Beyond the balcony, the rooftops of the citadel stretched out around her, the slate tiles and twisting crenulations falling slowly away to the city of Ardath. A thin haze clung to the city, but through it she could just make out the red-brick walls of the merchant quarter. The distant ring of bells carried from the three-pronged spires of the temple. Slowly the ringing faded, and was replaced by the sounds of the waking city.

A lump rose in Alana's throat as she listened to the shouting voices and clip-clopping of hooves on the brick streets. Down amongst the people was where she belonged, amidst the chaos and the noise. Not up here, surrounded by stone, amidst the trappings of the Tsar's power.

She stood at the marble railing and looked into the courtyard six storeys below. Basalt and limestone cobbles wound outwards from the central fountain in a spiral pattern, and small shrubs grew around the edges of the courtyard.

A sudden resolve came over Alana, and carefully she climbed up onto the railing of her balcony. The wind swirled around her, threatening to drag her to her death. Her stomach plummeted into her boots as she looked down and saw how far it was to the ground. A sudden weakness took her. Her legs shook as she crouched down and gripped the railing with both hands. Struggling for breath, she clenched her eyes closed.

What are you doing?

Alana shivered. She didn't know the answer. The wind caught in her bedclothes and her heart lurched as she wavered on the edge.

"What are you afraid of?" she heard herself ask. "You don't exist, Alana."

Tears burned in her eyes, but releasing the rail she straightened. Her throat contracted as she looked down into the courtyard. The spiral pattern seemed to be spinning, and she wavered on the edge, the edges of her vision turning dark. Fists clenched tight, she sucked in another breath. Her heart beat slowed, and her fear receded, giving way to the awful emptiness.

"*Alana!*" a voice yelled from behind her. Over her shoulder, Alana saw Quinn appear in the alcove. Eyes wide, he stood frozen to the spot, hand outstretched. "What are you doing?"

"I'm sorry," Alana whispered, tears blurring her vision.

Before he could stop her, she closed her eyes and allowed herself to topple backwards.

Her stomach lurched as she began to fall, and the wind howled in her ears. Air rushed around her as she screamed, the breath catching in her throat. She kept her eyes closed tight, waiting for the *thud*, the final flash of light as she struck hard stone, for her life to go howling into the void.

The shrieking of the wind seemed to grow louder. It whirled around her, catching at her clothes, clawing at her hair, and somehow the sense of falling began to slow. Time stretched out, until unable to resist any longer, Alana opened her eyes. She gasped as she found herself hovering just a few feet above the cobblestones. Terrified, she thrashed against the wind that still buffeted her. Abruptly the vortex suspending her mid-air dissipated, and she fell the last few inches to the ground.

Air rushed from her lungs as she struck the cobbles. Gasping, she rolled onto her side and clutched her stomach, her lungs straining for breath. She was still struggling to breathe when Quinn dropped from the heavens, his cloak whipping around him as gusts of wind, summoned by his Sky magic, slowed his fall.

He blinked as he touched down, flicking a glance back at the tower. "Well, that's a new trick…" he muttered. Shaking his head, he crouched beside her. "Alana, are you okay?"

Alana cursed as she finally caught her breath. Pushing him away, she pulled herself to her feet. "Why did you save me?" she shrieked, shoving him hard in the chest.

He stared back at her. "You don't know what you're doing, Alana," he replied. "This isn't you."

"I know that!" she yelled, swinging on him. She jabbed a finger at his face. "How do you think it feels, finding out that everything you've ever known is a lie? That everything I am is some…some construct?"

Reeling back, Quinn held up his hands in supplication. Her words trailed off as she sucked in a breath. Her chest still ached from the fall and her heart was racing, the panic building within her. Wheezing, she staggered, her legs beginning to tremble. Alana slumped back to the ground and drew her knees up against her chest.

Seating himself beside her, Quinn placed a tentative hand on her back. Alana flinched, but this time she did not pull away. In that instant, her hatred and fear of Quinn seemed small beside the desolation within.

"Just breathe," he murmured, rubbing her back. The silence stretched out, but when he finally spoke again, his voice was soft, reassuring. "I'm sorry. I should have come sooner. Your fath– the Tsar, he thought it best to give you your space."

"Why is this happening to me?" she croaked, trying to keep herself from sobbing.

"It is…difficult to explain," Quinn said. "But I'm here now. Maybe I can help."

Alana closed her eyes, still struggling to control her breathing. Quinn's hand moved across her back in slow circles, his warmth and presence strangely comforting. The thought gave her pause. This was the man who had hunted her and her brother across the Three Nations. She had fought with every ounce of her strength to escape him, yet he had just saved her life with his magic. Sitting with him now in the quiet of the courtyard felt strangely warming, and she shivered at the familiarity of it.

"Are you okay, Alana?" he asked into the silence.

Shaking her head, Alana glanced at him. The sight still set her heart racing, but she fought the instinct to run. "Quinn… please…help me?"

He nodded. His hand slid beneath her arm and he pulled her up. "Come with me."

Alana obeyed, taking his shoulder for support. She felt strangely exhausted, as though her plunge from the balcony had stolen away the last of her strength. If not for Quinn, Alana wasn't sure she could have made it back inside, let alone up the long stairway to her room.

Still in her nightclothes, she allowed herself to be led through the winding corridors and endless courtyards of the citadel. There were fewer guards now than on the first day she'd woken, though she hadn't bothered to ask anyone where they'd gone. Those they did pass kept their eyes fixed straight ahead. Even so, Alana's cheeks warmed with embarrassment. The silk nightgowns she'd found in her clothes trunk barely went down past her waist. In the life she could remember, Alana would never have worn such tight-fitting bedclothes, but here there'd been little else to choose from.

Alana's thoughts were jerked back to the present as warm air touched her cheek. Blinking, she looked around, surprised to find herself in a sprawling lawn and garden. Beyond the short-cropped grass and twisting rosebushes, the outer walls of the citadel towered overhead, the dull grey stone standing out in sharp contrast to the vibrant colours below.

Pathways of red sandstone and blue marble twisted away from where they stood, threading their way through the green lawns and passing beneath archways of flowering vines. Despite the icy winds of winter beyond the citadel walls, the air here carried with it the touch of summer. The trees dotting the gardens were in full blossom, the reds and yellows and blues of their flowers seemingly aglow with magic.

Despite the warmth, Alana found herself shivering. She knew this garden, had seen it in the dreams that had plagued her during her flight across the Three Nations. She had seen herself and her brother here, running across the lawns, playing in the distant trees.

"I know this place," she whispered.

Quinn smiled. "That's good." Taking her hand, he led her onto the lawn.

Alana was barefoot, but the grass was soft beneath her feet. Closing her eyes, she savoured the touch of sunlight on her skin, the warmth of the air, the distant chatter of laughter. Looking around, she sought the source. To her wonder, a troupe of children came running across the grass, closely followed by a woman in a sunflower yellow dress. Scarlet hair bobbed as she ran, her pale skin aglow with the morning sun. She wore no jewellery except for a pair of emerald studded silver bracelets, and there was a smile on her face as she watched the children.

The smile fell from the woman's lips as she saw them. Leaving the children to their play, she wandered over. Alana started to speak, but before she could get a word out, the woman swung on Quinn.

"She shouldn't be here," the woman hissed, her voice taut with anger.

Quinn's eyes flashed and he stepped forward, placing himself between Alana and the woman. "Afraid of an audience, Krista?" he asked coolly.

She glared at him, eyes narrowed. "Never," she snapped, "but the children do not need the distraction. The boy, Liam, is taking his examination this week."

"We will not interfere, Krista," Quinn said with a smile. "Now, I suggest you get back to your charges. They seem to have wandered off."

Krista glanced around and swore when she saw the children disappearing through an archway. She took off without another word.

Chuckling, Quinn turned back to Alana. "You'll have to excuse Krista."

Alana hardly heard him. One of the children had caught her attention. She started after them, eyes narrowed, trying to catch another glimpse of the boy. She could have sworn she recognised him. The breath caught in her throat as the boy she'd spotted glanced back. For a moment he stared at her, a frown on his young face, then he turned and disappeared through the arch.

"That was the boy from the stepwell," she whispered.

Quinn rested his hand on her shoulder. "His name is Liam."

Alana shook her head, tears welling in her eyes. "What is this?"

"The truth," Quinn murmured.

Her breath coming in ragged gasps, Alana looked into Quinn's eyes, seeking some sign of deception. He stared back at her, his face soft now, his forehead creased with concern.

Gone was the steely glint of the Stalker who had chased her across the Three Nations. From the depths of her memories, she heard again the question in her dreams.

Are you ready, Alana?

She closed her eyes. For weeks she had fought the truth, clinging to the belief the Tsar and his people were evil. According to his laws, all Magickers were to be brought to the citadel. Once taken into custody, they were never seen again. The day her brother's magic had woken, she had *known* they had to flee, or face death. But now…now everything was wrong.

The boy she'd seen was the same one Quinn had arrested in the stepwell so many weeks ago. He should have been dead, and yet here he was, healthy and alive, happy…

A sob tore from her lips as the last of her resistance crumbled. "Why is this happening to me?"

"Your magic," Quinn said.

"*My*…magic?" Alana whispered. Her mouth opened and closed as she struggled to find the words to reply. "My…no… that's not possible."

Clutching her chest, she staggered back, struggling to keep herself upright. Before she could fall, Quinn grasped her firmly by the shoulder.

"It's the truth, Alana," he said as she steadied herself. Taking her hands in his, he held them tight. "You have the power to alter minds."

Silently, Alana shook her head. Her hands slipped from his grip as she sank to her knees. Wrapping her arms around her chest, she locked eyes with Quinn, silently beseeching him to take back the words.

Instead, he knelt beside her, unblinking. "We believe that, somehow, your magic went wrong," he continued inexorably, "that you lost control, and wiped away the memories of yourself and your brother. Your power must have imprinted another…reality over your own consciousness."

"How is that possible?" Alana croaked.

"I don't know," Quinn murmured. "I have never seen you lose control before. All I can tell you is that you disappeared with your brother on his sixteenth birthday. We searched for you, locked the city gates and sent out men to search the streets. But for weeks, there was no sign of either of you. Not even your father, with all his power, could find you."

"It wasn't until I sensed Earth magic near the northern gates that we picked up your trail. I didn't know it was you though, not until that night in Sitton Forest."

Alana closed her eyes, struggling to comprehend, to make sense of this new reality. She thought back to their escape from the city. A cold breeze blew across her neck as she recalled her conversation with the ship captain, how he'd suddenly changed his mind and allowed them to depart.

"How…how can…" she trailed off, fighting back tears.

"I'm sorry this happened to you, Alana," Quinn said. He paused, taking a breath. "But…you were happy here once. You had a place, a role in this world."

Tears welled in Alana's eyes. "I don't remember…"

Quinn smiled. "Then let me show you," he whispered, offering his hand.

Trembling, Alana stared at him a moment. Fear spread through her chest as she wondered what fresh revelations Quinn had in store for her. It seemed that every word from his mouth further unwound her sense of self, making a lie of everything she believed in. A yearning rose within her, to flee back to her room, to hide beneath the blankets and block out the world.

Yet there was no running from this truth. She could hide no longer. Swallowing back her terror, Alana reached out and took his hand.

2

Devon fell in with Kellian as they left the tavern. He was aware of his friend's irritation, but couldn't help but grin as he caught the man's eye. After all, the unconscious men in the tavern were hardly his fault. Knowing it would be recognised, Devon had left his warhammer *kanker* at the inn, but in the end it hadn't mattered: as much as he'd wanted to lay low, Kalgan was a small place nowadays, and his reputation amongst the survivors of the war was well-earned. Whether they succeeded in finding Enala's contact tonight or not, they would have to leave the city by morning, or risk being hunted down by a mob of vengeful townsfolk.

Thinking back to the wily old priest, Devon found himself wishing Enala had joined them on this quest. Recalling that last day in the gate tunnel of Fort Fall still filled him with awe. With fire and sword in hand, Enala had sliced into the Stalkers like a scythe through the wheat fields of northern Lonia. Only the arrival of the Tsar's Red Dragons had prevented her victory. As it was, they'd been forced to flee on the back of a Gold Dragon the old woman had summoned.

Devon would never forget that wild flight; yet as they'd

soared high above the mountains, it had been sorrow, not joy, that had filled his heart. They had escaped, but Alana had been left behind, trapped in the vile clutches of the Stalker lieutenant, Quinn.

His heart twitched at the thought of Alana, of what she must now be suffering for his failure. If only he'd managed to kill Quinn, things might have ended differently. Instead, a crossbow bolt had torn through his shoulder, all but incapacitating him. The wound would normally have taken months to heal, but after their escape, Enala had directed the dragon to a temple high in the Northland mountains. There, they had discovered an order of priests dedicated to the Goddess, Antonia. Several of the men and women there had possessed the healing magic of the Earth, and had quickly set about tending to the wounds of their visitors.

The hairs on Devon's neck stood on end as he recalled the soft green light that had seeped from the hands of the priests. His pain had fled at its touch, his wounds stitching themselves together before his eyes. Within minutes he'd been whole, without so much as a scar to remind him of the desperate battle in Fort Fall.

The healers had taken more time with Alana's brother, Braidon. The wound in his stomach had been deep, and the boy was barely clinging to life when the priests reached him. Hands raised, three priests had gathered in a circle, their power forming a glowing dome of green around the boy. For hours they had stood thus, unmoving, their eyes closed and brows creased, features like stone.

Devon's worry had reached a fever pitch by the time they finally lowered their hands. Shuffling forward, he'd barely dared to breathe as he searched for signs of life in the young man. Only as the last of the green light faded away did he glimpse the gentle rise and fall of Braidon's chest, and that the wound in his stomach had vanished.

Even now, Devon could hardly believe he'd witnessed such a miracle. During the war, he'd watched the Tsar's Magickers decimate the Trolan army with their power. Yet there were few healers amidst their ranks, and their powers were never wasted on regular soldiers. Thinking of friends he'd lost to lesser wounds than the one Braidon had taken, Devon felt the familiar anger stirring.

After the temple, Enala and her Gold Dragon, Dahniul, had flown them further into the mountains, to the hidden city of Erachill. It was there Devon had announced his decision to return to the Three Nations, and save Alana from the clutches of the Tsar.

To his surprise, Enala had readily agreed, though she had left it up to Dahniul to decide whether the dragon would carry them. He could still remember the dragon's soft voice in his mind, after asking why he would risk such a quest. Devon's response had been simple and to the point.

Because I do not desert my friends.

A rumble had come from deep in the dragon's chest, and Devon had felt an odd warmth spreading through his mind, even before the reply came.

Then I will take you.

Afterwards, Kellian had been quick to announce he would be coming as well, hopeless though their mission seemed. Devon had tried to dissuade his friend, but there was no changing the man's mind once it was made up, and two days later they'd left the mountain fortress on dragon back.

Enala had joined them for that first length of the journey, directing Dahniul south and west across Northland until they reached the northern coast of Trola. The dragon had landed near the ruins of Straken. There, priest and dragon had bid them farewell.

"The Tsar will sense me if I journey further with you, my friends," Enala had told them. "Now he knows I live, he will be searching for me. He won't be taken by surprise again, and even I don't have the power to fight the creatures he will send."

So Enala and Dahniul had bid their farewells and soared back into the northern skies, to Erachill and the boy they'd left behind.

Devon found himself smiling as he thought of Braidon. The boy had wanted to come as well, to help save his sister, but he'd found the rest of the party aligned against him. No one wanted to face Alana's wrath if she discovered they'd allowed her brother to return to the Three Nations. As it was, it was a relief to know Braidon remained in Northland, safe beyond the reach of the Tsar.

"Master that power of yours, Braidon," Devon had told him. "Then we'll see."

He wondered how Braidon's training was progressing beneath Enala's watchful eye. Bright as he was, the boy seemed to be struggling in the days before Devon and Kellian had left. The loss of Braidon's sister had left him despondent. His eyes were often distant, his mind far away in another world. Devon prayed to the Gods he could find a way to save Alana and reunite the two siblings.

"We're close." Betran's voice from the road ahead snapped Devon back to the present.

Looking around, he shivered. The streets were dark, most of the buildings just crumbling remnants of the ancient structures which had once decorated the Trolan city. Here and there lights flickered, the dim lanterns of the few residents piercing the gloom. Above, the sky was black, the stars hidden by clouds. Even so, he could sense Kellian's tension beside him.

"Where are we heading?" Kellian asked, keeping his voice low.

"The bathhouses," Betran replied. When Kellian muttered something choice, the man shrugged and replied, "Can't rebuild a civilisation without bathhouses."

Devon chuckled, but Kellian caught him by the arm and pulled him back as Betran moved on. "Are you sure we can trust this man?" he hissed.

"Probably a bit late to be asking that now," Devon replied with a grin. When Kellian only glared at him, he elaborated. "If he'd wanted trouble, he would have already taken us down some darkened alley and had his friends waylay us. Now come on, if I smell half as bad as you, we're both in need of a bath."

He continued down the street to where Betran now stood beneath a bright cluster of lanterns. Kellian grumbled something unintelligible behind his back, but a moment later his friend's footsteps followed after him. As they approached the building, a wooden door swung open and a burly man stepped out into the street. Folding his arms, he studied the three of them, then settled his gaze on the Trolan.

"What's this, Betran?" he rumbled. "Last I heard you couldn't afford a barber, let alone a bath." The man waved a hand in front of his face to emphasise his words. "Certainly smells like it."

Betran bristled, but Kellian stepped forward briskly before their companion could find the words to respond. "Betran here was just showing us the way. We're new in town."

Taking a breath, Betran collected himself. "They're here to see Godrin."

The doorman narrowed his eyes. "He's not taking visitors."

"We're friends," Kellian said quickly, then in a voice no louder than a whisper: "Enala sent us."

For a second it seemed the doorman had not heard. He stood still as a statue, the muscles of his neck and shoulders bulging. Devon tensed, readying himself for a fight, but before he could move the guard silently turned and stepped back into the establishment. Leaping forward, Devon jammed his foot into the doorway to keep the man from locking them out.

Inside the bathhouse, the guard glanced back and raised an

eyebrow. "Are you going to stand in the doorway all night, or are you going to come inside?"

Devon blinked. Beneath his beard, he felt his cheeks grow warm. Giving a gruff nod, he stepped through the doorway, followed closely by Betran and Kellian. Inside they waited as the door was closed and bolted behind them, then followed the guard down a long corridor leading into the earth.

The temperature rose as the corridor ended abruptly, giving way to a circular chamber with a domed ceiling. On the other side of the chamber was another stone corridor, but elsewhere wooden booths lined the room. Most had their doors closed, but the guard gestured to one that still stood open.

"Cloaks, clothes and boots in there, please. You'll find towels and slippers inside," he said.

Grinning, Devon shared a glance with Kellian and Betran. "Right boys, who's first?"

"I'll wait out here," Betran said quickly, his eyes flickering nervously towards the exit.

Devon couldn't fault him for his worries—no doubt he'd get the blame if things went wrong with Godrin. He was about to agree with the Trolan, when the guard spoke again.

"You'll join your friends, Betran," he said in a tone that brooked no argument.

A strained silence followed. Feeling the tension rising, Devon glanced at the guard, then shrugged. "Well, we'd best get to it boys!" Grinning, he stepped into the booth.

After a moment's hesitation the others followed. The small wooden room sported a single bench and hooks for their clothing, but it was clearly designed for two occupants at the most. A lot of grunting and shuffling followed as they fought to remove their clothes in the cramped quarters, before quickly wrapping towels around their waists to hide themselves.

Finally, they stepped back out into the stone chamber and locked the door behind them. Entrusting the key to Kellian,

Devon looked around for the guard, feeling more than a little exposed with only a towel to cover him. It wasn't the being naked that bothered him, so much as the sudden sense of vulnerability. It was one thing to walk into danger unarmed—it was something else entirely to do so without even a thread of clothing on his back.

The guard appeared from the corridor that presumably led deeper into the bathhouse, his expression still unreadable.

"Ready?" he asked, his voice echoing off the stone ceiling.

Devon nodded, and the man turned on his heel without another word. They followed him a short way down the corridor, until he stopped in front of a heavy metal door. He undid the latch and heaved it open. A cloud of steam billowed out, and the guard gestured them inside.

One by one they ducked through the door and entered the sauna. Through the steam, Devon glimpsed a circular stone bench in the centre of the room. Several men lounged there, laying with their backs to the stone or sitting in silent contemplation. Around the edges of the chamber were more ledges, along with stone bowls and steel faucets. Sweat dripped from Devon's forehead as the hot air swamped him.

As they moved further inside, the guard's voice came from behind them. "Cross the room and go into the next chamber. You'll find a thermal pool. Godrin is waiting for you there."

An ominous screech came from behind them as the door swung closed, followed by the muffled *click* of the latch being locked. Despite the heat, a chill slid down Devon's spine. Doing his best to ignore it, he straightened his shoulders and walked around the stone bench in the centre of the room, taking care not to trip over any outstretched limbs.

The doorway took shape from the steam as he approached the far side of the chamber. Sweat trickled down his brow as he stepped through, eager to leave behind the scrutiny of the half-naked men. The walls narrowed around him as he entered a corridor, then widened again into a secondary chamber. Here, the ground ended abruptly in the clear waters of a steaming pool. It was difficult to see more than a few feet into the rippling waters. As he came to a stop a voice called out to them in a Trolan twang.

"Devon, Kellian, how pleasant of you to join me. I heard you were dead."

"I've been hearing that a lot," Devon replied with a grunt.

Laughter carried across the water. "Come, join me. You must be weary after your travels."

Devon shrugged, and removing his towel, stepped into the water. He winced as the heat engulfed his leg, reminding him of the blows he'd taken in the bar, and he paused. Kellian stepped past, a weary smile on his face. Walking down the steps into the bath, he sank beneath the surface, only to reappear a few seconds later. Silently he raised an eyebrow at Devon.

Muttering under his breath, Devon steeled himself and followed his friend into the scalding water. A splash came from behind him as Betran did the same, and together they walked forward until they were submerged up to their waists. Slowly the heat became more bearable, and Devon found the aches in his muscles beginning to fade.

Kellian had already disappeared into the steam, and gritting his teeth, Devon chased after his friend. Back in Ardath, Kellian had been wealthy enough to afford luxuries such as the bathhouses. Devon usually had to make do with washing himself in the pig trough nearest the *Firestone*. Ahead, Kellian reappeared, but he was no longer alone.

Lounging on the other side of the pool was a man almost as large as Devon himself. He sat with the water up to his chest, bulging arms stretched out on either side of him, an amused smile on his clean-shaven face. Muscles along his shoulders rippled as he lowered his arms and stood, his hawk-like brown eyes studying them intently. Devon shivered as they settled on him.

"Well, if it isn't the Butcher of Kalgan," the stranger said softly.

"I take it you're Godrin."

The man nodded. "I hear you have a message for me from Enala. You had better hope it's important. Your life depends on it."

Devon glanced around them, but the steam hid the rest of the room from view. As far as he could see, they were alone. Even so, the hairs on the back of his neck tingled, and his heart beat quickened.

Forcing a bravado he didn't quite feel, Devon smirked. "Sorry to disappoint you, but we're the message."

Godrin's brow deepened as he looked from Devon to Kellian. "You'd best explain," he said. As he spoke, he raised a hand. Movement came from behind him as two men stepped forward, crossbows in hand. "Or I'll be sending you back to Enala in pieces."

3

For Braidon, the weeks since the final confrontation at Fort Fall had dragged by with excruciating slowness. Each day he waited for news of his sister, for word of her public torture and execution at the hands of the Tsar. With each passing hour he could feel his anxiety rising, the strain of expectation slowly tearing him apart. His nights were spent tossing and turning, his thoughts consumed by the awful things the Stalkers might be doing to Alana.

Yet still there was nothing, not a single whisper of her fate. It was as though she had vanished off the face of the continent.

Often Braidon would find his thoughts drawn back to the last battle, to what he might have done differently to save Alana from the Stalkers. But those final moments were little more than a blur now. From the moment the crossbow bolt had torn through his stomach, he could recall only glimpses, of Quinn laughing and Alana crying out in agony, of flames burning in the darkness, and a golden dragon soaring through icy skies.

Only when the warming light of the healers had touched

him did the memories resume, drawing him back to the agony of a reality without his sister. He had woken with a cry in the quiet sanctuary of an Earth Temple. For a moment he'd thought himself back in Sitton Forest, in the ruins of Antonia's temple. But as his vision cleared and he saw the light fading from the hands of the priests surrounding him, he'd realised the truth.

He was no longer in the Three Nations, no longer under the influence of the Tsar. He was finally free.

And Alana had given her life to make it so.

Exhaustion had taken him then, and he'd faded back into the darkness. When he'd woken next, he'd found himself here, in the strange city known as Erachill. Hidden deep in the mountains of Northland, it was difficult to know where the city itself ended and the original caves began. Even now, as he wandered down the winding corridors of the city, he could only wonder at the centuries of toil it must have taken to construct such a place.

Ahead the light was growing, the flickering lanterns giving way to natural sunlight. He breathed a sigh as he stepped out into the open, his chest swelling with relief to have open space around him. Above the cliffs stretched up a hundred feet, the worn granite pockmarked by dozens of caves identical to the one from which he'd just emerged. Around each opening, blocks of marble formed great facades of polished white, each engraved with runes and glyphs depicting the rooms hidden within. Great staircases had been carved into the cliff-face, winding their way up between the caves without so much as a banister for safety.

Shivering, Braidon turned his gaze to the distant flood-plains of Northland. They fell away below him, the rocky slopes of the mountain giving way to open ground. With winter now gripping the continent, snow blanketed the land as far as the eye could see, broken only by the occasional rocky outcrop. Above the mountains the sky was grey and beginning to darken, the heavy clouds promising the approach of yet another winter storm.

Hoping there was still time before it struck, Braidon set out across the rocky slopes, taking care to avoid patches of ice as he searched for the flash of green robes that would reveal his mentor's location. The mountain winds had already blown the slope clear of snow, but the going was precarious, and it was a few minutes before he finally saw her. She was in her favourite spot, seated atop a ledge with her legs hanging out over the five-hundred-foot drop. Swallowing hard, Braidon picked his way towards her, coming to a stop when he was still a few feet from the edge.

"You're late, boy," Enala said without looking up.

"Sorry, Enala, I...was distracted."

She glanced back at him, her eyes creased with sadness. "You were thinking of your sister." When he didn't reply, she went on. "Devon and Kellian will bring her back, Braidon. You must have faith."

"Faith?" he asked. His eyes burned, but remembering his sister's strength, he refused to show his weakness. "They don't even have magic. What chance do they have against the Tsar?"

"They saved you…"

"*You* saved me, Enala," he snapped. Taking a breath, he tried to quill his sudden anger. Shaking, he crouched down on his haunches and looked across at her. "Maybe if you'd gone with them…"

Enala shook her head. Her wrinkles seemed to have deepened since she'd returned from Trola, and her sapphire eyes were weary when she looked at him. "He knows I live now, young Braidon. He will be searching for me. If I went with them, it would not take long for him to find me. Then my powers would matter little."

Despair swelling in his chest, Braidon looked away. A

strained silence fell between them as Braidon looked out over the plains, where the soft flickering of lightning burned in the distant clouds.

"Shall we begin then?" he said abruptly.

The old priest looked at him closely. "Are you sure—"

"I'm fine," he snapped, cutting her off. "The sooner I master my useless power, the sooner I can be rid of this place."

Enala pursed her lips, but he turned away, unable to bear her pity. He heard her sigh. "Very well. You know the process. I will observe you while…"

"Fine," Braidon grunted.

Seating himself, he crossed his legs and closed his eyes, doing his best to force thoughts of the old woman and his sister from his mind. His lungs swelled as he sucked in a breath, then exhaled. Concentrating on his breathing, he sought the peace of mindfulness, to escape the pull of his body, the lure of emotion, the strain of his memories.

Yet even as he did so, he felt the chaos pressing back, the past rising up to haunt him. A pang came from his stomach, and his hand drifted unconsciously to where the crossbow bolt had struck him. Not a mark remained, but amidst the darkness, the memory felt fresh, an almost tangible thing, piercing his consciousness.

He shuddered, but with an effort of will, released the memory. It drifted back out into the void as he forced his mind back to his breath.

In, out. In, out.

The darkness swirled as more memories rose to assail him. He saw again their arrival on the back of Dahniul, felt the thrill of flight and the wonder of the beast's power. Thought to be extinct in the Three Nations, a few dragons had apparently survived in the wild lands of the north, descended from those that had fought alongside mankind against the dark Magicker Archon a hundred years prior. Bound by an ancient treaty between the Gold Dragons and the king of Trola, the creatures only allowed royal descendants to ride them. Fortunately for Braidon and his friends, Enala was such a descendent—perhaps even the last one left living.

Realising he'd been distracted again, Braidon tore his thoughts away from the noble beasts. It did not take long, though, for his undisciplined mind to wander again, and he found himself thinking of the escort that had met them as they'd landed beneath the cliffs of Erachill. Armed soldiers had marched out to surround them, before leading them deep into the bowels of the city. Enala they had treated with reverence, but Braidon and the others they had looked on with anger and suspicion.

Then the Queen had come, with her steely green eyes and a crown of twisted iron upon her head. Grey had streaked her auburn hair, but she carried about her such an authority few would dare challenge her.

Braidon shivered at the memory, and releasing it, plunged deeper into his subconscious. Something was flickering in the darkness now, a white light that seemed to radiate from all around. The sight of it sent a shiver through his spirit and he pulled back. An image formed in his mind, of his sister, a smile on her face, her eyes dancing with amusement.

Alana.

Pain sliced through him at the thought of her. He shuddered as memories flashed by, and he watched again her desperate battle against Quinn. He'd tried to save her, had tried to use his magic to drive back the Stalkers. Only then had he learned the truth: his magic was a sham, no more than a fancy trick with the light to create illusions, harmless.

Braidon fled into the darkness, seeking now not inner calm, but to escape the memories, to forget that final glimpse of Alana as she was dragged away by the Tsar's Stalkers.

And in the darkness, the white light grew. Only when

Braidon finally recovered his senses did he realise it was all around him, brilliant and shining, hemming him in. Terror filled his soul as he realised he was lost, trapped amidst the swirling powers of his magic. If it engulfed him, he would be lost.

He spun, searching the white, seeking the darkness. A speck appeared far above, impossibly distant, unreachable. Gathering himself, he raced towards it. The light swirled, circling and drawing nearer. Claws reached out to tear at him, and he screamed as the icy hooks dragged him back. His flight faltered, and he watched with despair as the light folded in on itself, gathering all around, twisting and changing, until the great shining form of a Feline rose before him.

Braidon opened his spirit mouth to scream as the Feline loomed. The creature took a step towards him, jaws agape, teeth reaching out to tear him asunder, to hurl his soul into the void. Should it succeed, he would be consumed, his body reduced to an empty husk to be controlled by his magic. He would become a demon.

With a roar, the beast leapt…

…only for a shining red inferno to spring into life between them. As the Feline struck the blaze, it screamed, the white light flickering and falling back, the creature shrinking as it retreated.

And then Braidon was back in the real world, his cries echoing off the nearby cliffs as he threw himself back from the awful fangs…

"Braidon, calm yourself!" He froze as a steely hand gripped him by the wrist.

Blinking, he found Enala sitting alongside him. His terror fled, replaced by the sickening despair of failure. Tearing his arm from the old woman's grip, he stood abruptly and swung away. A loose stone lay nearby and he lashed out at it with his boot, sending it soaring out over the ledge.

"*Damnit!*" he screamed.

"Braidon, stop, you're okay–"

"I'm *not* okay," he snapped, turning on Enala, "I'll never be okay, not with this…this *thing* inside me."

"It is a part of you, Braidon," Enala replied, "and you were closer that time."

The anger left Braidon in a rush. His shoulders slumped as he lowered his gaze to the ground. They had been at this for two weeks now, but still he felt no closer to mastering the magic within him. Whatever Enala said, he continued to fail at the final step. When his magic appeared before him, his courage would fail and he would flee into the darkness until Enala intervened. One day, he knew the creature would catch him…

"Fear is its only weapon, Braidon." Enala's voice cut across his thoughts.

"What's the point, Enala?" he asked bitterly. "Why does it even matter? Everything I do is just an illusion!"

"There is always a point, Braidon. There is no *just* when it comes to magic." She sighed, her eyes taking on a faraway look. "I knew a Magicker once, with powers like yours. She could manipulate the light to conceal herself, become invisible. I've never met anyone as brave."

"Who was she?"

Enala grinned. "A Baronian thug who tried to kill me on more than one occasion."

Braidon's head jerked up. "What?"

Enala smiled. "Life isn't always as simple as it seems, young Braidon."

Still confused, he shook his head. "What happened to her?"

"She gave up her life to save us from Archon's demon."

Braidon was lost for words. He swallowed, staring into the aged face of the woman standing opposite him. The years had turned her hair white and wrinkled the once youthful face, but her eyes shone with power and an ancient wisdom. Even so, it was easy to forget the things she had seen, the dangers she had faced in her long life.

"How have you lived so long, Enala?" he asked suddenly, the question slipping out before he could bite his tongue.

Enala's laughter bubbled across the clifftop. Gently, she eased herself back to the rocky ground and gestured for Braidon to join her. They sat in silence for a moment, looking out at the approaching storm. It was a long time before Enala answered, and a cramp was beginning to form in Braidon's leg when she finally spoke.

"Truthfully, I don't really know why I have lived this long. It was the same for my brother. He told me once that it happens for one in a thousand Magickers, that occasionally the magic will grant its wielder extended life. Or perhaps it came from our...interaction with the Gods. Although for Gabriel..." She trailed off.

For a second Braidon thought he glimpsed tears in her eyes, but she looked away before they could fall.

"Enala?" he said. Leaning forward, he placed a hand on her shoulder. "Are you okay?"

Enala smiled, all trace of tears vanished. "Do not concern yourself with the sorrows of an old woman, young Braidon," she said. "There is so much behind me now, Gabriel seems little more than the memory of another woman at times."

Braidon swallowed, not understanding, but hearing the grief behind her words. Sensing this was not a topic the old woman wished to speak of, he changed the subject.

"What was she like? Antonia?" he asked, remembering the legends. "You met her?"

Enala chuckled. "'Met' would be putting it lightly."

"And were the legends true? Was she really as powerful as they say?"

"She is an enigma," Enala replied, her wrinkles deepening

as she smiled.

"Is?" Braidon asked, a tingle running down his spine. He sat up, suddenly alert. "She's gone though, isn't she?"

"Her body, yes. Like all the Gods, she gave up her physical form after the battle with Archon," she answered. "But they never truly left us."

"What do you mean?"

"The Gods existed long before our priests devised a way to channel their spirits and power into physical form," Enala replied, "and they exist still. Their spirits are all around us: in the light of a sunset, in the earth beneath our feet, in the wind and the rain and clouds. They are the spirits of the land, the balance to our world. The source of all magic."

Braidon clenched his jaw as he realised what she was saying. "But they cannot help us."

Enala threw back her head and laughed. "You are an insightful student, young Braidon, I will give you that." Her eyes danced. "But still not entirely correct. Even in spirit, the Gods are not impotent. It was Antonia, after all, who sent me to find you."

"Antonia? Truly? How is that possible?"

"Let us just say, the Gods are inside some of us, more than others."

Braidon frowned. Sensing he would get no more information on the subject, he changed tactics. "But why would she care about me and my sister in the first place?"

Enala sighed. "I do not know the answer to that," she replied. Her eyes grew distant as she looked out over the plains of Northland. "But I have a feeling we will find out before the end. Now come, we'd best return to the city. The storm is almost upon us."

She stood and started off towards the cliffs of Erachill, leaving Braidon to scramble to his feet and chase after her, a dozen questions still clambering within his mind for answers.

❧ 4 ❧

Alana followed Quinn through the corridors of the citadel, fully dressed now, her sword thumping gently against her side. The blade made her feel more at ease, though she knew it would be pointless attempting to flee. The guards no longer tailed her, but there were eyes everywhere, and she doubted she'd make it as far as the gates before someone stopped her.

Regardless, she could not run, not while a million questions still filled her mind. She caught a glimpse of herself in the shining breastplate of a nearby guard. The hackles rose on her neck as she saw the cool eyes staring back at her. She quickly turned away. Even her own reflection seemed foreign to her now.

Who are you?

Casting aside the question, she looked up in time to see Quinn push open two double doors and make his way into a large hall packed with long wooden tables. Men and women were walking along the rows between the tables, and along the far wall cooks were serving food over a steel counter. Following Quinn into the dining room, several of the occupants looked up at their approach. Whispers spread around the room, giving way to a hushed silence.

Alana clenched her jaw as she felt the eyes of everyone on her. She glanced at Quinn, her mouth suddenly dry. "They know me?" she hissed beneath her breath.

"Of course," Quinn replied. "You were their teacher."

"Their…teacher?" Alana stuttered. A sudden laughter bubbled up from her chest, emerging as a half-muted snort. Struggling to control herself, she gasped the next words. "What did I *teach?*"

"Magic," Quinn said.

"Oh…" Alana trailed off. She opened her mouth, then closed it again, lost for words, struggling to comprehend what Quinn was saying. The men and women in the room were staring back at her with a mixture of awe and surprise, their silence absolute. Most wore ordinary clothing, though a few sported the red cloaks of soldiers.

Beside her, Quinn was still speaking. "Your father placed you in charge of the young Magickers. You taught them how to reach their magic, trained them to be strong enough to master it."

Alana tore herself free of her shock. "Taught them to use it? I didn't even know I had magic until an hour ago!"

"That's not true, Alana. Deep down, you know that. Look around you, this is the truth. This is who you were—and will be again!"

Shaking her head, Alana stumbled back a step. Chest tight, she wanted to scream, to tell him leave her alone, to stop with his lies, but before she could speak, a tentative voice came from behind her.

"Alana?"

Heart racing, she swung towards the voice, reaching for her sword hilt. Behind her, the young man who'd spoken jumped back. Raising his hands, he gaped at her, eyes locked to the half-drawn sword.

"Who…who are you?" she gasped.

The young man blinked and glanced over her shoulder at Quinn. His plain face was heavily tanned, and long black hair tumbled down around his shoulders. He was dressed for the cold in a plain white tunic of homespun wool and heavy black pants. Alana was sure she'd never seen him in her life.

"My apologies, young Bodrum," Quinn said, stepping up alongside her. "Alana's magic has…backfired. She has—temporarily—lost her memories. I brought her here to see if her old students could help jog them."

"Oh!" The young man turned to Alana, his mouth hanging open. Then he seemed to remember himself, and clamping his jaw shut, offered his hand. "My apologies, princess! My name is Bodrum, you were my teacher a few years back. You… taught me to master my magic over the Earth."

Still struggling to contain her own shock, Alana stared at his outstretched hand for a second too long, noticing he wore the same silver and emerald bracelets as the teacher she'd met in the gardens. Finally, she reached out and took his hand.

"It's nice to…meet you?" she said.

A grin appeared on his face. "It's good…to see you again," he said. "I…never got to thank you for your help. I did not appreciate your teaching at the time, but you…you gave me the strength I needed to survive."

Alana smiled despite herself. "I'm glad I could help you, Bodrum."

Nodding, the young man walked away. Alana made to speak with Quinn, but before she could get a word out, a young woman appeared. She smiled, words tumbling from her mouth so quickly Alana struggled to keep up. She was saying something about how long it had been since Alana had last been around the citadel, and how good it was to see her again. Alana noticed she seemed nervous, her eyes constantly flickering to Quinn, her hands deep in her pockets.

Alana hardly managed a "hello" before the woman darted off again. Another student quickly moved in to take her place. Before Alana knew it, she was stammering through explanation after explanation, even as more students gathered around to await their turn. They were all studiously polite, keeping their distance, bowing and curtseying, speaking in respectful tones and never questioning how she could have lost control of her power.

As the crowd finally started to thin, Alana found herself feeling unexpectedly alone. While every student had offered her their thanks, there was a stiffness about the way they approached her, as though they were speaking out of obligation rather than gratitude. All kept a respectful distance, offering token apologies when they discovered her predicament.

When the last of them had left, Alana could only shake her head in confusion. Their thanks had at first lifted her, yet she found herself wondering why none of them had seemed anything more than just students to her. Had she not befriended any of them, not inspired anything but respect and professional courtesy?

Hugging her arms to her chest, she turned and found Quinn watching her.

"Are you okay?" he asked.

She scowled, growing irritated by his constant concern. "I'm fine," she snapped.

He nodded, though she could see in his eyes he did not believe her. Even so, he dropped the subject and taking her arm, led her across the room to an empty table. As they seated themselves he waved to a nearby servant, sending the man scurrying across the room in search of food. A tray of roasted lamb and stewed vegetables appeared a few minutes later, followed by two tankards of ale.

"Your favourite…once," Quinn said, gesturing to the food and drink.

"I guess some things don't change." The tankard was halfway to Alana's lips when she glanced up and found Quinn watching her. A familiar flash of anger reared inside her, but remembering his earlier kindness, she pressed it down.

Hesitantly, she tilted her tankard in his direction. "Cheers."

Quinn smiled and lifting his own drink, clinked it against hers. "Cheers."

Meeting his eyes, Alana took a long swig of the bitter ale, enjoying the cool liquid in the heat of the dining hall.

"What do you think?" Quinn asked.

"It's good," Alana replied, though she knew he wasn't talking about the ale. When he only raised an eyebrow, she sighed and went on. "I don't know what to think of all this, Quinn. I'm…sorry I've been so hard on you. I know you're only trying to help but…it's just all so overwhelming."

"I know…" he began, but she raised a hand and he trailed off.

"You have to understand, just a few days ago I thought all the Magickers…captured by the Tsar were dead. And now it turns out I was *teaching* them?"

Quinn laughed at that. "Yes, I guess I can see how that would be confusing."

Alana shook her head. "I don't understand though: why haven't the people been told what happens here? About what happens to the Magickers who are brought to the citadel?"

"Because they cannot know their children live." Alana made to speak, but at a look from Quinn, closed her mouth again. After a moment he went on. "It is one of the reasons they are brought here. Once, before the Tsar, magic was ungoverned. It was chaos. Wild magic was free to wreak havoc across the Three Nations, taking lives at random. There is a legend in my hometown, about a boy who once levelled our town and brought its community to its knees. Such power cannot go unchecked."

"Yes, but that doesn't explain why you allow—"

"Please, let me finish, Alana," Quinn interrupted her. She saw the pain behind his eyes. Gritting her teeth, she nodded, and he continued. "As I was saying, before the Tsar, people with magic were free to exploit their powers, to take advantage of the powerless, to destroy the lives of others, usually without repercussions."

"The Tsar's rule has changed that. After he was crowned, he passed laws to protect the people from exploitation by Magickers. Those who used their powers to harm others were brought before his judgement, while the benevolent were allowed their freedom. It worked for a while—until a General overthrew the Trolan king and led an uprising against the Empire. Hundreds of Magickers stood with him. Their powers enacted a terrible price, and while ultimately the rebellion failed, their treachery convinced the Tsar that the price of free magic was too great."

"And so magic was outlawed. Those Magickers known to the crown were brought here and offered a choice: imprisonment, or service to the Tsar. So it has continued with every new Magicker we discover."

"But that doesn't explain why the people can't know what happens to the Magickers you capture!"

Quinn sighed. "They cannot know, because the children cannot know of their lives before this place."

"What…" Alana trailed off as realisation struck her, her stomach curdling. She stared at Quinn, open-mouthed. "I wiped their memories," she breathed.

"Yes," Quinn said solemnly. "The children are made to

forget their past, so they will never be tempted to use their magic to benefit their former families."

"No wonder you wanted me back so badly," she croaked, the words catching in her throat.

Quinn reached across the table and placed his hand on hers, but she flinched away. He looked at her, a frown on his lips. "It's more than that and you know it, Alana," he said. "Your father loves you, and your brother too. He would do anything to protect you."

"Oh?" Alana snapped, on her feet now. "Is that why he sent his dragons? Can you honestly say he wasn't trying to kill us with those beasts?"

"He was…desperate. He thought you were lost to him."

Alana swallowed. "So he ordered us killed, rather than let us escape."

"No…he only wished to stop you," Quinn said quickly. "He would never have seen you harmed, Alana."

Alana stared down at him, trying to judge the truth behind his words. She could still remember her terror as the scarlet creature dropped from the sky, still recall the searing heat of its flames, the stench of rotting meat and burning ash. Looking at Quinn now, seeing the pain in his eyes, Alana knew he would never have sent such creatures to kill her. Yet her own father had. Or was Quinn telling the truth? Had the dragons only ever been meant to stop them?

The anger left her in a rush as she slumped back into her chair. She stared at her food for a moment, the roast lamb and vegetables still untouched. Absently, she picked up a fork and began to push them around the plate. Memories swam before her eyes, of Quinn and Devon, her brother and Kellian. The faces of her students followed, one by one, and she felt the weight of guilt on her shoulders. She had stolen their families from them, robbed them of their pasts.

Who are you?

Yet even as the question rang in her mind, she found herself looking around the dining hall, watching the other Magickers as they sat together. Many wore smiles on their faces, and most seemed at peace, content with their place in life. She shivered, wondering if they could sense the hole in their lives, the abyss she had left within them. Or had her spell been a gift to them? Had her magic released them from the pain of loss, of being separated from their parents forever?

Across from her, concern lurked in Quinn's eyes. In a flash of intuition, she realised the compassion he'd shown her today had been far more than that of a servant. With the students, she had wondered why none of them had seemed to really know her, why they had been distant, indifferent to her loss. Now, as she looked at Quinn, she realised he had been the only one to show her true kindness since arriving in this cold palace. And she knew there was something more between them, something he had not yet revealed.

The question came unbidden to her lips before she could stop herself. "Who are you to me, Quinn?"

He smiled then, his eyes alight. "I am *your* teacher, Alana."

5

"Well, I'm waiting." Godrin stood with his arms crossed, eyes glowering as he watched them.

Devon studied the crossbow men standing behind the hulking crime lord, trying to judge the distance between them. On flat ground he might have risked charging Godrin, but waist-deep in the bath, there was no way he would be fast enough. Letting out a long breath, he smiled at the mobster.

"Really, is this any way to treat friends?" Kellian spoke before Devon could. Moving in front of the others, he gestured to the archers, who quickly redirected their crossbows at him.

"Friends?" Godrin spat the word like he'd swallowed poison. "Do you know how many of my countrymen lost their lives to his hammer, Kellian? To *your* blades, for that matter?"

"Eighty-six," Devon interrupted. "Now ask how many friends I lost to Trolan swords."

Godrin sneered. "They got what they deserved, as will you. If this is all the Butcher of Kalgan has to say for himself…"

"My friend, please, do not be so hasty!" Kellian cut in. Holding up his hands, he continued smoothly. "We did not come here to rehash the past, though no doubt we could debate for hours who was responsible for the war. No, we came to talk of the future, of a chance for Trola to regain its former glory."

The man froze at Kellian's words, his eyes narrowing. "And how exactly do two Plorsean rebels propose to accomplish such a task?"

"By bringing down the Tsar, and the Empire with him."

"Ha! You must think me a fool, Kellian. Do you think you can tempt Trola into a war it cannot possibly hope to win? We would be crushed in the first battle. And then where would my people be? The Tsar would slaughter or enslave the survivors. Trola would truly be doomed."

"I took you for an intelligent man, Godrin. Can you not see that Trola is doomed regardless? You hardly have the people to till the fields or man your ships, and any progress you make is crippled by the Tsar's taxes. How long before your people starve? Two years? Three?"

"We are Trolans. We will survive."

"You will die as paupers in your own country," Kellian snapped. He paused, and a sly smile spread across his lips. "Or you can join us, and fight for your freedom."

"I will not drag my people into another war."

"Who said anything about a war?" Kellian retorted.

"How else do you intend to free us from the Empire?"

"By assassinating the Tsar. Without his magic, without the dragons and demons, the Empire would be sundered. Trola and Lonia could be free once more. Northland would support you, send aid to your freedom fighters, as your nations once did for them."

Godrin stared at them, lips pursed, expression unreadable. Then he began to laugh, softly at first but quickly growing louder, until the sound of his mirth echoed from the stone walls. "Assassinate the Tsar?" he gasped. "A brilliant plan—if not for, how did you put it, the magic, demons and dragons that protect him!"

"Enala believes there is a way to defeat him—if we can get close enough to the man."

"Then the old woman has finally lost her mind," Godrin snapped, the laughter dying in his throat, "and anyone mad enough to believe her is a fool."

"Fools we might be," Devon said, wading up alongside Kellian, "but at least we're not cowards, wallowing in the former glory of a fallen city."

"What did you say to me?" Godrin hissed, lurching forward. Behind him, the archers raised their crossbows. The steel points of the loaded bolts glittered in the lantern light.

Ignoring the weapons pointed at his chest, Devon laughed. "You heard me! I called you a coward, Godrin. You're nothing but a washed-up commander, using your power to prey on the same people you claim to care about, to terrorize the same citizens who once looked to you for protection. You call me a butcher, but at least I never betrayed my own people!"

"Terrorize…betray…" A vein bulged on Godrin's forehead as he sputtered out the words. "How…dare…you?"

Devon took another step forward, his voice dropping to a whisper. "Tell me, Godrin, how did you survive the battle for Kalgan? I know for a *fact* the Tsar burned everyone in the city to death. So how did an entire *cohort* survive?"

Baring his teeth, Godrin stepped forward, so that he stood eye-to-eye with Devon. "We ran," he spat. "I told the King the war was lost, that we had no choice but to surrender ourselves to the Tsar's mercy. He refused. So I took my cohort, along with any citizens who would follow us, and commandeered a ship. The city fell two days later, but we were already gone."

"So you left your comrades to die?"

"Yes," Godrin said quietly, his eyes flashing, "and I would do it again. Because of me, there is still order in Kalgan.

Without my men, the city would still be a wasteland, a battle-field to be fought over by the survivors."

"Or you might have tipped the balance for Kalgan, saved the city from destruction."

"Do not mock me, Devon," Godrin replied. "We were both there. You know there was never a chance. The Tsar had already destroyed most of our forces in the Brunei Pass. The city was doomed from the moment the Tsar marched across the border."

A strained silence fell across the baths then, as the two warriors stared at one another. Devon was close enough to reach Godrin now. One quick rush, and he could use the man as a shield against the archers, giving his friends a chance to flee. But he made no move to attack. Instead, he reached out and placed a hand on the man's shoulder.

"I cannot change the past, my friend," he said, "but for what it's worth, I am sorry for what became of your people, and the part I played in it. It is a regret I will carry with me forever."

Godrin bowed his head, and Devon felt a shudder go through the former soldier. "Why are you here, butcher?" he whispered at the steaming waters. "And do not entertain me with tales of freedom and toppling empires."

Sucking in a breath, Devon glanced at Kellian. His friend shook his head, but when Devon returned his gaze to the Trolan warrior, the lie he had planned turned to dust on his tongue. "To rescue a…friend," he said instead.

Chuckling, the man straightened. "And for this friend you would go against the might of the Tsar?"

Devon grinned. "What's the point of being friends if you wouldn't walk through hell for one another?"

Godrin stared at him for a moment, the hate still lurking behind his eyes. Taking a breath, Devon moved alongside the man and sat on the stone bench running the length of the pool, exposing his back to the archers.

"You are a strange man, butcher," the former General said.

"If we are to be friends, I would prefer to be called Devon," he replied.

"Devon…" Godrin said, a pained look on his face. He shook his head. "I'm beginning to regret entertaining this meeting. I should have had my guards cut your throats and toss you in the harbour."

"And doomed your people to a slow extinction," Kellian interrupted.

"Perhaps, but they still would have thanked me for it." He started to laugh. "As it is, if word gets out you left my bath-house alive, my own days will be numbered."

"Then you're not going to kill us?" Quiet until now, Betran burst into life. "Thank you, sir!"

Godrin stared at the young man for a moment, his eyes dark. "Betran." He said the man's name like a curse. "Don't think I've forgotten your part in this."

Betran shrank before the former General's gaze, retreating into the pool until he almost vanished into the steam. Shaking his head, Godrin turned his attention back to Devon and Kellian.

Kellian spread his hands. "You didn't answer the man's question."

"And you have not told me how you plan to rescue this friend of yours. Or how you think you can kill the Tsar."

"He is not the all-knowing, all-powerful immortal he would have you believe, Godrin," Kellian insisted.

"No?" Godrin asked.

"No," Kellian replied, "because we're still here. He sentenced the two of us to death, sent his Stalkers and demons and dragons to hunt us down, and yet here we are. Is that not enough to make you curious?"

Godrin stared at the two of them a long while, his hands trailing in the waters to either side of him, as though weighing up their fates. Devon's patience finally snapped.

"Look, sonny," he growled. Pushing himself to his feet, he climbed from the pool. The archers bristled, the crossbows rattling in their grip. Contemptuously he turned his back on them and glared down at the crime lord. "It's been a long night and my bed is calling. If you're going to try and kill us, get it over with. But I promise you, I don't die easily." He turned and glared at the two bowmen. They took a collective step back.

"You're a bold man, Devon," Godrin growled.

"Bold? Not really." Devon laughed, the sound booming from the stone walls. "Reckless, maybe. A few weeks ago I thought my time had finally come, but Alana and her brother saved me. I owe her for that. Now, are you going to help us, or not?"

Godrin's face was grim, his eyes hard, but suddenly his face split, and he threw back his head and laughed. "By the Three Gods, I think I could have liked you, Devon. If you hadn't marched with an army into my country and slaughtered my people, we might have been friends. As it is, I think that I will help you. You're right, the Tsar is not immortal. It's time we proved it. I'll march with you to Ardath. I have contacts there, might be they know a way into the citadel."

"We'll be glad for the company," Devon replied. He glanced behind him at the bowmen, who had finally lowered their weapons. "Hope you'll be leaving your friends behind, though."

Climbing from the water, Godrin offered his hand, which Devon took in his meaty grip. "What was your plan if I'd refused?"

"Kill you, and anyone else that got in my way. March up to the gates of the citadel and demand Alana's return." Devon shrugged. "I like to keep things simple."

Godrin blinked, his eyes showing surprise for the first time. Twisting, he looked down at Kellian, who was still in the pool with Betran. "He's not serious?"

Kellian smiled. "Devon is the most stubborn man I've ever met." Climbing from the bath, he joined them. "Luckily for him, he usually has the strength to back up his words."

Shaking his head, the Trolan looked from Kellian to Devon.

Devon grinned. "Admittedly, General, I'm hoping you have a better plan."

𝕊 6 𝕊

Q uinn paused outside the giant oak doors to the throne room and took a moment to collect himself. The day had been long and strained, beginning with Alana's precipitous plunge from the balcony. Remembering her tumbling backwards over the railing, he suppressed a shudder. In that instant he had thought her lost, but unexpectedly, his magic had come to her rescue. As his heart had lurched in his chest, his magic had rushed from him, drawing in the air currents and wrapping them around Alana.

It was an ability he had not known he'd possessed, though he had heard rumours of Storm Magickers who could fly with the winds. Either way, it had saved Alana, and by extension himself. He shuddered, imagining the Tsar's rage if his daughter had succeeded in taking her own life. No, had Alana died, Quinn's life would have been forfeit—and it would not have been an easy death.

Still, it had worked out in the end. The shock of her near-death experience seemed to have snapped Alana out of her depression—at least long enough for Quinn to talk with her. Reticent as she was, it was difficult to tell whether he'd succeeded in getting through, but she had at least seemed calmer when he'd left her.

He smiled then, remembering their fiery argument in the dining hall. However much Alana fought against it, he could see much of his former student in the young woman. As they'd spoken he'd caught glimpses of the Alana he'd known—of her calculating mind and dogged determination to hunt out the truth. And at the end, the fire in her eyes when she'd accused the Tsar of trying to kill her...he could have been looking into the past, when they'd spent long afternoons arguing over the best methods of tutoring young Magickers.

Letting out a long breath, Quinn pulled himself back to the present. He nodded to the royal guards stationed outside, and one pushed open the doors. Squaring his shoulders, Quinn marched after him, while inside the throne room the guard announced his arrival.

"Your majesty, Lieutenant Quinn has arrived."

Beyond the doors, the throne room was empty but for the ring of guards surrounding the dais. Ignoring the man who'd announced him, Quinn strode across the room, his footsteps muffled by the line of red carpet leading up to the throne. The guards at the base of the dais parted as he approached. Striding up the steps, he dropped to one knee.

"Lieutenant, Krista tells me you have been showing my daughter her former pupils." The Tsar's voice came from the throne, soft and dangerous.

His mouth dry, Quinn swallowed. "She was...upset. I thought it best to show her some of her former life."

"Did I not tell you she was to be left alone?"

Quinn climbed to his feet. He stared into the Tsar's crystal blue eyes, seeking some hint of emotion, but the man's expression remained unreadable. Though not a tall man, the Tsar was powerfully built. His jet-black hair was streaked with grey, but he showed no other outward sign of aging. He had first been crowned King of Plorsea some fifty years ago, yet he looked no older than forty, and not for the first time, Quinn found himself wondering at the man's true age.

"With respect, sir," Quinn began, clearing his throat, "if I had not acted, she would now be dead."

The Tsar did not move, but Quinn thought he detected a slight tremor to the man's brow. "Explain."

"She...threw herself from the balcony," Quinn said in a rush. "I was just in time to catch her with my magic. But afterwards, I thought it best to...take precautions as to her state of mind. I showed her the gardens and children, then took her to the Magicker's quarters, introduced her to some of her former students. She...seemed to...take the new...information well." He stammered to a stop beneath the withering glare of the Tsar.

A strained silence hung in the air, and Quinn found himself shrinking before the man on the throne, as though his very essence was being drawn from him. Clenching his jaw, he forced himself to look into the icy eyes.

"You overstep yourself, Lieutenant," the Tsar said. He paused, and a smile spread across his face. "But you have done well. Again, I find myself in your debt."

Quinn bowed his head. "It was my pleasure, sir," he said. "You know I have always been...fond...of your daughter."

A soft chuckle echoed from the tall marble walls. "If she can be saved, perhaps she will finally return the affection."

Heat spread across Quinn's cheeks, and clearing his throat, he changed the subject. "What about your son? Have you heard anything from the Queen?"

"My spies tell me he lives," the Tsar replied, "but my emissary has not yet reached their capital."

"He will be returned," Quinn said. "She will not dare risking war for a single boy."

"No, though she would dearly love to defy me." The Tsar chuckled. "How are preparations proceeding for the invasion?"

"You have a force of ten thousand foot soldiers and two thousand cavalry gathering on the northern shores of the lake. Half the guard have already been shifted into their wartime regiments. In addition, you have a force of almost a hundred Magickers trained in warfare, and a dozen demons at your command. As you know, only three Red Dragons remain under your control. They have not fared well in captivity."

The Tsar waved a hand. "Should we need more, I will fetch them from Dragon Country," he growled, though his smile did not waver. "So we are ready to march?"

Quinn hesitated. "Within the week, I think," he said. "Your generals tell me they still need time to organise provisions, and restore war time discipline to the troops."

"No matter," the Tsar replied, "it gives us time to secure the release of my son. Once he has been returned, Northland will fall, and there will be nowhere left for the treacherous Magickers to flee."

"What of the priest who attacked me? If the Queen has more Magickers of such power—"

"There are no more like her," the Tsar said, cutting him off. He rose to his feet. "And I will see her dead before the end. Now be gone, Quinn. After her…adventures today, perhaps it's time I visited my daughter."

A lana paced across her room, her thoughts far away, lingering on memories that hovered just beyond reach. Fog swamped her, but through it she could sense the truth, taunting her with its unseen knowledge. Without it, she felt helpless, forced to trust Quinn's words. And trust had never come easily for her.

Or had it?

Confused and frustrated, she slumped down onto a velvet sofa.

"It's impossible," she murmured to the empty room.

Anger flared in her then, feeding strength to her weary body. Determined, she sat up, seeking another way. Quinn had told her that only she could unlock the secrets of her mind, but without her power she had no way of doing so. She gritted her teeth at the impossibility of the task set before her.

Yet she knew there had to be a way.

Then she remembered the ancient Tillie, and how she'd begun teaching Braidon meditation to control his power. Alana had attempted it herself, and found herself surprisingly adept at the exercise. An image flared in her mind, of the angry ball of red she'd discovered within while in the trance. She shivered, imagining it inside her, its twisting tendrils tied in unending knots, and the secret hidden within.

Could that be where she'd hidden her memories?

Alana sucked in a breath. Meditation was dangerous for those with magic—she had seen as much with her brother. Tillie had warned them what happened to those who lost control, that magic could overwhelm its user and take control. But what other choice did she have but to try? There was no other way—she had to find what lay hidden within that ball of light.

Besides, she knew now how she'd mastered the exercise so quickly, why her brother had progressed much faster than Tillie had expected: they had done it before, in another life. When they'd entered the trance, their subconsciousness had taken over, propelling them into the depths of their minds as they had apparently done so many times before.

Lowering herself to the floor, Alana closed her eyes. She focused on the rise and fall of her chest, the soft whistle of each inhalation, the thumping of blood through her veins. Memories drifted in and out of focus: of Devon, *kanker* in hand, as he fought the demon; then his face in the darkness, as they spoke of their past, and future, on the plains south of Fort Fall; and finally, the racing of her heart as his arms wrapped around her in the midnight pools.

Alana released her breath. The air slowly emptied from her lungs, and with it the thoughts of Devon drifted away. Darkness swelled, before her brother's smiling face shimmered into view. Terror gnawed at her stomach as she watched him fall, a crossbow bolt in his stomach. Quinn insisted he still lived, that the wound had not been fatal, and had been healed. Despite her mistrust, she clung to that hope. The thought of her brother free gave her strength.

Concentrating, she turned her thoughts back to her breath,

imagining the air flowing through her, filling her chest and arms, her legs and head. Strength flowed into her weary body, swirling and growing, even as her consciousness expanded. Beyond herself, she sensed tremors of power twisting on the air. Instinctively she knew it was the workings of other Magickers within the citadel.

Her curiosity was piqued, but there would be time for that later. Turning from the vibrations, she forced her mind inwards, and suddenly found herself floating amidst an infinite darkness.

Alana shivered as she looked around, utterly alone amidst the black. Not a spark shone amidst the dark, not a star or candle to light the way—until she turned and saw the distant spark of red.

The sight did nothing to quell her fear. Instead it grew, swelling until it was all she could manage not to go fleeing back to the confines of her body.

Are you ready, Alana?

Quinn's words echoed through the void, and she saw again the way he'd looked at her in the dining hall.

I was your teacher, Alana.

His words had rung true, yet she sensed there was more, something he had not revealed. A part of her yearned to scream at him, to demand the answers he continued to with-hold. Yet she knew now the only way she'd ever unravel the lies and half-truths was to restore her memories.

To do that, she would need to face the terror within.

Releasing a breath, Alana concentrated on the speck of red. Fear still clung to her soul, but gathering herself, she drove towards it, racing through the darkness like a fish through an endless ocean. The light appeared before her, growing larger, clearer, until it loomed like a sun, flickering from red to orange to raging blue.

She hovered before it, sensing the emotions radiating out

from the tangled knots, the hidden thing lurking within. She touched her spirit hand to a thread. A wave of hatred swept through her. For a second Alana thought she would drown in it, but closing her eyes, she allowed it to wash over her. Slowly it dissipated, like a wave crashing on a sandy shore.

As the hatred faded, Alana took hold of another string and sent it whirling out into the darkness. This time it was fear that touched her, piercing her core, adding fuel to her mounting terror. She clenched her teeth and fought on, turning the ball with her mind, determined to unwrap the convoluted emotions and reveal the mystery inside.

Time passed, and the ball grew smaller, spinning faster. Flecks of light shot off into the darkness, where they drifted like stars, flashing red and orange before finally vanishing as though they'd never been.

Finally, she sensed the end was near. Only a few strands remained now, though when she reached out to pull them clear, she felt a new wave of terror strike her. More powerful than anything that had come before, it overwhelmed her. With a scream, her spirit turned in the darkness, preparing to flee.

Are you ready, Alana?

The question came again—and this time, she found her answer.

Yes!

Crying out in triumph, Alana pulled the last strands clear.

The red bindings went flashing out into the void, and a new light bathed Alana. In that second, Alana knew she'd made a terrible mistake. It was not her memories hidden amidst the tangled emotions, nor the woman she'd once been; it was the magic that had stolen them away.

Now it reared up before her, its glow not the red or orange or blue of her emotions, but the deepest green of the Earth. Terror froze Alana in place as the magic reared back on itself, twisting and morphing, its cries of release echoing through the darkness.

Alana watched as a dread Feline took shape, its giant maw open wide, its claws stretching out to engulf her tiny spirit. Pain sliced through Alana at their touch, unlike anything she'd ever experienced. She opened her mouth to scream, but in the void her cries went unheard. Agony engulfed her, driving away her strength, crushing her spirit. She found herself falling, even as the beast rose, tearing her soul from her body and flinging her into the darkness.

Back in her room, Alana's eyes flickered open, but it was no longer Alana who looked out. A soft glow bathed the carpets as the grey of her irises gave way to green. As though by a will of its own, her head turned, the magic within gazing out at its surroundings. An awful smile touched her lips, and laughter whispered from her throat.

Slowly, tentatively, her body stood, the magic in control now. Finding its balance, it strode to the outer doors and threw them open. Two men stood guard outside. Their eyes widened at her appearance, the green glow of her eyes lighting the corridor.

"Princess?" one asked.

The magic did not reply, but stepped in close and placed a hand to the man's chest. At its touch, his eyes glazed over, and before his companion could react he drew his sword and drove it into his comrade's chest. Crying out, the dying man fell back, clawing at the bloody wound.

The magic laughed as the guard died, his screams echoing loudly in the narrow corridor. Then the magic turned its gaze on the other. Immediately, the man reversed his blade and drove it into his own stomach.

Elation swept through Alana's body as the magic started down the corridor. Within, its power was spreading, harrying the spirit of the girl who'd dared command it. Power burned through the girl's veins, magic joining with blood. Within, it could feel the girl's strength fading, the flames closing on her spirit.

In the corridor, two men came running, drawn by the screams of their fellow guards. Seeing their princess, they staggered to a stop, mouths wide as they stared at the dead men behind her.

A touch to their chests, and the two began to hack at each other with their swords. They died screaming as the magic continued on, its power growing, spreading out beyond its mortal host. When the next men came into view, it no longer needed to touch them. One look into the girl's emerald eyes, and they turned and leapt on the guards who came close behind them.

"*Alana!*"

The magic spun as a voice came from behind it. A man stood in the corridor, a glowing sword in one hand, his face hard as granite.

"Alana!" he called again.

Somewhere deep within, Alana heard her name echo through the void. Turning, she saw a blinding light shining in the darkness. At its touch, her fear fell away, and she saw the awful green retreat. She shuddered, clinging to it like a lifeline in stormy seas. Her name came again, echoing through her consciousness, feeding her strength. She clambered upwards, fighting back the claws and teeth of the awful Feline.

In the hallway, the man advanced, glowing sword held tightly in one hand. It flashed once, then again, the glowing green of Alana's magic falling back before it. His jaw was set, his blue eyes flashing with untold power. Yet still the green light shone from Alana's eyes.

"Alana!" he called again, despair in his voice now. "Come back to me!"

Within, Alana heard the call. Gathering her strength, she

tore herself free of the last bindings trapping her in the dark. With a scream, she shot towards the white, as the beast roared its frustration. The green flickered around her, its grip on her body loosening. She could hear her name echoing from all around her now, and she followed it like a beacon, reaching out, grasping it with all her strength…

Alana gasped as she found herself suddenly back in her own body. Shuddering, she staggered sideways into a wall. The strength went from her legs and she slid to the floor, her eyes falling on the bloodstained carpets, on the broken bodies lying nearby. Her throat contracted as she struggled to breathe. Slowly, she toppled sideways to the floor, unable to even lift a hand.

Staring up at the gold inlaid ceiling, Alana groaned as agony spread through her limbs. Darkness swirled at the edges of her vision, as from somewhere nearby she heard her name called once more.

Teeth clenched, she fought to remain conscious. Overhead, the face of the Tsar appeared, his brow creased in concern. "Alana," he said, his voice shaking. "You're back. You're safe."

Alana tried to reply, to ask what had happened to her, but her mouth would not open. The pain spread as her muscles cramped. Her vision turned to red, and she would have screamed, had any part of her body been able to move.

"Be calm," the Tsar said, sounding calmer himself now. Reaching down, he gently closed her eyelids. "You're safe now. Sleep."

At his words, a soft white swirled in Alana's mind. The pain faded and the darkness rose to claim her. This time, she surrendered to it without a fight.

❧ 8 ❧

Braidon shivered as he followed Enala out into the shimmering light of dawn. Blinking, it was several moments before the world clicked back into focus. The air outside was crisp and cold, and he found himself standing in a narrow box canyon, stretching only a few hundred feet in either direction. Behind them, the familiar stairs wound their way up the granite cliff-face to the other tunnels.

On the cliff facing them, however, there was only one opening, though it was as large as all the others combined. Huge marble columns lined the entrance, supporting the intricately carved façade. Three small ledges had been cut into the stone surrounding the cave mouth, each supporting a statue of blue marble. In the centre stood a towering man, hair long and eyes distant. Another man stood alongside him, while on the right stood a woman, her face strangely familiar.

Braidon frowned, studying the statue, trying to place the woman. But Enala was already disappearing into the cave mouth, and shaking himself free of his curiosity, Braidon followed her.

Inside, he paused again, though the darkness wasn't as

great as he'd expected. A thousand candles sparkled within, and he couldn't help but marvel at the size of the cavern he found himself in. A scarlet carpet stretched down the centre of the polished stone floors, terminating some fifty feet away in three large alters.

On either side of the cavern, the rows of stone columns from outside continued, holding up the vaulted ceiling, where an artwork of stunning scale had been painted. At the end of the room he recognised the three figures from the statues outside. Here though, they were bathed in light—green and blue and white—and he realised now they were depictions of the Three Gods. Light flew from their outstretched hands, over hordes of painted men, women, and monsters, to strike a singular figure depicted above the entranceway.

Braidon swallowed as he looked on the likeness of Archon. Black magic swathed his slim body, his pale face and dark eyes looking across at the Gods, alight with hatred. Averting his eyes, Braidon looked around the rest of the room, glimpsing tiny alcoves and other statues. Rugs covered the stone floor, and here, men and women knelt in silence, their eyes fixed to the altars at the front of the room.

"What is this place?" he found himself asking.

"A shrine to the Three Gods," came Enala's reply. "After the fall of Archon, the Northerners had it built here, at what was once the heart of his power, to celebrate their freedom."

"I thought the people of Northland fought *for* Archon."

"They did," Enala said sadly. "But not all did so willingly. Though they were descendants of the banished, the people here were never the true enemy. They only wanted what was best for their families, for an escape from the vile creatures that stalked their land, from the wasteland that was this nation."

"It doesn't look like such a wasteland now."

Enala smiled. "Before the Gods departed, they spent much of their time in Northland, healing the land of Archon's

magic, driving the monsters back into their holes. After their…
disappearance, the kings and queens of the Three Nations
continued their work."

"That was how they built Erachill?"

"No. Erachill has always been here, though it was hidden
from the peoples of the Three Nations for centuries. Even now,
few know of its existence, since most trade with the Three
Nations is conducted on the coast. It is the final bastion of the
northern people, carved from the mountains where their
ancestors first took refuge from the beasts."

Braidon shivered, thinking of the terror the people must
have felt then, forging a new life for themselves in the barren
lands. From what he'd seen there was little fertile land even
now, with much of the northern continent full of towering
mountains and harsh steppes.

"Take off your shoes." Enala said, pointing to his boots,
then to a pile of shoes beside the entranceway.

Noticing she'd already removed hers, Braidon quickly
followed suit. With that done, Enala led him across the room to
a quiet rug in front of one of the altars. Sitting beside her,
Braidon glanced at the altar, noticing the vines and strange
creatures carved into the stone.

"Why is the temple dedicated to all three of them?" he
asked, nodding at the Three Gods depicted overhead.

"Why not?" Enala smiled. "The Northerners saw the truth
at the final battle of Fort Fall. Separate, the Gods could do
little to halt Archon's reign—it was only when they came
together that he was defeated."

"What really happened back then?" Braidon asked, still
studying the mural on the ceiling. "There are so many tales
now, no one seems to know the truth. I thought it was you and
your brother who destroyed Archon, with swords the Gods had
imbued with their powers."

Chuckling, Enala shook her head. "Perhaps it seemed that

way to some," she replied, "but no, we played little part in the end. It was the Gods themselves who cast Archon into the earth, finally destroying him."

"And what about you, Enala? How did you come to be here? You were a legend, a hero amongst our people. But you and your brother, you disappeared."

Enala sighed. "After we…returned, my brother and I were supposed to be the heirs to the Trolan throne. But after everything we'd been through, we didn't want it. Eric left with Inken for southern Plorsea. I married my love, Gabriel, and eventually followed them. Together, the four of us made our home in a forest far from the outside world, and for a time, we were happy. Sometimes a king, queen or council would send emissaries, asking for our help with some problem or another, but for the most part we kept to ourselves. They were good years. It wasn't until my thirtieth birthday that I began to realise something was different. That Gabriel was aging, while I was not."

Braidon watched the lines on Enala's face deepen, her eyes beginning to shimmer. He said nothing, but reached out and squeezed her wrinkled arm. She nodded, a smile brightening her face, and went on.

"He was nearing sixty when his heart gave out. By then, I only looked like a woman in her thirties. After his death, our home was no longer the same, and I returned to civilisation, but there was almost no one left who remembered me. I was a remnant, a relic from a time long since passed, when Gods and Archon strode the land. So I left, took my sorrows and wandered the lands beyond the Three Nations."

"Did you not have children?" Braidon asked.

"We had a son, a year after Inken and Eric gave birth to a boy of their own. They were fast friends, but I learned long ago a life of isolation is not for the young. They left when they were still in their teens, and forged lives of their own. By the time I returned...I thought it best not to interfere with what they had built for themselves."

"And so you came to Northland?"

"Eventually. It was here that I finally found a people who had need of my...skills. I made a new life for myself in the northern wilderness, slaying creatures and helping to make the land safe. With other Magickers, we finished the work the Gods had started, lifting curses from the land, bringing rain and prosperity."

"While the Tsar conquered the Three Nations," Braidon murmured.

"Yes." At his words, Enala's eyes had taken on a haunted look. She grew very still, and when she spoke, her voice was little more than a whisper. "He wasn't always like that, you know. The leaders of the Three Nations raised him up as a peace bringer, to unite their troubled peoples. The laws he passed seemed just, placing limits on how magic could be used, on the harm it was capable of."

"But he changed?"

"Perhaps," Enala replied, "or perhaps we only saw the truth too late. He always hated magic. I wonder now, whether those early days were part of some greater plan."

"Why does he hate magic?" Braidon whispered. "He is a Magicker himself."

"No," Enala replied, "he was not born with the gift."

"But...that's not possible. The Tsar is the most powerful Magicker in the Three Nations!"

"Yes. But he found another way..."

Braidon sat in stunned silence for a moment. "How?" he finally managed to gasp.

Enala did not answer immediately. She sat looking up at the painting of the Gods, the lines on her face making her look all of her hundred plus years. When she finally spoke, Braidon jumped, his heart beginning to race.

"He came to me once, in happier days, before Gabriel had passed. He wanted to know more about our tale, about what had truly happened during the days of Archon. He asked me what became of the old king of Trola, whose magic had been devoured by Archon's curse."

"What are you talking about, Enala? Which king?"

"King Jonathan," she murmured. "The traitor king, who would have doomed us all to regain his magic. He tried to steal mine, took me to Witchcliffe and tried to rip it from my dying body. Eric stopped him."

Braidon swallowed. A pit had opened up in his stomach, but he forced himself to ask the question. "What does any of this have to do with the Tsar?"

Enala's ancient eyes turned on him, and he saw the pain there, the weight of regret. "The Tsar was not born of magic. All the power he has, he tore it from the broken shells of other Magickers."

A terrible silence fell over the temple. Looking around, Braidon saw the other worshipers had vanished, leaving them alone in the great hall. He shivered, his breath coming in ragged bursts as he thought of all those Magickers who'd been taken before the Tsar. Had he truly murdered them all to feed on their magic?

But if that was the truth…

"Why did no one stop him?" The question tore from his lips, echoing loudly in the hall, growing louder, until it seemed an accusation, hurled into the face of the woman who'd saved him.

"They tried," Enala whispered, "but it was already too late. My brother was the last to face him. Had I known what he intended to do, we could have faced him together. Instead, Eric stood alone against the darkness of the Tsar."

"What happened to him?" Braidon breathed.

"He died."

❧ 9 ❧

Devon's teeth rattled in his skull as the horse trotted along beneath him, its two-beat gait sending vibrations up his spine. He'd never been much of a rider, and a dull ache was already growing in the small of his back. Resettling himself in the saddle, he eased back on the reins, slowing the beast to a walk.

Three days had passed since the meeting in the bathhouse, and now the mountains of the Brunei Pass stretched high above them, their white-capped peaks glistening in the afternoon sun. Away to his right, the Onslow River raced past, its white waters surging over unseen rocks and boulders. The land around them was barren but for a few scraggly bushes, the cliffs to either side stretching up over five hundred feet. Any army passing between Trola and Plorsea had to venture through this gorge—and many thousands had died over the centuries in battle for its possession.

Now though, it belonged to the Tsar and the Empire, the old borders drawn between the Three Nations little more than remnants of a time long passed.

Devon sighed as the riders in the lead picked up the pace.

Urging his horse after them, he thought of the road ahead. The last time he'd passed this way had been at the end of the war, when the triumphant Plorsean army had marched home. It had been a stark contrast to his first passage through, when every inch of ground had been paid for in the blood of fallen soldiers.

Looking at the land now, he could almost hear the screams, smell the blood, see the anguish on the faces of the dying. Shivering, he realised his hand was clenched around *kanker*. The great warhammer rested on his pommel, the runes carved into its steel head shining in the afternoon sun. Its elm haft was smooth in his hand, comforting, but he forced himself to release it. Their Trolan companions were hostile enough as it was, without him brandishing the weapon that had killed so many of their comrades.

He turned his gaze back to the horsemen riding ahead of him. Despite Devon's suggestion, Godrin had brought along five of his own men. They said little, other than to voice their disgust at riding with Plorsean soldiers. Devon couldn't blame them, but he'd seen the hurt in Kellian's eyes. The man was used to being liked—it was part of the reason he'd opened an inn after his retirement—and their hatred did not sit well with him.

Devon smiled as he watched his friend. Kellian was riding between Godrin and the young Trolan, Betran. After their meeting in the bathhouse, when the crime lord had told them of the men he'd be bringing with him, Devon had offered the man another Gold Libra to accompany them as far as Ardath. Despite the loss of his brother during the war, the young man had proven more than trustworthy, and Devon had a feeling another loyal sword wouldn't go amiss on the long journey to Ardath.

Ahead, Kellian looked back. They shared a glance, and his friend pulled back on his reins and rode back to join him.

Devon kicked his horse forward and they fell in step together, a dozen paces behind the Trolans.

"I don't like it," Kellian said, his words muffled by the *click* of steel-shod hooves on rock. "I don't trust Godrin, certainly not his men. He could be leading us into a trap."

"If he'd wanted us dead, he'd have killed us back in the bathhouse, old friend," Devon replied reasonably. "Besides, if he plans to betray us, he should have brought more men." He rested his hand on *kanker* with a grim smile.

Kellian rolled his eyes. "You're growing arrogant in your old age, Devon," he snorted. "Even with Betran, we're still outnumbered two to one."

"We faced worse odds in Fort Fall," Devon said.

"And if not for Enala, we would have died," Kellian snapped. "Anyway, he doesn't need to fight us. We're riding for Ardath—if he wishes, he could deliver us straight into the Tsar's hands. Did you think of that?"

Devon shrugged. "It crossed my mind. But I don't see what other choice we have. Without his contacts, we have no way of reaching the citadel, let alone getting inside. Our faces are known in Ardath, we wouldn't make it through the gates without being spotted."

"I have contacts of my own," Kellian growled, but when Devon raised an eyebrow, he only shook his head. "You're right, though, they couldn't get us through the gates—maybe into the citadel if we were lucky. But I still don't like it."

"Enala trusts him, remember," Devon added. "If Godrin had betrayed her, the Tsar would have known she was alive before Fort Fall."

Kellian sighed. "You're right, of course. Still, it just seems wrong, trusting the Trolans. What reason do they have to help us?"

"Freedom," Devon murmured, his eyes sweeping out over the canyon. They fell silent for a moment, remembering the final battle, the surging of men and horses, the crackling of magic and the clash of steel.

"Remember when the Trolan's broke?" Kellian asked suddenly. Devon nodded, and Kellian went on. "I thought it was done then, that the Tsar would sue for peace with Trola, and we'd return home."

"If only."

Kellian chuckled. "If only. Now there's the two most useless words, if ever I heard them. If only he'd sued for peace. If only we'd defied him. If only the Gods would return."

"You're in a cheerful mood this evening," Devon said dryly. He trailed off, his mind turning to Kellian's last statement. "You ever wonder what happened to them?" he asked finally.

"The Gods?" Kellian replied. He shrugged. "Probably got tired of settling our childish bickering."

Devon's laughter echoed from the cliffs. At last he shook his head, his mirth dying away. "Perhaps they'll return when the Three Nations are finally at peace. Either way, we're on our own now. Not much point dwelling on the past."

"I disagree," his friend said. "There is *every* point wondering about the past, about the way the world has changed since the departure of the Gods. They say the days before Archon were a golden age, that the Gods ruled over the Three Nations as though we were all one people."

"Ay, and now we have the Tsar."

"He is the most powerful Magicker the world has seen since Archon," Kellian agreed. "But many would consider him a force for good. Has there not, largely, been peace since he united the Three Nations?"

"Until the civil war," Devon grunted.

"Ay, we have seen the darkness he wields over men and women. But remember, back in Plorsea, he is still seen as the saviour, the man that prevented a Trolan army from marching on our homeland. The atrocities we committed in his name took place far away. They are nothing but tales and rumours to them, easily forgiven. Especially when seen through the lens of peace."

Devon fell silent, his heart heavy with remembered guilt. "I will not forget them, nor forgive myself for what I did."

"Nor I," Kellian said, "but how do we make them see? And even if we win, without the Gods, how do we prevent another such tyrant coming to power?"

"We fight," Devon said, resting his hand easily on the head of his hammer. "Whether we can win or not doesn't matter, so long as we make a stand. You said 'if only' is nothing but useless words. I agree. But when we marched on Trola, when we sacked their cities and slaughtered their inhabitants, I knew it was wrong. If only I'd made a stand then, perhaps my soul would be clean. But I did not, and while I cannot change it, I will never allow myself to fall in with such evil again. I will stand against the Tsar, even if it means my death."

"I will be with you, Devon," Kellian said, his eyes shining in the dying light. "To the end."

Silence fell at their words, so that the only sounds in the valley were the distant echoes of falling stones and the *clip-clop* of their mounts. Above, the sun disappeared behind the line of the cliffs, plunging them into shadow. They were high in the mountains now, and without the sun the temperature fell rapidly. Shivering, Devon pulled his woollen cloak tighter about himself. Ahead, the ground was still clear of snow, but despite the dry winter, the pass at the end of the valley was likely to be frozen over.

"I'd prefer to live though," Kellian added suddenly.

Devon saw his friend's face split into a grin. He raised an eyebrow. "You have a plan?"

"Call it a backup plan," Kellian said lightly. "In case *kanker* isn't as powerful as we hope."

Devon looked at the fabled hammer, his stomach tightening. He hadn't told Kellian, but Enala had come to him before they'd left. As though able to read his mind, she'd asked if he planned to use the hammer on the Tsar. When he'd nodded, she'd sighed, and told him there was little chance that such an attack would succeed. The Tsar's powers were too great—but there was no need for the others to know that.

Forcing a smile to his lips, Devon chuckled. "Only time will tell, old friend. But *kanker* has yet to see an enemy it could not best."

"You as well, Devon," Kellian added. His smile grew, and Devon felt a pinch of guilt at the deception.

Shaking it off, Devon pointed at the way ahead. "I'd say we have another three days until we reach Ardath. Want to fill me in on this plan of yours?"

"No," his friend replied, brushing a strand of black hair from his face. After the long weeks on the run, his usually well-trimmed hair now stretched halfway down his neck. "Not this time. I wouldn't want to spoil it for you."

"Ha! Well, I'm sure we won't need it. Godrin has a plan…"

"Which he also won't share," Kellian replied, his face hardening. "Whatever you say, I don't trust him…"

"And we've come full-circle," Devon cried, throwing his arms in the air with a dramatic flourish. Kellian scowled, but Devon only laughed and kicked his horse into a trot. "I'll leave you to your worries, Kellian. At this point, even the Trolans sound like better company than you!"

"Fine, but send Betran back, will you?" Kellian's voice carried after him.

Devon raised a hand to show he had heard, then directed his horse forward to where the six Trolans were riding close to the river. The men's faces darkened as he approached. He grinned, knowing each of them would rather drive a dagger through his back than fight alongside him. But then, in his short life he'd seen his fair share of friends become enemies. He saw no reason why the reverse could not happen as well.

"Betran!" he shouted as he rode up. "Kellian would like to speak with you!"

The young Trolan raised an eyebrow. "Why?"

"Didn't ask, sonny. But I'm all out of coin, so if you want your pay you'd best get down there quick."

Betran nodded, a smile on his face despite Devon's sardonic words. "He get sick of your company, big man?"

Devon laughed. "I may be broke, sonny, but I can still give you a thrashing. Now get out of here, before I pull you off that horse and teach you some manners!"

Chuckling, the Trolan tugged on the reins, turning his horse to the side of the trail to wait for Kellian to catch up. The others rode on, Godrin in the lead. Devon pulled his horse alongside the crime lord.

"So how's that plan coming along, Godrin?"

"None of your business," he snapped.

A strained silence fell across the group as they continued up the mountain trail. The sky was growing darker with each passing minute, the air colder, yet no one suggested they stop and set up camp. The men stared straight ahead, their eyes steadfastly fixed to the distant peaks. With a sigh, Devon turned his gaze to the path, and let the silence deepen.

Well, maybe not these enemies.

❧ 10 ❧

Pain dragged Alana back from the darkness. Opening her eyes, she clenched her fists and moaned, feeling the burning of her muscles in every inch of her body. It was as though she'd swum the length of Lake Ardath and returned without rest. A tremor shook her as she tried to sit up. Cramp tore into her forearms, and she collapsed back to the sheets, a scream on her lips.

Movement came from nearby and the curtains around her bed were pulled back. She flinched as the Tsar appeared at her bedside. Her stomach turned to ice, before an image flickered into her mind—of a man standing before her, glowing sword in hand, calling her back from...

Alana cried out as she sensed her magic stirring. Clutching her arms around her, she fell back on the bed, her heart thudding hard against her chest. She shook her head, feeling the glowing green beast as it slowly lifted from its slumber.

No, no, no!

"Alana!" the cool voice of the Tsar sliced through her panic. His eyes trapped her gaze as he gripped her arm. "Take a deep breath. Calm yourself!"

Still struggling for breath, Alana found herself obeying his orders without question. Exhaling, her lips quivered as she sensed the magic roiling inside her. Tears welled in her eyes, but she took another breath, seeking to calm her racing heart.

"It cannot harm you unless you touch it," the Tsar said softly, seating himself on the bed beside her. "It wants you to panic."

Alana shook her head, her fear rising once more. "It took control…"

"But you took it back!" The Tsar growled. "Even without your memories, you are my daughter still."

For the first time, she noticed the crinkles around his eyes, the warmth in his smile. Impulsively, she reached out and gripped his hand. "Thank you for saving me."

"I am your father," he said simply.

His words shook her, but this time she did not look away. "It's really true?"

He nodded, and she closed her eyes, the last of her doubt crumbling away. A fresh resolve rose within her, a need to discover the rest of the truth. But she knew now she could never do it alone—the magic would destroy her. It was like a caged animal, waiting for its moment to strike.

She looked up into the face of the Tsar—of her father. "Will you help me find myself?" she asked. "I…I can't do it alone."

The Tsar watched her for a long while, his face impassive, eyes unreadable. Finally, he nodded. "I will do what I can."

"Thank you," Alana whispered. She hesitated, still feeling the power swirling in her chest, the awful ache of her body. "Can it be now?" she added. "I can…feel it, seeking a way back. I'm afraid…"

The Tsar squeezed her fingers. "Of course. Come, let us sit on the sofa. It will be more comfortable—and more seemly."

Alana nodded and pulled herself from the bed. As her legs

took her weight, the muscles knotted and screaming, she fell against the Tsar. His powerful arms went around her waist, lifting her back up, and with his help she made it to the couch. He lowered her down and sat beside her, his eyes touched with concern.

"You are sure you wish to do this now?"

"Yes," she insisted, biting back a moan. Her hands were locked in claws, her forearms aflame. "It has to be now."

"Very well." He held out his palms. "Take my hands, and we will face the beast together."

A shudder ran down Alana's spine as the image of the green Feline formed in her mind. "I...I don't know if I can!" The words tumbled from her in a rush. Tears formed in her eyes, but she blinked them back.

"I will be beside you." The Tsar's voice was calm, powerful, and she found herself drawing strength from it.

Taking a deep, shuddering breath, Alana nodded. "Okay."

Before she could lose her nerve, she closed her eyes and began to breathe rhythmically. As she meditated, the Tsar took her hands in his own. Warmth spread from her fingertips and along her arms, expanding to wrap around her chest. At its touch, the fear left her. Anger rose to replace it, a rage at her own weakness, at her failing to master the power within her.

She was Alana, and she feared nothing!

The tangled threads of emotion were gone now, torn asunder by her meddling. Without the cage to bind it, her magic was free, its green fire flickering amidst the void. It rose before her, the Feline taking shape as an awful roar shook her consciousness, sending cracks through her newfound courage.

Fire burning in her heart, Alana faced the beast. It padded towards her, its claws spread, extending to grasp her. But now she felt no fear, no terror of approaching death. Only anger that this creature should think her prey.

As the beast approached, it started to shrink, each step

seeming to take from its power. When it finally reached her, the Feline was no longer a monster, but a kitten, tiny and impotent. Smiling at its weakness, Alana reached down and lifted it into her arms...

In a blinding flash, the world around Alana exploded. She found herself hurtled back, her consciousness sent tumbling through the void. Images flashed amidst the darkness, and she perceived a thousand, thousand memories in the blink of an eye, each at once familiar and strange to her.

Alana saw herself, standing on the banks of the lake and hurling herself into the freezing waters, her strong strokes as she swam the circumference of the island Ardath. Then she became a young girl, sitting in a courtyard with Quinn, seeking the pathways to her magic. The images changed again, and she found herself watching the familiar dream as she fought her father, the clash of steel blades, then the pain as the Tsar's sword flashed down, slicing through the flesh and bone of her arm. Her consciousness had fled, only to return hours later, her severed limb whole once more.

The memories continued, becoming a flood that threatened to wash her away. She saw herself with the Magicker children, shouting orders, batting at them with cane and magic, sending them sprinting through the gardens until they collapsed from exhaustion. She took a cold delight from their pain, remembering the years she'd suffered at the hands of her father.

Dark emotions assailed her, and Alana felt herself sinking, her sense of self overwhelmed. Within, another consciousness was stirring, a woman at once her, and yet wholly different. Alana cried out as the woman rose, fed by the memories. Desperately, she sought something, anything that might anchor her to the person she knew herself to be.

A moonlit image flickered into view, of the night she had spent with Devon in the pools beneath Fort Fall. She clung to it, to the feel of his hands around her wrists, the desire in his eyes, the rush of blood to her head.

Then the image of a woman flashed into view, red-haired and brown-eyed. She stroked Alana's cheek.

I love you, my daughter.

The image changed again, and she saw the woman that was her mother dying in her bed, blood staining the satin sheets. Silence fell over the room as the midwives stood back. Then a piercing scream echoed from the walls, her new-born brother crying out for life.

Grief and love swirled through Alana, and her grip on the memory of Devon faltered—then was swept away. With a cry, Alana found herself sinking, falling, drowning in the memories of another life.

Yet still they continued, each flickering recollection filling in another piece of the jigsaw. Bit by bit, the true Alana reasserted herself, taking form from the darkness, restored by her power. The green light of her magic began to rise, but almost by instinct, she reached out and crushed it down. The magic was not her master, but a slave to be used as she saw fit.

Finally, the rush of memories slowed, and as the last of them snapped back into place, she was complete.

When Alana opened her eyes again, she was no longer the renegade who had fled the capital with Devon and Kellian, but the Daughter of the Tsar, the warrior, the Magicker. A smile spread across her face as she found her father seated beside her.

"Father," Alana said, pulling herself up on the sofa. "Thank you for your help."

His face remained impassive. "Has my daughter returned to me?"

Alana's smile faded, and brow creasing, she turned her eyes inwards. For a moment there was nothing—then with a jagged flash of images, she felt that other self. The girl's cries echoed blindly in the darkness of her consciousness, desperate, despairing. Disgust welled in Alana as she studied the pitiful creature she had become without her memories. Shivering, she tried to recall how her power had been set free but to her surprise, she found that memory still lost to her.

Devon? Kellian? Help me!

Laughter came to Alana's lips as the girl's voice carried up from the void. Summoning her magic, its power still weakened by the girl's stupidity, Alana sent bands of fire down to wrap around her counterpart. A single scream echoed through her mind, followed by a deathly silence as the girl succumbed to her imprisonment.

Opening her eyes, she looked at the Tsar. "I am here, father."

Jaw clenched, the Tsar nodded. "I am glad," he said softly, "for we have much to discuss."

Alana nodded, the girl's memories of the last few weeks surfacing. "We have a new enemy. The woman, Tillie. Who is she, truly?"

"An old enemy, from before your time," the Tsar replied.

Reaching out a hand, he drew her to her feet. Alana swore as pain shot through her legs, and again she cursed the foolish girl who had taken control of her body. Pushing aside her father's hand, she straightened, embracing the pain, becoming one with it.

"I thought all your enemies were dead."

"So did I," her father said, "but I should have known she would not go quietly to her death. I fear her hand is behind much of the strife we have suffered this last decade. You know her true name."

Alana eyed her father, thinking quickly, running over the list of those who'd stood against her father through the years. He had told her of them all: Caelin and May, Nikola and Darien, Eric and...

Realisation came to her in a rush. There was one woman whose end her father had never spoken of, though she should have been long dead by now. Frowning, she thought back to the woman she'd known as Tillie. The old woman had spoken of times, of people that she could not possibly have known.

Not unless…

"It was Enala," she said, looking into her father's eyes.

"Yes," her father replied, "somehow, she has returned from the dead to defy me."

A third voice echoed from across the room. "Then we will find a way to make her pay."

11

"Then we will find a way to make her pay," Quinn heard himself say.

On the sofa, Alana and the Tsar looked up, their eyes widening as he entered the room. Their surprise was short-lived though, and smiling, Alana rose to greet him.

Quinn had been across the lake checking on preparations for the army, and had only heard of Alana's attack on his return to the city. Fearing the worst, he'd headed straight for her residence, and had overheard the end of their conversation while he'd approached the open door.

"Teacher," Alana said, laughter in her eyes as she placed a hand on his chest. "Thank you for rescuing me."

A lump lodged in Quinn's throat as he felt the warmth of her fingers through his woollen shirt. He stared down at her in stunned silence, and she laughed out loud. Lowering herself down on the sofa opposite her father, she gestured for Quinn to sit.

"You...have returned?" he said, finally finding his words as he sat alongside her.

"I have, thanks to you, *teacher*." She said the last word playfully, even as her hand drifted down to rest on his thigh.

Quinn shifted on the couch, suddenly uncomfortable. He did his best to ignore Alana's close proximity, the sweet cinnamon scent of her hair, the warmth of her hand…

"You said it was Enala?" he all but shouted. "How can that be? She must be well over a century old by now."

"The woman worked with the Gods to destroy Archon," the Tsar replied. "Who knows what secrets she discovered? She disappeared when I was first coming to power. I always thought she would return to defy me, but even I had long thought her dead. Her reappearance is concerning, though it may also prove to be an opportunity."

"How so, father?" Alana asked, sitting up.

"Her knowledge after a century of life must be vast. She may hold the key to unlock the final secrets of magic."

Quinn's chest tightened as he remembered facing off against the ancient priest. "She bided her time well," he mused. "I sensed no magic from her in Sitton Forest, nor on the docks of Lon. Not until she attacked my men at Fort Fall. By then, my own magic was too weak to fight her." He cursed. "I should have saved my strength…"

"Nonsense," the Tsar growled. Quinn looked up at the man's tone. "Had you not used your magic to power the sails of your ship, you would never have reached Fort Fall in time to save my daughter. Besides, if you'd fought Enala, she would have destroyed you, magic or no."

"I have bested fire Magickers before," Quinn argued.

"Not *this* fire Magicker," the Tsar said. "You think you have the knowledge to outsmart a woman who has lived for over one hundred years? Especially after she spent most of them fighting demons and dragons and Magickers far more dangerous than yourself!"

His mouth dry, Quinn shook his head. Alana laughed, and

her hand trailed lightly over the fabric of his leggings. "Do not look so sad, teacher," she said. "You saved my life, after all."

"Yes, Quinn, you did well, despite the odds. Enala must have known I'd have sensed her if she'd used her magic sooner —and indeed I did. Sadly, even Fishibe and her kin could not reach you in time to save my son from their clutches."

"Does he truly still live?" Alana asked quickly.

Quinn saw the concern in her eyes. Her teasing momentarily forgotten, he reached out an arm and hugged her to him. "He lives," he replied. "We received word from our spies in Erachill—he was healed at an Earth Temple not long after our...fight."

He felt Alana relax, the worry falling from her face. "That is a relief." Her eyes hardened. "Did the Stalker who shot him survive the battle?"

A chill spread through Quinn's stomach at the look on her face. In the chaos, he had shouted an order without thinking, and one of his men had loosed a crossbow bolt at the boy. Fortunately though...

"No," he said quickly. "Enala...killed them all."

"A shame," Alana said with a sigh. "I would have liked to hear his screams as he died. I hope the witch took her time with him."

"I..." Quinn began, then decided it was best to remain silent.

"Yes, if it comes to moving against the Queen to get him back, your Stalkers had best retain their discipline this time. I won't see my children harmed." Quinn gritted his teeth at the man's hypocrisy after ordering Fishibe and her kin after Alana. Smiling, the Tsar went on. "And what of you, my daughter? Do you remember...why your magic took your memories?"

Beside him, Alana sighed. "No," she said, "I have searched my mind, but there is still a mist over the months before I woke in the stepwell. I cannot remember how it happened, or what Braidon and I did in the first few weeks after we vanished."

The Tsar waved a hand. "No matter. They will return, or they won't. What matters is you are yourself again. We will need all our strength in the coming months."

"What of Devon and Kellian?" Quinn asked. He felt Alana tense at the mention of her former companions and glanced sidelong at her, but she was staring at the Tsar and he couldn't tell what she might be thinking.

"They have left Northland and flown to Trola on the Gold Dragon. Enala only followed them as far as our northern shores before returning to Erachill. The two are entirely untalented, however, and I was unable to track them from there. But I believe they are heading here, to rescue you, Alana."

"It seems my...other self, worked quite the spell on the hammerman," Alana said, smirking. "More fool on him. I take it appropriate measures have been put in place to stop them?"

"Even better. My magic may have lost them, but I received word last night they have encountered one of our agents in Trola. A team of Stalkers has been sent to welcome them back to the Three Nations."

Quinn's head jerked up at that. "They have? Why was I not told?" he said, a little too sharply.

The Tsar held Quinn's gaze for a long moment, the sapphire eyes boring into him. Finally, he swallowed and looked away. A dry chuckle came from the Tsar. "After your... recent battles with the hammerman, I thought it best to send Darnell's pack."

"Darnell?" Quinn growled. "You think her Stalkers have the skill to take on a warrior like Devon?"

"They had better," the Tsar replied, his voice like ice, "or they'd best die trying."

Sensing the conversation had come to an end, Quinn swallowed back his anger and nodded. "You know best, my liege," he said stiffly.

"I do," the Tsar replied, "and you'd do well not to forget it."

Silence fell over the room, and a chill spread through Quinn's stomach. Suddenly the Tsar laughed, a grin appearing on his face. "Besides, after everything the two of you have shared, I doubt you would have brought him back alive, Quinn." His voice hardened, the smile falling from his lips. "And I would rather like to meet the man who thought he could steal my children from me."

Despite himself, Quinn shivered at the glitter he saw in the Tsar's eyes. Since the hammerman had first joined the army, he and Quinn had shared a mutual rivalry. And despite his magic, Quinn had far too often found himself finishing second-best to the giant warrior. Even while hunting him, Quinn had always been a step behind. Now though, no force in the Three Nations would compel him to switch places with the hammerman.

On the opposite sofa, the Tsar let out a long sigh and climbed to his feet. "Well, I have kept you long enough, my daughter," he said, brushing the greying locks of his hair from his face. "There is much to be done and my attention is needed elsewhere. I will leave you in the tender care of your teacher."

With that, he turned his back and left, the heavy doors swinging shut behind him. Alone now with Alana, Quinn swallowed as he found her staring at him. Looking into her eyes, he sought the girl he remembered, the one he had sat with for so many long evenings, who'd he'd trained and taught to use her powers.

"Is it truly you, Alana?" he asked quietly.

"Almost," she whispered.

12

S itting on the couch facing Quinn, Alana had never experienced such turmoil. All her life she'd known exactly who and what she was—the Daughter of the Tsar, born to rule the Three Nations. Her father's enemies were legion, and as his oldest child, one day they would be her enemies too. Weakness had never been an option.

Yet as she'd sat listening to her father discuss his plans for Devon and Kellian, she'd felt that other side of her stirring. A lead weight had settled in her stomach as they spoke of the capture of her former companions, her heartbeat quickening. She knew her father well, and it was unlikely either would be treated to a quick death.

They are nothing to you! she told herself.

They are important to me! another voice echoed from the depths of her soul.

Gritting her teeth, she turned her eyes inwards, finding the shivering consciousness of her other self hovering in the void of her mind. The spirit of the girl flinched back from her, but too slowly, and Alana's magic swept out to encircle her.

You are nothing! she growled, watching in satisfaction as her magic dragged the other girl back down into the darkness.

The confusion went with the girl, and opening her eyes, she smiled at Quinn. His eyes were locked on her. The intensity in his gaze made the breath catch in her throat.

"Is it truly you, Alana?" he asked.

Somewhere far away she could still hear a voice crying out, and for an instant the scraggly face of Devon drifted across her thoughts. Her rage flared and she tore the image away, hurling it into the abyss along with the foolish girl. Licking her lips, she looked across at Quinn.

"Almost," she whispered, brushing a strand of hair from his face.

His eyes closed at her touch, but she paused, noticing the blood on the sleeve of her white cotton shirt. Realising she was still wearing the same clothes from when her magic had taken control, she cursed and stood. Quinn's eyes snapped back open, but ignoring him now, she crossed to the trunk at the foot of her bed and pulled it open. She picked out a woollen jerkin and brown leather pants, and tossed them on the bed.

"I'm glad you're back, Alana," Quinn said, coming up behind her and placing his hands on her shoulders.

She smiled, enjoying the warmth of his touch, but shrugged him off. Turning, she looked up at him. "It seems I am in your debt yet again, teacher," she murmured. She drew circles on his chest with her finger, a sly smile coming to her lips. "How can I ever repay you?"

Quinn swallowed visibly, and she felt him trembling at her touch. When he said nothing, she laughed and took a step back. Slowly she began to unbutton her bloodstained shirt. His eyes widened.

"Alana, what are you doing?"

Alana's smile broadened. Deep in her mind, she could hear the voice screaming again, and felt a slight stirring in her stomach, as though a part of her recoiled at the thought of Quinn's touch. But it was weak, already fading. With a sense of triumph, she unclipped the last button and pulled off her shirt, tossing it to the floor.

Quinn stood open-mouthed before her, his eyes wide, drinking her in. Seven years her senior, Quinn had been like an older brother to her when she was young, having come to the citadel when he was a boy to dedicate himself to the Tsar's service. He had taught her to climb and fight, to wield her magic against her enemies. Many were the bruises she'd sported from sparring with him, yet it had been Quinn who had given her the strength to withstand her father's private lessons.

She had never thought of him as more than a mentor, even as she'd noticed his feelings changing as she'd grown older. A new light had come into his eyes, a fire that had driven him to chase her across the Three Nations and restore her to life. Thinking of that fire now, viewed through the memories of her…softer self, Alana felt a lust of her own.

More than that though, she wanted to restore her sense of self, to mark a line in the sand. Watching the flickering memories of the other Alana, she sensed the growing love she'd felt for the hammerman, Devon. It was a strange, distant sensation, and one she had never experienced before. She didn't like it, didn't like the way it stole away her control, as though her destiny was no longer her own.

But she knew how to kill it, knew how to crush the last hopes of her other self.

Half-naked now, Alana smiled up at Quinn, her eyelashes fluttering. "Do you not like what you see…teacher?"

There was naked lust in Quinn's eyes as he looked on her, yet still he hesitated. "Alana…" he murmured, "what is this?"

Alana reached out and grabbed Quinn by the collar of his shirt, pulling him close. He had stopped shaking now, but a soft moan whispered from his throat as she moved against him. Standing on her tiptoes, she pressed her lips to his ear.

"You have always wanted me," she whispered, her breath hot. "I see it now, watching my memories afresh, the burning in your eyes."

"I...I..." Quinn's words fell away as Alana's fingers trailed down his front, plucking at his buttons as they went. He stiffened as she slid her hands inside his shirt, playing with the hair on his chest.

"You brought me back, *Quinn*," Alana continued. "Saved me, stopped me from betraying everything we've worked for. How can I ever repay you?"

"Alana..."

"I think I know how to start."

Her lips moved from his ear to his neck, and she nipped at his flesh, savouring the groan that rumbled up from his chest. Suddenly his arms were around her waist, drawing her in, gripping her tight. Feeling the warmth of his chest against her, she yanked his shirt open, tearing the remaining buttons clear. He released her then, dragging it from his shoulders and hurling it across the room.

Stepping back, Alana took a moment to savour his naked chest, her eyes lingering on his hulking shoulders, his chest, his arms. Then he was stepping in close again, leaning down, and she was lifting her mouth to meet his, and they were kissing. His hands pulled at hair, drawing her in deeper, and her tongue darted out, tasting, teasing. She shuddered as he cupped her breast, and groaned, feeling him harden against her. Gasping, she kissed him back, her lust rising with a fierce, violent need.

Suddenly an awful horror swept through her, a swirling disgust, and then Devon's face exploded in her mind. She cried out, thrusting Quinn back from her as she staggered across the room. The strength went from her legs and she slid to the ground, the pain flaring as she felt again the cramping muscles of her weary body. Within, she sensed the other part of her rising, her revulsion sweeping out, filling her.

"Alana, are you okay?" Quinn shouted, his voice slicing through her thoughts.

"*Get out!*" Alana shrieked, hardly hearing him. Her power roared, chasing the girl back into the darkness.

She gasped as the girl's emotions fled, leaving her feeling strangely, sickeningly alone. Tears stung her eyes and she quickly blinked them back. Shaking her head, she looked up and saw Quinn standing over her, bare-chested with open shock written across his face.

Rising, Alana shook her head, dismissing the last traces of the girl from her thoughts, and then stepped towards him. He retreated, lifting his hands as though to fend her off. "Alana, what was that?"

"Nothing." She scowled. "Just the witch that took my body. She's gone now."

Before he could slip clear, she darted forward, catching him by the wrist. With a tug, she pulled him forward, so that they stood close together once more, mere inches separating them. But she could see the hesitation in his eyes now, the rejection on his lips. She gripped him tighter, her mind turning inwards. Her magic was still weak, but she allowed a trickle to touch him, muting his fears.

Quinn shivered, his eyes glazing for a moment, before he blinked, a grin coming to his face. Lifting a hand, he brushed a lock of blonde hair from her face. She could feel his desire, his need to take her, and savoured in it. With a sense of euphoria, she leaned up and pressed her lips to his, and felt the last of his barriers give way.

Locked together, they stumbled backwards across the room, until she felt the wall pressed up against her back. She gasped as Quinn moved his mouth to her neck, and felt the soft bite of his teeth. Her fingers tightened in his hair, and she drank in the pain she sensed in him. Then he paused, pulling back for a moment. She was surprised to see the concern in his eyes once more.

"Are you sure you're okay?" he murmured.

Alana only laughed. Gripping him tight, she pushed him backwards. He retreated, though this time she did not release him. She directed him towards the bed, waiting until he was close, then shoved him hard in the chest. He toppled backwards onto the soft mattress.

"Not yet," she said, as she joined him.

Straddling him, she began to unbuckle his belt.

13

"**D**amnit!"

Surging to his feet, Braidon stumbled and tripped over the candles scattered about the room. Two toppled to the floor and flickered out on the cold stone. Cursing again, he crouched and righted them, though his hands were shaking and it took two attempts to fit them back into their copper holders.

"You must have patience, young Braidon," Enala said, her voice carrying across from where she still sat cross-legged on the floor.

He swung on her, teeth bared, angry words tumbling from him in a rush. "I've *been* patient!" he snapped, "but I can't do it, it's too much, it's…impossible!"

Enala's expression was untouched by his screams, her eyes shining in the candlelight. "It is not impossible," she answered, rising to her feet. "Remember back in Lonia, when your magic was threatening to take control? You mastered it then, found the peace to turn it back. You can do so again."

"That was different," Braidon growled. "I hardly knew

what I was doing. I didn't know there was some...*demon* inside me, waiting to tear me apart."

"It is *nothing* to you, Braidon," Enala replied. "Why can you not see that? Only your fear makes it real."

Braidon turned away, bitterness rising in his throat. All his life he'd lived in his sister's shadow. She was the strong one, the warrior, their father's favourite. Then had come his magic's emergence, flickering into life on his sixteenth birthday, and everything had changed. His memories of that day were strangely blurred, indistinct, but he could remember feeling pride as his power came to life. Even the threat of persecution could not change the fact he finally possessed something his sister did not.

But even that had been a lie. The battle in Fort Fall had shown him the truth of things, had revealed the lie that was his magic. His power accounted to little more than circus tricks, illusions to fool the senses, ultimately worthless.

Braidon had thought to use his power to save his sister in Fort Fall. Instead, as always, she had been the one to save him. And she had been stolen for it. Even now, the knowledge ate at him.

Looking at Enala, he felt lost. "I can't do it."

For a moment he glimpsed disappointment in the priest's face. She quickly masked it with a shake of her head. There was a long pause, and then she smiled, the wrinkles falling from her cheeks. "We shall see, young Braidon. But for now, I think it best we take a break. Come, it is past time I showed you more of the city."

Braidon had little desire to do anything but curl up in his bed and hide away from the world, but Enala was already moving away, and he had little choice but to follow her. Together they wandered from the stone chamber that served as their meditation room, out into the long corridors of the mountain city. The ground was smooth beneath their feet, seamless, as though the rock itself had been shaped by some immortal hand.

Enala led him deeper into the city, along pathways Braidon had never seen before. Those they encountered as they walked payed them little attention, though a few stopped to greet Enala. It was clear she was well-known here, a legend amongst the residents. Slowly the crowds grew denser, until at last they emerged into a grand cavern some three-hundred-feet wide. Two-hundred-foot walls towered over them, ending abruptly in open sky.

Braidon struggled to hide his shock. Before him was a marketplace that would rival even the bustling bazaars of Ardath and Lon. Alcoves cut into the walls boasted dozens of stalls, while others had been set up in rows spanning half the cavern. Their vendors lounged in hammocks behind the counters, many dozing as they waited for customers to find them.

Men and women thronged the alleyways between the stalls, pausing to purchase fresh bread and produce, meat and fish. Braidon could hardly believe the wealth of goods on hand. Amongst the stalls in sight, he could see blankets of Lonian wool, wooden furniture boasting of Trolan origin, even incense and spices from the south of Plorsea. Until now, he'd thought Northland to still be a poor nation, its development hindered by the centuries of strife under Archon's rule. Never had he thought to see goods from his homeland so far north—yet now he could only marvel at the industry of it all.

"This way," Enala called. Blinking, he found her waving from across the way.

Following her, they moved away from the market stalls and out into the open. The sky was bright and clear, and Braidon smiled as the sun's rays touched him. The air was cool, but within the cavern they were protected from the winter winds. The ground sloped downwards, until it disappeared into the waters of a natural spring. Braidon was surprised to see a dozen children floating in the water, their youthful voices echoing loudly from the sheer cliffs.

"Aren't they freezing?" he asked.

Enala laughed. "I think you'll find the water quite pleasant. The spring is fed from deep inside the earth, where the natural fires keep it an agreeable temperature all year round."

They had reached the edge of the pool now, and crouching down, Braidon ran his hand through the water to confirm the priest's words. While not hot, it was a great deal warmer than the air outside the city. Straightening, he joined Enala where she had seated herself on the rocky shore.

"They're like you, you know," she said softly.

Braidon followed her gaze out to where the children were playing. He frowned. "What do you mean?"

"Most of them are Magickers, or the children of Magickers. All of them came here from the Three Nations to escape persecution by the Tsar. The Queen takes them in, gives them a home, helps them to master their powers."

Braidon looked at the children with fresh eyes. There was a dozen in total, the oldest around eighteen, the youngest maybe ten. All wore broad smiles as they tossed a leather ball between them. There was a great splash as one of the older boys dove, catching the ball and then plunging beneath the water. Laughter followed as he surfaced spluttering.

Braidon grinned at the sight. Then a sadness crept over him, his thoughts turning to his own lonely childhood. For as long as he could remember, Alana had been his only companion, though she had often been...away with their father. He couldn't recall ever playing with other children like this, though why...he could not remember.

"Would you like to join them?" Enala asked.

A lump formed in Braidon's throat. Suddenly his heart was racing, his shoulders tense with anxiety at the thought of introducing himself to so many new faces. He clenched his fists against the stone, his eyes flickering between Enala and the crystal waters.

"I…" he started, but before he could complete the thought, a voice shouted from behind them.

"*Enala!*"

Braidon jumped, swinging towards the newcomer, his hands forming fists to fend off an attack. He lowered them again when he realised there was no one close by. A moment later, he spotted the speaker, still some fifty feet away, but closing in fast. It was a woman. Two men in chainmail shadowed her, swords sheathed at their sides. Braidon swallowed hard as he recognised the woman from his first night in the city. She wasn't wearing the iron crown, but there was no mistaking the aura of authority she carried.

Beside him, Enala calmly rose to her feet as the Queen reached them. "Your majesty," she said, "what brings you to the bazaar?"

The woman came to a stop before them, her green eyes flickering from Enala to Braidon. "Take him," she snapped, gesturing at the men behind her.

Braidon cried out as the men surged forward. Taken by surprise, he had no chance to resist. The first struck him hard in the stomach, driving the wind from his lungs and dropping him to his knees. The second man stepped in, grabbing his arms and pinning them behind his back.

Gasping, Braidon swayed in the man's grip. An awful heat spread through his chest, his magic stirring, rising through the depths of his consciousness. Fear flared inside him, but it was too late to cool the flickering glow, and he felt a rush as the power flowed from him.

Blinding light flashed across the cavern and a great *boom* echoed from the cliffs, igniting screams from nearby. A shout came from behind him as the hand holding Braidon loosened. Anger took him then, and he surged backwards against his attacker. The sudden movement sent the man stumbling. As his hands came free, Braidon spun and slammed his fist into the man's stomach.

Lights were still flashing around them, appearing overhead and rushing away, sizzling through the air like fireworks. Nearby, the marketplace had descended into chaos as people rushed to and fro, unaware the light show was nothing more than an illusion. Even the Queen had retreated, her hands raised over her face to protect her eyes.

But now the other guard had found his courage. Drawing his sword, he advanced on Braidon with murder in his eyes.

Before the man could reach him, Enala stepped between them, her eyes burning red.

"*Stop this!*" Her words rang out, slicing through the chaos.

The guard froze at her command, his eyes suddenly fearful, and Braidon saw that Enala's hands were aflame. Beyond her, citizens were stumbling around the bazaar, their faces twisted in terror. Shame filled him then, his anger dying away. The light went with it, and silence fell once more over the cavern.

Weariness swept through Braidon. Sinking to his knees, he watched as the Queen straightened, her hands falling to her side. He swallowed as their eyes met, and the strength of her rage washed over him.

"Take. Him," she spat, pointing a trembling finger at Braidon.

Her men hesitated, still shocked by the sudden display of magic, and Enala quickly barred their way.

"What is the meaning of this, Merydith?" she growled. The fire in her hands had died away, but now her eyes shone with a rage to match the Queen's.

"Get out of my way, Enala," the Queen snapped. "This does not concern you."

"The boy is under my protection," Enala replied, her voice

trembling. "And you will answer to me if you wish to harm him."

"Harm him?" came the Queen's reply. "The boy may have brought about the destruction of my kingdom—and you worry about my *harming him?*"

Braidon could only look in confusion from the Queen to Enala. Her words made no sense to him. Surely she couldn't mean the Tsar intended to invade Northland because Enala had given him refuge?

"What are you talking about, Merydith?" Enala asked, the anger falling from her voice.

The Queen sucked in a breath, her hands shaking. "The boy is not who he would have us believe, Enala," she said softly.

"What?" Braidon gaped, but the two women ignored him.

"What do you mean?" Enala asked for him. "Who could he be that the Tsar would threaten war with us?"

The Queen closed her eyes, a pained look coming over her face. "His emissaries just arrived. Unless we return him, they claim the Three Nations will march north with all their strength. They're claiming we have kidnapped the Tsar's only son."

Braidon's mouth dropped open. The colour slowly drained from Enala's face, her skin turning a paled grey. The old woman swayed on her feet, and it seemed as though she had aged ten years in a matter of heartbeats. Reaching out, she gripped the Queen's arm.

"What did you say?"

The Queen stared at Enala, her frown softening. Then she looked across at Braidon, and he saw the hate lurking behind her eyes. "I'm saying Braidon is the Tsar's son, Enala. I'm saying he has betrayed us all."

❧ 14 ❧

That evening Devon and Kellian made camp beneath the cliffs, taking advantage of a small crag to shelter them from the cold winds sweeping down the valley. As darkness fell, they lit a fire against the cliff-face, so that its heat would be reflected back on them.

After eating a meagre stew of toughened beef and tubers, Devon wandered away from the others. His mind was distant and he was in no mood for company. Seating himself on a boulder some distance from the camp, he stared out over the moonlit valley. Images rose from the vaults of his memory. It had been here, in this valley, that he'd first tasted glory.

In those early days, victory had been far from assured, flitting above the heads of the armies like a firefly, always just out of reach. The Plorseans had battled for every inch of ground, forcing the Trolans back with nothing but sheer bloody-minded determination. Devon had stood at the front, his hammer rising and falling like death itself, smashing his way through the Trolan line, a giant amongst men.

Back then, there had been no doubt in his mind of the

Tsar's righteousness, of Plorsea's right to govern the Three Nations. But that had been before the destruction of Kalgan, before the razing of cities and the slaughter of innocent civilians. Before he'd brought shame to his ancestors.

Now, looking out over the former battlefield, he felt only sadness. In the moonlight, the boulders lining the valley shone a ghostly white. He could almost imagine them to be the souls of fallen men, doomed to wander these faraway mountains, forever in search of home.

"I hear them too."

Devon jumped as a voice spoke from behind him. Betran appeared in the moonlight, his eyes distant as he looked out over the valley. Devon was surprised he hadn't heard the little man approaching, and he felt a flicker of irritation at the intrusion on his solitude. It faded as he untangled the Trolan's words.

"Hear who?" he asked.

"The ghosts," Betran shivered. "How many lives have been lost here, in this pass, do you think? How many generations of young men and women have marched to their deaths, their lives lost to the futility of war?"

"They say twenty thousand met here, when the Tsar marched against your…people."

"Ay," Betran replied, "and before that? Ours was not the only battle these lonely peaks have witnessed." He sighed. "My brother will have no shortage of company in the afterlife."

Devon's throat tightened, and he eyed the man, seeking some sign of anger. But there was only sadness on the Trolan's face. He glanced down at *kanker*, his guilt swelling. "You two were close?"

Betran shrugged and took a seat on the boulder next to Devon. "He was my younger brother. I marched to look out for him, more than anything. Little good it did him." He smiled ruefully. "I didn't even see you coming. One moment we were pressing your line back, the next minute you and that hammer of yours had broken our ranks, and my comrades were streaming back around us. Kieran, fool that he was, tried to stand his ground. He was dead before I could reach him."

"I'm sorry," Devon whispered, but the little Trolan only shook his head.

"I think it must be the folly of the young, to want to test their skills against their fellow man. Maybe that's why our nations have been so cursed with war."

"A depressing thought," Devon mused. "You think that means another war is inevitable?"

There was a long pause before Betran answered, and when he spoke, there was an edge to his voice. "What choice do we have?" he murmured. "I'm thirty-five, with a wife and son, but since the war there's been no work. Of the little I do earn, most goes towards the Tsar's taxes. When you showed up, my family was a week away from starvation."

"And you believe a war with Plorsea will free you?"

"No." To Devon's surprise, there were tears on the Trolan's face now. "We would be crushed. But I can sense the hate in my people, even in my own son. One day soon it will spur them to rise up. And the Tsar will return with his armies, with his demons and his dragons, and destroy us once and for all."

Devon swallowed, struggling to find the words to reassure the young man that they could change things. Before he could speak, another voice came from the shadows. "You're wrong, Betran."

Godrin came wandering across the rocky slope. He looked from Devon to Betran before seating himself alongside the Trolan. His hand gripped Betran's shoulder, though his eyes were fixed on Devon. "Your son is right to hate the Plorseans," he said quietly, "and one day, we *will* make them pay for your brother's life, and all those other lives they stole."

Devon saw the hate in the Trolan's eyes. Godrin had

agreed to this mission partly because of Enala, partly because they offered him a chance to strike at the Tsar, and save his nation from a long, slow death. But that had done nothing to change his heart. The hate remained, festering, tainting his mind with thoughts of revenge. Seeing it, Devon wished he had the words to mend the fracture in the man's heart, to restore the unity that had once existed between the Three Nations. But Kellian was the one with the silver tongue, and all Devon could do was sit there in silence.

"And what will that achieve?" Betran spoke up, his voice touched with sadness. "My brother will still be dead, but the hate will have spread. When you're done, some young Plorsean will be left to nurse the hatred in his heart. Then one day he will return to take his revenge on the foul Trolans who killed his loved ones."

"It won't be like that."

"How can it not, when you talk only of hatred and revenge?"

"So when the time comes to free our nation, you will not be with us, Betran? Will you hide in the shadows while your comrades fight for your freedom?"

Betran turned cold eyes on the crime lord. "I will be there, Godrin. I will stand with my people and fight for our right to live, because I believe the Tsar is evil, and evil must be countered wherever it is found. But know this—the day you march on Plorsea, the day the war turns from liberation, to conquest, I will stand against you. And I will implore our people to do the same. Unlike you, I remember our legends. I will not lead our nation into yet another act of folly."

Godrin snorted. "They are only legends, Betran," he said scornfully. "Told to scare unruly children. Or do you truly believe these mountains once came alive, and consumed entire armies?"

"Maybe not, but I choose to see the message behind the words. War has no victors, only survivors. And I will not be a part of it. Should the day come, I will return to my home, and hold my wife and child in my arms. I will do my best to live with love in my heart, and hope that is enough."

"I believe the legends are true," Devon said, as a quiet settled over the mountain slopes. With the mention of the past, his thoughts had turned to Enala, and the tales that were still told of her. Realising the other men were staring at him, he scratched his beard and went on. "Before all this started, I thought the same, that the stories were just that—stories. But in the last few weeks, I have witnessed trees come to life, have fought with a demon and escaped a dragon's flames. I've met a woman over a hundred years old, who fights like a wraith. And I've seen Trolans unite with Plorseans in the hope of freeing their nation." He paused, eyeing the others, a grim smile on his lips. "After all that, who's to say these mountains couldn't eat an army or two?"

Silence fell over the others at his words, and he turned away, looking back out over the valley. He knew the legend of which they spoke. It dated back to a time long before Archon's reign, when the Great Wars had been fought between Lonia and Trola. The conflict had consumed the lands now known as Plorsea, turning them into lifeless desert. Legends told that a final battle had been fought here, in Brunei Pass. But as the two great armies came together, the surrounding cliffs had snapped closed, entombing thousands in solid rock.

Devon suppressed a shiver at the thought of the towering cliffs closing in on him. Within the pass, there would be nowhere to run, no hope of survival. Five years ago, he had barely given the legend a second thought, but now the old tale sent a shiver down his neck.

The voices from the campfire had quieted now, and Devon

was beginning to feel the weight of the day's travel. Yawning, he stretched his arms and stood, sheathing *kanker* on his back. Bidding the two men goodnight, he started towards the camp. The fire had burned low now, and there was little light. Squinting in the darkness, he was still searching for his bedroll when a distant *thud* carried down the valley.

Turning, he scanned the gloom in search of the source. The ground lay open around them, but the moon's light was shrouded in cloud. He could see no sign of movement below them, but as he looked up the valley, he caught a flicker of movement near the cliffs at the top of the pass.

Abandoning the search for his bedroll, Devon wandered back down to where Betran and Godrin still sat talking. They looked up at his approach, their mouths opening to question him, but he waved them to silence. Straining his ears, he listened for further signs of movement, and caught another *thud*, as of a horseshoe on stone.

Silently, Devon lifted *kanker* from his back. The other two rose to stand alongside him, their eyes focused on the darkness at the top of the valley.

"Someone's coming," Devon whispered.

"I know," Godrin said, before something hard struck Devon in the back of the head.

Stars flashed across his vision and he found himself suddenly on his knees, the strength flowing from him. *Kanker* slid from his hands as he swung to see Godrin standing over him. Betran lay on his stomach nearby and for a moment, Devon thought he was dead. Then a low moan whispered through the night, and Betran shifted, his hands curling into fists, but he did not rise.

Devon tried to summon the strength to stand, but the movement caused his vision to swirl. He swayed on his knees as Godrin loomed above him. There was a pause as their eyes met. The man raised his fist for another blow. Devon tried to defend himself, but his arms only lifted weakly in response. Snarling, the Trolan batted them aside, then hammered his fist into Devon's face.

There was a flash of light, followed by a rush of colour—then darkness.

Quinn's mind was far away as he walked the ramparts of the citadel, consumed by thoughts of the night before. The meeting with the Tsar had been frustrating, especially after learning he'd been passed over to lead the pursuit after Devon. His frustration was tempered by what had come next, though he could still hardly believe it.

After years spent watching her grow, after the long lessons in magic and watching her as a young woman take lover after lover, Alana had finally come to him. While he was some seven years her senior, Quinn had always felt a shared attraction between them, a tension that neither had quite dared break.

Last night, that barrier had been shattered, the two of them making love long into the night. Even now he rejoiced in their shared passion, savoured the sight of the young woman standing before him naked. Her momentary confusion had given him pause, but at her touch his hesitation had vanished, and he'd spent the rest of the night in a state of ecstasy, their lips locked together, their bodies entwined...

Feeling himself growing aroused, Quinn clenched his jaw and forced his thoughts to other matters. He had risen with the dawn, leaving the still-sleeping Alana to her rest, and headed to the walls for his morning rounds. Relieved of his duties with the Stalkers, the Tsar had placed him in charge of the citadel's defences, along with reporting progress on preparations for the Northland invasion.

When he looked out over the lake, Quinn could just make out the foothills that hid the gathering men. By now, the army would be nearing twenty thousand men and women—a force unlike any the Three Nations had seen in generations. It would be needed if they were to take the north. The Queen's nation spanned more land than the Three Nations combined, and after centuries of poverty, the generosity of their southern neighbours had finally allowed Northland to grow, becoming a power in its own right.

And how did they repay us? Quinn wondered to himself.

Since the Tsar's decree outlawing magic, the Queen had given refuge to hundreds of Magickers. Her motives were obvious—by aiding them today, she joined their power with hers, making her nation a force to be reckoned with. Little good it would do her; the Tsar planned to neutralise the threat before the Queen could exploit her budding force of Magickers.

Quinn paused on his patrol to inspect the uniforms of two guards standing in the northern gatehouse. They stood to attention at his approach, eyes fixed straight ahead as he scanned their chainmail and spears. Quinn drew their swords from their sheaths one by one, inspecting the blades for nicks or rust, but there was not a spot to be seen. Nodding, Quinn moved on, his thoughts returning to the Northerners.

The biggest risk from the northern invasion was if Lonia or Trola rose up behind the invading army. Already, Stalkers stationed in Trola were reporting unrest amongst the common folk. If the Tsar marched north with most of his forces, there would be little to stop an uprising. Boosting the garrison stationed in Kalgan might squash thoughts of rebellion, but they could ill afford to waste the soldiers.

No, it would be better if the threat were neutralised before it ever began. He made a note to talk with the new Lieutenant of the Stalkers about rounding up potential ringleaders. The mob would quickly disperse if their leaders were taken.

Reaching the eastern tower, Quinn considered taking another round of the battlements, but dismissed the idea. The men and women guarding the walls were chosen from the best of the city guard. They needed no instruction from him on how best to defend the citadel. All carried the standard spears and short swords of the Plorsean army, and many were also equipped with crossbows. It would take an army to storm the citadel. Even if Devon and his friend managed to evade Darnell's Stalkers, they would meet a quick death if they tried to reach Alana here.

Thinking of the young princess, Quinn's heart beat quicker, and he headed down the nearest stairway from the ramparts. It was still early, and they had been up late into the night. Perhaps she was still asleep, her naked body draped in the silken sheets...

"Quinn!"

Quinn started as a voice shouted out from the ramparts above him. He was surprised to find Krista there, her eyes aflame with anger as she started down towards him. He watched her come, his arms folded and face expressionless.

"What is it, Krista?" he asked, trying to keep the irritation from his voice. He did not appreciate the delay.

"I hear Alana has...returned," she replied, stopping on the step above him. "Is it true?"

Unable to keep the smile from his face, Quinn nodded. "The Tsar helped restore her memories. The true Alana is back with us."

"How very exciting for you," Krista said, her voice like acid. "but where does that leave me?"

Quinn raised an eyebrow. "What do you mean?"

"The young Magickers. What is the Tsar's plan for them?" Krista asked, then continued before Quinn had a chance to respond. "Because I won't stand by and let her take them from me!"

Despite her best efforts, fear lurked behind Krista's eyes. He could well understand it. Alana's return put her position at risk. As the Tsar's daughter, Alana was used to getting what she wanted—or taking it by force, if necessary.

But Alana had made no mention of the young Magickers or Krista the night before. He doubted she would be interested in such trivial matters while her brother was still missing.

"Alana has other things to occupy her right now," he replied gently. Then his face hardened, and stepping up beside her, he gripped her hard by the wrists. "But you should not be concerning yourself with the mind of the Tsar's daughter, Krista. You should be with your charges."

To his surprise, Krista sneered. "From what I hear, you should take your own advice, Quinn."

Anger flared in Quinn's chest at her words, and tightening his grip on her wrist, he pushed her backwards. They were still halfway up the steps to the ramparts, some twenty feet above the ground. The colour drained from Krista's face as she stumbled, her feet slipping on the edge of the stone stairs. Quinn felt a warm sense of satisfaction as he held her there, suspended over the edge. With a sharp tug, he pulled her back and sent her sprawling against the wall.

"I suggest you return to your charges, Krista," he growled. "Before I am forced to report your negligence to the Tsar."

Krista climbed slowly to her feet, her eyes glittering with rage. The soft crackle of lightning came from her fingers, but he only grinned, and after a long moment the energies died away.

"I won't let her take them from me," she said, her voice hoarse. "The Tsar praises strength. If she tries to interfere, I'll show her just how strong I am."

Quinn smirked. "Do as you will, teacher," he replied. "The Tsar will judge you in the end."

With that he turned and continued his way down the stairwell, leaving Krista to her impotent anger.

❧ 16 ❧

Devon woke to the rhythmic thump of horse hooves beneath him. His head throbbed with every step, and his mouth tasted of dust and vomit. Groaning, he tried to sit up, and found his hands had been tied to the saddle horn. Cracking open his eyes, he stifled a scream as light sliced through his skull.

"Ah, the cowardly hero awakes at last!"

Devon swayed in the saddle as he looked around for the speaker. A woman rode alongside him, her black cloak and pants marking her as a Stalker. The gold diamond-shaped brooch of a captain shone from her breast as she smiled sweetly at him. She patted the haft of his hammer, which she had lying across her lap.

"Thanks for the trophy. I'll be the envy of every regiment with this hanging from my mantle!" She threw back her head and laughed. "Hell, I can't wait to see the look on Quinn's face when I ride through the gates of Ardath with you in tow."

The stars dancing across Devon's eyes were fading now, and staring at the woman, he struggled to place her. She was young, probably no older than twenty-three years, but she carried about herself an arrogance he'd come to expect from the Tsar's Stalkers. Her auburn hair was tied back in a long ponytail, and her copper eyes watched him like a hawk, as though she still expected him to resist. Prominent cheekbones and a tanned complexion suggested she came from southern Plorsea, though she spoke with the sharp accent of someone raised in Ardath.

It took a long time for Devon's sluggish mind to realise he didn't recognise her. That was not surprising—while most of the Stalkers had been promoted up from those who'd campaigned in Trola, the army had numbered in the thousands—there was no way Devon could have known them all. Transferring his gaze to the rest of their company, he found Kellian on the horse behind him, still slumped unconscious in his saddle. There was no sign of Betran, but further back Godrin and his men were riding at the rear of the column.

Anger clenched around his stomach as he stared at the crime lord. He scowled at the woman riding beside him. "And to whom do I have the pleasure?"

"Captain Darnell, at your service," the woman replied.

His head still pounding, Devon forced a smile. "Nice to meet you, missy," he murmured, "but I doubt you'll earn much respect for arresting an unconscious man. Why don't you hand me back my hammer, and we'll see how well you really fight?"

Darnell grinned. "And I suppose you expect to be set free should you triumph?"

"Only seems fair," Devon grunted.

"Thanks, but I think I'll pass." She pointed a finger at Devon's chest. Around him the temperature plummeted as though a bucket of ice water had been thrown over him. His teeth began to chatter as she went on. "And if you try anything, I'll turn you into an icicle."

His hands tied to the saddle horn, all Devon could do was grit his teeth and nod. After a long moment, the woman clicked her fingers, and the cold vanished, the warmth of the morning sun returning. Chuckling to herself, Darnell heeled her horse forward. As she moved away, the thump of hooves came from behind Devon. He narrowed his eyes as Godrin rode up beside him.

"So much for bringing war to the Plorseans," he growled.

"It's a complex business, politics," Godrin replied genially. "I considered your plan, Devon, truly I did. But this is the only way Trola survives—by proving our loyalty to the Tsar, and living to fight another day."

Devon studied the man, searching for some hint of remorse, but there was no telling what lay behind his hard eyes. "What drivel," he said at last. "I know your kind. Always looking out for yourself, willing to sink to any level, so long as you get to live. I should have known better than to trust a general who would abandon his people in their time of need."

Godrin's face darkened. "I saw a chance to *save* my people."

"You saw a chance to save your own skin," Devon spat.

"And what of you, Devon?" Godrin growled. "You sit there talking of honour, but you never had any intention of liberating my people. You only wanted to rescue your precious friend. For that you expected me to set aside my enmity, to ignore the crimes you committed against Trola? Make no mistake, *friend*, you are the enemy. When I return to Trola, my people will celebrate your death."

"If that were true, why did you not kill us back in Kalgan? You could have made a display of it, followed in the Tsar's footsteps, and staged a public execution."

"Ay, but then word would have gotten back to Enala and the Queen." He shrugged. "As I said, politics are complicated. Northland and its agents are a growing power. I could not afford to alienate them. And besides, death is too good for you,

Devon. I want to see you *humbled*, for you to watch as everything you've ever loved is destroyed."

Tasting blood in his mouth, Devon spat on the roadside.
"You are a little man," he said. "With such little ambitions."

Godrin's eyes flashed. "I hope the Tsar brings out this girl
of yours and kills her in front of you."

Devon shook his head. "And what has this revenge cost
you? What happened to Betran? Did your betrayal require his
death, too?"

"Fool though he is, I have no grudge against him," Godrin
replied, suddenly unable to meet Devon's eyes. "We left him
unconscious by the fire. It was all I could do for him. No doubt
he'll find his way home, and be the safer for it."

"Glad to see hatred hasn't entirely blinded you to reason."
Kellian's voice came from behind them. Devon's friend was
sitting up now, a purple lump the size of an egg swelling on his
forehead. Swaying in his saddle, he frowned at Devon, his eyes
still slightly unfocused. "You know, I hate to say it..." he
began.

"Then don't," Devon growled, his head still pounding.

Kellian scratched his chin, turning to Godrin. "So what's
the plan now, Trolan? Hand us over to the Tsar and claim the
reward—then what? You think your little deception will keep
Enala from learning of this?"

"The woman isn't all-knowing," Godrin shot back.

"Might be she's not." Kellian nodded, then gestured at the
men riding around them. There were almost twenty black-
cloaked Stalkers, plus Godrin's men. "But with all these eyes,
she'll hardly have to be all-knowing to find out your role in
this."

Around them several of the Stalkers chuckled. Godrin
narrowed his eyes. "You talk too much, little man."

Before Kellian could react, the Trolan's fist swept up and
struck him hard in the face. With his hands bound, Kellian had

no way to defend himself, and he reeled back. Only his bindings kept him from falling to the rocky ground.

Godrin raised his hand to strike Kellian again, but Devon dug his heels into the side of his mount. The horse was well-trained, and it surged forward, bringing him alongside Godrin. As the two horses came together, Godrin's mount flinched away, jostling Godrin. As the man wavered, Devon drove his shoulder forward, catching the Trolan in the small of his back and flinging him from the saddle.

The sharp *thud* of metal and flesh striking the ground echoed through the pass. Around them the Stalkers drew rein, bringing the party to a stop, as on the ground Godrin coughed and groaned, struggling to his feet. He looked up and caught Devon's eye. Snarling, he reached for his sword.

Devon laughed down at him. "Come on then, sonny! Come cut me down, show me how much of a man you are!"

For a moment he thought the Trolan would do it. Godrin stood trembling on the trail, his knuckles turning white as he clenched his blade's hilt. Then a Stalker pushed his horse between them. "Something the matter, Trolan?" he asked gruffly.

A strained silence followed as Godrin turned his hate-filled eyes on the Stalker, before he finally shook his head. "No problem, *sir*," he said, spitting the last word. He climbed back into his saddle and kicked the horse hard, sending it cantering to the head of the party.

"You know, I'm liking your plan less and less," Kellian commented.

Devon glanced at his friend. His cheek was already beginning to turn purple. Devon's heart sank, his mind turning over as he sought a way out. With a feeling of dread, he realised they had already reached the top of the pass and were descending into Plorsea. Time was running out. Around them the mountains were quickly giving way, the cliffs widening out into the plateaus of western Plorsea. The river still flowed away to their right, but its waters had now split into several channels separated by gravel banks. Ahead, the land still sloped upwards, but the incline was gentle, barren rock turning to open grassland.

"Least we're still heading in the right direction," Devon grunted.

Kellian chuckled dryly. "Ay. Our enemies are no doubt quaking in their boots." He paused, his eyes flicking back the way from which they'd come. "Do you think they really left Betran alive?"

"I can't see why not," Devon replied noncommittedly.

"Good…I liked the man," Kellian said. "Would have been a shame if our folly had left his son an orphan."

Devon nodded. "Ay, I have enough Trolan lives on my conscience."

"How about you stop worrying about the past, and start thinking of a plan that'll get us out of this, old boy?"

"I thought you didn't like my plans."

"True," Kellian mused. "Well, *I* suggest we wait to make our move until the citadel. Since, well, for now we're going in the right direction." He nodded to the way ahead.

Devon groaned as he saw they'd topped a rise, revealing the land for miles around. The river wound away from them, its channels merging and deepening until a single waterway threaded its way past the buildings of a settlement. The plain grey walls and slate roofs gave it an ugly look, of a place that did not quite belong; but then, Onslow was not known for its beauty. The town sat on the trade route between Trola and Plorsea, at the furthest navigable point of the Brunei river before it entered the mountains.

The docks were almost as large as the settlement itself, though there were only a few ships at berth. Times had been hard for the little town since the fall of Trola, and few traders would bother to risk a shipment to the impoverished nation in the middle of winter. At the end of the docks, a ship sat at anchor sporting the jet-black sails of war.

"At least they were kind enough to send us a welcome party," Kellian said.

❧ 17 ❧

Alana strode across the soft grass, her eyes fixed on the trees ahead. The distant laughter of children called her on, drawing her through the ever-blooming roses, through archways and along mosaic paths. Finally, she glimpsed movement through a low-lying hedge, and angled herself towards it.

As she walked, her mind drifted back to the night before, and the long hours spent in Quinn's embrace. His lovemaking had been clumsy and rushed, his hands trembling as he held her. But she had enjoyed his wild, animalistic grunts, the rush of heat through her stomach, his power as she straddled him.

More than anything, Alana had savoured the screams echoing from deep within her mind, the revulsion rising up from that other part of herself. The crumbling of the girl's hope had been ecstasy.

Yet afterwards, there had only been a hollow emptiness in her stomach, a feeling of dissatisfaction she couldn't quite explain. Even as she lay in Quinn's embrace, Alana had felt strangely alone. When he'd risen early in the morning, she had pretended she was asleep, and he had left without a word. Only with him gone did the strange emotions dissipate. A short while later she had risen, determined to reclaim her old life, to restore her purpose in the world.

Now, walking through the gardens, she paused to watch the scene before her. Children were running freely across the lawns, broad smiles on their faces, their voices raised in joy. Only a few were sitting on the nearby benches, their eyes closed in concentration. She could sense the slight flickering of their magic from where she stood, weak and untamed. None were practicing with sword or bow.

Anger touched her as she watched the woman responsible for the chaos. The teacher Krista sat with two children on the benches, her watchful gaze on the children at play. She wasn't even attempting to direct those dedicated enough to be practising their magic.

Alana shook her head, disgust rising like bile in her throat. How would these students ever grow to serve the Tsar, to master their magic, when their teacher did not even care enough to prepare them?

Clenching her fists, she marched towards them. With her eyes on the children, Krista did not notice her approach until the last second. She was smiling as she turned, but the joy fell from her face as she saw her rival.

"Alana." The woman stood, her stance widening as if to brace herself. "I heard you were well."

"I am," Alana replied. She stepped past Krista and looked out at the children. "You may go now."

A stunned silence followed. Then a hand gripped Alana's shoulder and spun her around.

"*What?*" Krista snapped.

"I said you may go," Alana said, staring at the woman. "Are you deaf as well as stupid?"

Krista tensed, her teeth showing as her lips drew back into a snarl. "I'm not going anywhere," she hissed. "I was given this appointment by the Tsar himself, when you…fled. You can't just waltz back in here and–"

"Yes, yes, yes," Alana interrupted. "I'm sure my father thought it was a good idea at the time, appointing you." Her lips twisted in a cold smile. "But I'm back now. Your services are no longer required. In fact, I'd say they never were, looking at the damage you've done here."

A soft crackling drew Alana's gaze to Krista's hands. Blue lightning flickered between her fingers as the woman clenched her fists. "I said, I'm not going anywhere," Krista growled through clenched teeth.

Alana raised an eyebrow. "You would strike down the Tsar's daughter?"

"I will do what is necessary," Krista hissed. "I won't let you terrorise these children any longer."

Throwing back her head, Alana let her laughter roll across the gardens. The children nearby turned to stare, their eyes widening at the sight of the lightning dancing across their teacher's fingers. Alana allowed the smile to fall from her face.

"Your kindness will destroy them," she said. "You have allowed them to become soft. Now where will they be when it comes time for their exams?"

"I don't take orders from you, *girl*," Krista shot back. She lifted a hand and pointed it at Alana's chest. Lighting hissed along her skin without leaving so much as a mark. "Now go, before I make you."

Alana sighed, her shoulders slumping. "Very well."

As she turned away, she glimpsed the surprise in Krista's face. She paused, watching the tension drain from the woman, the lightning beginning to die. Instantly she spun back, her hand snapping out to catch the woman. Krista's eyes widened, the colour fleeing her face. She opened her mouth, a single word slipping out.

"No…"

Then Alana's magic flared, burning its way down her arm and into the other woman. A roaring sounded in Alana's ears as the power poured into Krista, scorching its way through her mind, tearing and rending at her consciousness. The woman began to shake beneath Alana's grip, her body growing taut, as though trying to flee. But there was nowhere left for her to run. Alana's power was within her, and there was no escape.

The thrill of her own power filled Alana as she chased down the woman's mind, harrying her spirit, tearing at the flickering light that was the teacher's consciousness. With every blow, she watched memories spill out into the void, to be consumed by the flames of her magic. Krista's spirit shrank, its flight slowing, allowing Alana's magic to engulf it. Swallowing it whole, she washed away the last of the woman-who-had-been-Krista, until only the stark emptiness of the void remained.

Finally satisfied, Alana released Krista's hand and stepped back. Her knees shook and a sudden weakness came over her. Gasping for breath, Alana staggered, and inwardly cursed her other self for wasting her power. Two days had now passed, and still her magic was as weak as a new-born fawn. Still, she was stronger than she'd been the day she woke, and more than strong enough to deal with one as weak as the teacher.

Smiling, Alana straightened and stepped up to the woman, inspecting her work. Krista stood there dumbly, her vacant eyes fixed on some distant point. Alana placed a hand on her shoulder, and the teacher blinked, the light slowly coming back into her eyes. Her brow creased as she found Alana standing in front of her.

"Who are you?" she asked. Then she staggered, clutching at her chest. "Who am *I*?"

Alana smiled to herself. To the woman, she said: "You are no one." Her voice was cold, and she showed no emotion in the face of the woman's distress. "And you should not be here."

"I'm sorry," Krista whispered, tears appearing in her eyes. "I don't know how I got here. I think…I think I am lost."

"Very lost," Alana agreed.

Taking the woman by the shoulder, she shoved her in the direction of the exit. Krista stumbled a few steps, and then sank to her knees, tears streaming down her face. "Where am I?" she cried.

Her patience wearing thin, Alana grabbed the woman by the wrist and yanked her back up. "Come on," she snapped.

Taking a firmer grip on the former teacher, she dragged her through the gardens, retracing her steps back inside. They wound their way through the citadel, Krista sobbing all the while, until they finally came to the gates leading out into the city.

The guards stood to attention when they saw Alana. "Your highness," one said, his chainmail rattling as he stepped up to greet her. "What brings…the two of you here today?" His eyes flickered nervously at the crying teacher.

Alana flashed the guard a cold smile. "Open the gates," she commanded. "Krista wishes to walk the city."

The man hesitated. The smile fell from Alana's face, and she stepped towards him. His face blanked, and she savoured his sudden look of fear; he was lifting the crossbar to the gates before she could take another step. The squeal of the steel hinges followed as the heavy wood and iron gates swung ponderously open.

Still with Krista in tow, Alana walked through, leaving the guards to stare after them. She led the former teacher several blocks through the cobbled streets before coming to a stop in a dark alley. The scent of urine wafted up from the stones beneath their feet, and not wanting to spend any more time in the filthy streets than necessary, Alana turned to Krista.

"This is where you belong, woman," she said coldly, releasing the former teacher's hand.

There was open fear in Krista's eyes now. The sun was hidden by the tall walls of the alleyway, and the temperature had barely risen above freezing.

"Where will I go?" she whispered.

Alana shrugged and started to leave, her thoughts already turning to the children waiting for her return. She would have to work them doubly hard now, to make up for the damage Krista had done. But the former teacher reached out and grabbed her sleeve.

"Please! Please…can you at least tell me who I am?"

Alana watched the tears streaming down the woman's pretty face. Her eyes were now shot with red, and her thin yellow dress would do nothing to fend off the winter cold. With her power bound deep within her, it was unlikely Krista would ever rediscover her magic. Without it, she wouldn't last a week outside the citadel.

A wave of pity swept over Alana as she looked on the wreck she'd left of the former teacher, and for a second she considered reversing the spell.

"It didn't have to be this way," she murmured.

Krista stared back at her, confused and fearful, already starting to tremble in the cold air.

Alana sighed. Shaking her head, she reached out to touch the woman, to undo what she'd done, when she sensed a wrongness within her. She frowned and turned her mind inwards, and found that other part of herself hovering in the void. Rage flared in her chest as she realised the girl's weakness had been corrupting her. Summoning her magic, she drove the foolish girl back into the darkness, and the pity faded.

Looking back at Krista, she felt only disgust at the woman's weakness. "Get out of my sight," she spat.

With that, Alana turned away. A cry came from behind her, but Krista made no move to follow her. Within minutes Alana was marching back through the gates of the citadel, the woman's sobs already a distant memory. Her mind was already on the task ahead, on the drills and punishments she would need to burn the weakness from her children.

She would begin with the blades, she decided. They would hack and slash at one another until their arms were dead and their bodies beaten black and blue. The first to drop would be sent before the Tsar, as an example to the others.

Alana was just crossing through into the first courtyard beyond the gates when she realised she'd forgotten something. She hailed the guards. "Gentlemen, be so good as to keep the riffraff out in future. I would be very displeased to see that woman back inside the citadel."

The guards saluted without hesitation this time, and smiling, Alana walked away. Whistling a soft tune, she wandered back through the citadel, already savouring the thought of the torments she had in store for her new charges.

❧ 18 ❧

B raidon paced quickly around the narrow room, the smooth stone walls seeming to draw closer with every lap he took. Flicking another glance at the steel panelled door, he wondered what was taking place behind it. Surely it couldn't take this long to sort out the misunderstanding. After all, the accusation by the Plorsean emissaries was patently ridiculous—he wasn't the son of the Tsar. His father was a...merchant.

He frowned, struggling to recall his past. The memories rose slowly, though they remained blurred and indistinct, as though viewed through a mist. He remembered his father as a giant of a man, a...traveller who he rarely saw. And then...nothing.

Groaning, he resumed his pacing. He'd been waiting more than an hour now, the pain of the blows he'd taken from the guards forgotten in the face of the Queen's revelation. He still couldn't believe she'd set her men on him—and on the word of some two-faced emissary! That she thought him capable of such deceit....

Braidon froze as the soft whisper of oiled hinges opening came from across the room. He spun, and watched in silence as the Queen and Enala entered the room. The Queen's expression was unreadable, and Braidon turned his gaze on Enala, seeking to find some sign of their decision.

His heart sank as he saw the sadness in her eyes.

"It's not true!" Before he could stop himself, his words were echoing through the chamber.

The Queen froze, and for a moment Braidon thought he saw uncertainty flicker across her face. Then the mask fell back into place, and she strode the rest of the way across the room.

"I'm afraid it is," she said coldly. "Though I understand now it was not you who practiced the deception, but your sister."

"What are you talking about? Alana is the Tsar's hostage!" Braidon shouted, his confusion turning to anger.

"That's not true." The Queen spoke over him, her eyes flashing a warning. Braidon bit his tongue, and she went on. "It seems Alana is a Magicker of some power. She used her magic to wipe your memory, to make you believe you were a simple commoner, instead of the Tsar's only son."

Braidon stood staring at them. "Wha…what?"

Her eyes shining, Enala knelt in front of him. "You are the son of the Tsar, Braidon," she said. Then she was reaching out, pulling him into her arms, holding him tight.

His chest constricted, and Braidon found himself lost for breath. He clutched at the old woman's back, struggling to make sense of the words, even as his mind began to spin. He saw again the images of his father, swirling in the mist, falling back into a void in the centre of his soul. And then he *knew*. The memories remained locked away, but he *knew* Enala's words were the truth.

"No," he whispered, clinging to Enala as though his life depended on it. "I…I don't want it, I don't."

"It's okay," Enala breathed, pulling back from him for a

moment. There were tears in her eyes, but she wiped them away.

A tremor swept through Braidon as he looked from her to the Queen. "I don't want to go back."

The Queen looked away. "You must."

"Still you persist on this path, Merydith?" Enala stood. "Can't you see the boy is terrified?"

The Queen did not back down. "I must!" she hissed. "If I refuse him, it will mean war. And we do not have the strength to stand against the Tsar's powers!"

"For years you have given refuge to renegade Magickers. Ask them for their help. They will not deny you!"

"No, they would not. But I gave them sanctuary without obligation—not to make them into an army. It would make a mockery of everything we've worked for."

"And this does not?" Enala snapped. "What makes Braidon any different from the others?"

"He does not face death," the Queen answered, her voice sad. "The emissary says the spell was a mistake, that his sister will reverse it. He will become himself again."

"No!" Braidon cried, scrambling back. "I won't!"

"The boy does not wish to go, Merydith," Enala said, stepping between them. "Will you truly take him by force?"

The Queen stared at Enala, fists clenched, eyes shimmering. "You would have me sacrifice a nation to save one life?" she whispered.

"I would have you hold to the morals your parents held so dear," Enala replied.

"We cannot win," the Queen said. "The Tsar commands tens-of-thousands, has Magickers and demons and dragons by the score. And then there is the man himself…"

"Northland is not without power," Enala reminded her.

"No, but we have no standing army, and our population is

too dispersed. It would take months to gather a force capable of matching him, longer still to train it."

Enala sighed, her eyes taking on a haunted look. Gently, she gripped the Queen's shoulder. "I cannot make this decision for you, Merydith. It is yours alone. But think on this—war is coming. If not today, then soon. The Tsar will not allow you to continue outside his rule. I know his mind. Sooner or later, he will seek to conquer the last bastion for magic."

Braidon watched as a strained silence fell between the two women. His heart thumped hard in his chest, and he was still struggling to breathe. Even so, his thoughts were becoming clearer now, his mind working hard to follow the conversation.

"Have you heard any news of Devon?" he asked suddenly.

The two women jumped, as though surprised to find him still standing there. After a moment, Enala shook her head.

"I have heard nothing. I'm sorry."

"Then I'll go," Braidon heard himself saying. The women's eyes widened, and he pressed on before his courage abandoned him. "Not with the emissary, but I'll go. If what you're saying is true, and Alana is really…the Tsar's daughter again, then Devon and Kellian are walking into a trap. We need to warn them."

"It doesn't need to be you, Braidon," Enala replied gently.

"No." Braidon paused, gathering his strength before continuing. "But I won't remain here while my sister is… imprisoned. You say she is there by choice, but I cannot believe that. And if Devon can't save her, it will have to be me."

Silence answered his words. The two women watched him, their eyes shining in the candlelight. Unable to tell their thoughts, Braidon looked away, his stomach tight with worry.

"You are a brave man, Braidon." He jumped as a hand settled on his shoulder. He was surprised to find the Queen standing over him. Gone was the hardness to her eyes, the anger and the fear. With a long sigh, she went on. "For what it's worth, you may remain in Erachill if your mind changes. I will not betray you to the Plorseans."

His throat tight, Braidon nodded his thanks, as Enala moved up alongside them. "She may not be the same woman you remember, Braidon."

"I know," he said, "but I still have to try."

Enala nodded, her eyes tearing.

"I will go alone if I have to," he said, a smile coming to his lips, "but it would be nice to have a dragon…"

The women blinked, then a grin split Enala's face as she started to laugh. "You will have one," she replied. "On one condition."

"Name it," Braidon answered.

"Master your magic, my child," the old woman replied, "and I will take you to Ardath myself."

Alana sighed as she sank into the velvet sofa, a glass of Lonian Red in hand. She was just about to take a sip when a *thump* came from the outer door to her quarters, followed by the soft squeal of hinges as it swung open. Quinn appeared in the doorway, his eyes sweeping the room before settling on Alana.

"Quinn," she said, a smile coming to her lips. After the long day she'd spent putting her new students through the wringer, he was just the man she wanted to see. "Come in, help yourself to some wine."

Wearing a smile of his own, he crossed to a cabinet on the wall and took out a glass. He filled it generously from the bottle on the table, then joined her on the sofa. "So, I hear you didn't waste much time…dealing with your replacement."

Alana sipped her wine, savouring the rich earthliness of the vintage, and she slid closer to Quinn until their legs were touching. "The woman annoyed me," she said simply.

Quinn laughed. "I'd best tread carefully then," he said, resting his hand on her thigh. With the fire keeping the cold of winter at bay, she had already changed into a loose fitting black skirt, its intricately knitted hem riding up above her knees. "I can't say I ever really liked her myself," he finished.

"I'm surprised you didn't deal with her then," Alana replied, enjoying the warmth of his touch as his hand slid higher, "after her show of disrespect on the battlements."

Quinn's hand stilled. "You heard about that?"

"Of course."

He sighed, glancing away for a moment. "Much as I might have liked to…remove her, I am not the Daughter of the Tsar," he answered carefully. "I have other matters with which to concern myself with, without starting a war with the other Magickers in the citadel."

Alana laughed. Leaning against him, she trailed her fingers up his chest, and looked up at him with playful eyes. "Has my father been keeping you busy?" she breathed. "Is that where you keep sneaking off too?"

Enjoying the slightly panicked look in his eyes, she lifted herself up until their faces were level, and pressed her lips to his. With a moan, he sank back into the sofa as she slid into his lap. Heat spread through her stomach as he stirred beneath her, his hands wrapping around her waist. Supressing a moan of her own, she bit his lip hard, the need swelling within her.

He flinched from the pain, but she held him tight, and a trickle of her magic seeped into him. Relaxing again, his eyelids flickered as a distant look came over his eyes. She grinned, enjoying her power over the man, before drawing her magic back into herself. Groaning, he blinked, coming back to himself. He almost looked surprised to find her straddling him.

Then a stiffness came over his face, an almost primal look, and Alana gasped as he tossed her down on the sofa alongside him. Before she could think, his weight was on her, pinning her down. A shock raced down her spine as he kissed her neck, and she wanted to scream for him to hurry, to tear apart her clothes and take her…

She fumbled desperately at Quinn's belt as he grabbed at her blouse and ripped it open. Buttons went scattering across the fur rug, and she moaned as his mouth slid down her body, his tongue circling her nipples.

Alana felt a rush of triumph as the belt came loose, then her hands were travelling down, gripping him tight, drawing him in…

Afterwards, they found themselves on Alana's bed, chests heaving, cheeks flushed. Still hot from their exertions, Alana lay back, content for the moment. But slowly the gratification of her triumph faded, replaced by a sudden emptiness, and the smile faded from her lips.

Quinn curled up alongside her, his muscled arms enfolding her in an embrace. The show of affection took her off-guard, especially after the way he'd taken her at the end. There had been an animalistic gleam in his eyes as he threw her down on the bed and flipped her onto her stomach…but now, as he kissed her gently on the cheek, she saw only warmth in his expression.

Devon's face drifted across her thoughts, and Alana felt a rush of irritation. Suddenly, she wanted nothing more than to be left alone. Wriggling clear of his arms, she struggled to keep her anger from showing. Within, she sensed no interference from her other self. Unable to pick the source of her disgruntlement, she lay back and stared at the mosaiced ceiling above her poster-bed.

"I saw the children earlier." Quinn didn't seem to have noticed her change in mood.

Alana was glad for the change in topic. "What did you think?" she asked. Recalling her efforts earlier with the young Magickers, she felt a warm sense of satisfaction. Krista had left a troop of weak and unruly children in her wake, but Alana was determined to turn them into the Battle Magickers her father needed. "They have a long way to go, but I think they can be saved."

Quinn grunted. "You don't think you might be pushing them too hard?"

"What?" Alana hissed, sitting up. Her irritation turned to anger as she swung on him. "How *dare* you?"

"Let's not have this discussion again," Quinn replied with a sigh.

"No, let's," Alana growled.

She rolled from the bed. Scooping up a nightdress, she slipped into the soft silk, though it did little to conceal her curves. Quinn stared back at her, a pained look on his face, but it did nothing to quell her rage.

"Alana..." he started, then trailed off. Silently he reached for her, but she pushed him away. "Alana...it's just....beating them, running them until they drop, that's not how I trained you."

"No," she answered coldly, "that is what my father taught me." Quinn said nothing, but seeing the defiance in his gaze, she went on: "You may have taught me how to control my power, but it was the Tsar who forged me into a weapon, who gave me the strength to resist my magic's call."

"You were already strong..."

"Not strong enough," Alana snapped. For an instant, she recalled the first time she'd reached for her power, the icy chills that had engulfed her as the emerald Feline rose in the void. Shivering, she forced the image away. "If it had been up to you, I would have been lost. The magic would have taken me, turned me, made me into a demon."

"So now all your students must suffer the same torment that you did?"

Alana laughed, the sound harsh in the stone confines of her quarters. "I am letting them off easy, compared to what my father subjected me to."

Quinn's eyes were sad now. "And what about your brother? Is that what you wish for him, when he returns?"

The retort died in Alana's throat, and she stood staring at Quinn, mouth open. Ice spread through her stomach as she imagined delivering her brother to the Tsar, the agony he would suffer, the fear and dread, and eventually, the awful hatred.

"What about the boy, Liam?" Quinn went on, taking a step closer. "I saw him in the corner of the dining hall, bruised black and blue, all alone. The others told me he is to take his examination tomorrow. I spoke with him—he's not ready, not even close. If he goes before the Tsar, he *will* fail."

"Then he will die, and my father will have another demon to serve him!" Alana screamed, her rage washing away all thoughts of her brother.

"You're condemning him to a fate worse than death."

"Get out," Alana roared, pointing at the doorway.

For a moment it looked as though he would refuse. Teeth bared, Alana stepped towards him, hand outstretched, her power bubbling in her chest. His eyes widened in fear, and before she could reach him, he spun and retreated through the outer doors. The *thud* of them closing behind him echoed loudly through her bedchamber.

Lowering her arm, Alana stared at the place where he had stood. The anger drained from her, slipping away until she felt only emptiness. Her shoulders slumped, and retreating to the bed, she dropping onto the satin duvet. Closing her eyes, she tried to bring back the anger, to feel anything but the awful void in her chest. But it would not come, and tossing and turning amidst the cushions, she drifted slowly into sleep.

❧ 20 ❧

Night was falling as the Stalkers led Devon and Kellian through the gates of the citadel. The day had been a hard one for both of them, sitting helpless on their horses as they drew ever closer to Onslow. The Stalkers had taken no chances with either of them. Kellian had been searched as he lay unconscious, all his knives taken from him. And not even Devon's prodigious strength could break their bindings. Even if they were to slip free, there were still more than twenty warriors and the captain's magic to deal with.

So instead, they had waited with growing frustration as they were loaded into the shallow-bottomed barge like sacks of grain. On the water, they had no hope of escaping, and the day had stretched out, the sun hot on their faces despite the cool winter breeze. Sailing upriver, Devon had watched as the waterway converged and broadened out into the great expanse of Lake Ardath.

Overhead, the black sails had creaked and groaned, a constant reminder of days long since passed, when Devon had first marched to war. The army had set off from Ardath with the rising sun, its scarlet rays staining the waters of the lake red. Standing on the deck of his ship, Devon had felt a thrill in his heart, a rush of joy as the trumpets sounded. Five years later though, there was only sorrow as he looked on the black sails of war.

Now, standing beneath the gates of the citadel, Devon couldn't help but wonder where everything had gone so wrong. He had been in his prime when the war ended, a warrior renown across the Three Nations. Fame and fortune had been his for the taking, if only he'd remained with the army. Instead, he had turned his back on his career as a soldier, and embraced a life of misery and despair.

Yet, as the gates swung shut behind them, he realised he felt no regret, and a smile came to his face.

"What are you grinning about, traitor?" Darnell snapped, coming alongside him. She was carrying *kanker* loosely in one hand.

Still smiling, Devon shook his head. "The folly of the young," he said.

Her face darkened and her fist lashed out to catch him in the solar plexus. His hands tied behind his back, Devon was unable to avoid the punch, and he doubled over, gasping for breath. But it was not the first blow he'd suffered that day, and after a moment he straightened with a laugh.

"You pack quite the punch, missy," he grunted, "but next time try putting your hips into–"

He broke off as she struck him again, a blow to the side of his head sending him reeling. Stars flashed across his vision and he almost fell, only the wall of the corridor keeping him upright.

"One more word, and you'll lose more than just your wits, traitor," Darnell said, her hand resting on the pommel of her sword.

This time, Devon decided to keep his mouth shut. Beside him, Kellian was in even worse shape than himself. His quick tongue had earned him several beatings on the voyage across the lake, but he had fallen silent now, his face a mess of purple and blue.

Marching deeper into the citadel, they followed the Stalkers through dimly lit courtyards and long marble hallways. Outside, the sun had dropped below the citadel walls, and here and there they encountered servants running about with fresh lanterns. As they passed through another courtyard, Devon glanced up and saw the stone lattices shielding the upper floors. Idly he wondered what unseen eyes might be watching their progress through the citadel, before they disappeared into yet another corridor.

Curiously, there weren't many guards in sight, though those they did see were heavily armed, their steel-plated armour shining in the lantern light. Most of their company had departed now: Godrin's men had remained outside while he continued with them, and most of the Stalkers had peeled off during their passage through the citadel. By the time they finally stopped outside a set of double doors, there was only the captain and two of her Stalkers left alongside Godrin. Together, they entered a white-walled chamber lined with steel doors.

One of the Stalkers entered one of the doors, while the other helped Godrin shepherd the two prisoners after him—though neither Devon nor Kellian attempted to resist. With their arms still tied behind their backs, they would be quickly overtaken if they did. No, the time to strike would be when their bindings were finally loosened.

Devon turned as the door clanged closed, watching their captors with a wary eye. The room in which they found themselves was unadorned but for several sets of chains hanging from the stone walls. There were no windows, and the only exit was the door through which they'd entered. His eyes were drawn to a single table set in the corner. Ice slid down his spine as he saw the implements laid out on the wooden surface.

"This isn't the dungeons," he murmured.

"You thought I would share my glory with the dungeon master?" Darnell replied, brushing a lock of hair from her face. Moving to the table, she unbuckled her sword belt and placed it on the table, then set *kanker* down beside it. "No, these are my private...quarters. Jarson, Olie, if you could introduce Devon and his friend to their new accommodations?"

Devon tensed as the two Stalkers moved forward, readying himself. This was their chance. They would have to loosen his and Kellian's bonds before chaining them to the walls; in that instant, there would be a moment when he could act. The Stalker to his right was a woman, almost as large as himself, while the man on his left was slightly smaller. Beyond them, Darnell and Godrin were standing too far back to interfere immediately. If he could down the two Stalkers, steal one of their weapons, he would stand a chance.

As the woman closed on him, he gathered himself, preparing to unleash bloody chaos the moment his bonds were loosened. But the moment the woman touched the ropes around his wrists, Darnell raised her hand. Before Devon could react, a sharp, piercing cold wrapped around his skull. Crying out, his legs crumpled beneath him, but the Stalkers caught him before he could fall. Through the agony, he hardly felt their jostling as they tore the ropes from his arms and shoved him up against the wall.

A sharp *click* sliced through the pain, and the cold vanished as quickly as it had come. He blinked, light dancing before his eyes, and he realised with dismay his arms had already been cuffed to the wall. Slumping against the cold stone, he watched in growing despair as the same procedure was repeated with his friend.

"And you have the gall to call me a coward," he finally managed to croak as the spell was lifted from Kellian.

Darnell only smiled. "One can only make use of the tools with which they were gifted." She said. "It is not my fault you chose to spurn yours, Devon. I know your story. You were blessed beyond all other warriors, a legend amongst the Tsar's soldiers, but you threw everything away." Stepping back, she shook her head. "Thank the Tsar I had a strong teacher, or I may never have mastered this power."

"Whoever he was, he sure did a fine job of turning out monsters," Kellian groaned, lifting himself to his feet and taking the weight off the chains now fastened around his wrists.

The captain smiled. "*She* is a great woman, and the daughter of the Tsar." She turned to one of her Stalkers. "Go and fetch Quinn, tell him I've brought him Devon. I can't wait to see his face when he learns it was *I* who finally brought the cowardly hero to justice!"

The black-cloaked Stalker nodded and left the room, the heavy wooden door slamming closed behind her. Watching her go, Devon strained against the chains holding him to the wall, testing their strength. The one holding his left arm seemed to move slightly; letting off the pressure, he stared at their three remaining foes.

The captain was no longer paying them any attention. She turned towards the table in the corner, then seemed to notice Godrin standing nearby. "Trolan, what are you still doing here?"

Devon pulled against the left-hand chain again as Godrin coughed. "There is the small matter of my payment, captain."

Darnell narrowed her eyes. "You'll get your gold, Trolan. But not now, it's late. Go back to your men, return in the morning. You'll receive your payment then."

"Do you think me a fool, captain?" Godrin murmured,

stepping in close. He gestured at Devon and Kellian. "The second I step through that door, my involvement in this whole affair will be forgotten."

"You overstep yourself, Trolan," the captain growled. Raising her fist, she opened her fingers. Blue light seeped across the room.

The sight gave Godrin pause. He stepped back, his hands raised in deference. "My apologies, captain," he said quickly. His eyes went to the other Stalker, who stood close to the prisoners, then back to Darnell. He lowered his hands. "It will be as you say. I shall return in the morning."

Darnell waited until he turned away before lowering her fist. Smiling, she faced Devon and Kellian. Gritting his teeth, Devon strained against his bindings, feeling the bolt in the wall beginning to give…

"Only one thing, captain," Godrin said suddenly, pausing at the door.

Growling, Darnell swung towards him, her hand coming up. "And what is tha–"

She never got to finish her sentence. As she turned, Godrin's hand whipped out, and a knife flashed across the room to bury itself in her throat. Darnell gasped, her hand reaching for the ivory hilt. Blood bubbled between her fingers as she tried to pull it free, but then the strength fled from her and she toppled silently to the ground. A pool of blood began to spread across the floor, almost black in the dim light.

"What the *hell?*" The one remaining Stalker stood stunned, looking from his captain to Godrin.

He scrambled for his sword as Godrin started towards him. The Trolan had left his sword at the gates, but he already had a fresh knife to hand. Steel scraped on leather as the Stalker drew his blade and roared.

Before the two men could meet, Devon yanked again at the weakening bolt. With a sharp *crack*, it came free. The Stalker had his back to the prisoners, but at the noise he glanced back, and Devon's fist crunched into his face. The blow sent him staggering backwards out of Devon's reach, straight into Godrin's dagger. Twisting the blade, Godrin dragged it back, and the man collapsed in a heap alongside his captain.

Leaning down, Godrin wiped his dagger clean on the man's shirt. Calmly he recovered a short sword and the keys from Darnell. Then, still smiling, he stepped towards Devon and Kellian.

"Time to be going, don't you think?"

21

"What the hell is going on?" Devon asked, gaping in disbelief at the bloody corpses on the floor.

Godrin shrugged. "You said you needed a way into the citadel. I arranged one."

"I didn't mean in bloody chains!"

The Trolan held up the keys. "Easily fixed."

Devon stared at them for a moment, then snapped. "Well what are you damn well waiting for?"

Feeling his anger mounting, Devon strained against the remaining chain holding him to the wall. When it wouldn't budge, he stilled, and a tremor shook him. Despite his earlier bravado, for a moment he had truly thought they were doomed, and the shock of that realisation was just beginning to touch him.

Godrin stepped towards them, then paused, his smile faltering. He glanced at Kellian, then back to Devon. "Sorry about the beatings…had to make it believable, you know?"

Devon bared his teeth. "Delaying isn't helping your cause. Now get these damn chains off of us!"

Godrin showed his hands. "Gladly!" He paused. "Just…

we're all friends here okay? No need to rehash the last few hours."

Straining his arms, Devon tested the remaining chain again, but there was no give in it. He let out a long sigh and looked at the Trolan. "Just get us out of here, before the Stalker returns with Quinn," he said, trying to keep his voice calm.

Godrin watched them a moment longer before apparently making up his mind. Moving forward, he unlocked the chain from around Devon's wrist, then moved to do the same for his friend. Kellian groaned, slumping slightly against Godrin before finding his feet. Rubbing his wrists, he pushed the Trolan away from him. Godrin stumbled back, opening his mouth to complain, but broke off when he saw Kellian sweep up a fallen knife.

"Hey, what—"

Kellian's empty fist caught Godrin in the jaw before he could finish the question. The blow sent the Trolan reeling sideways. His foot caught on the Stalker's lifeless body and he went down hard. Gasping, he rolled onto his knees and tried to rise, only to freeze as Kellian's blade touched his neck.

Kellian raised an eyebrow at Devon. "What do you think, should I kill him?"

Still on his knees, Godrin glowered at them. "Typical Plorseans, can't trust a single one of ya."

"That's rich, coming from you," Kellian snapped. His face was swollen, and a cut above his eyebrow was seeping blood.

"I did what I said I would," Godrin said coldly. "I never said it would be easy. You're lucky I got you this far."

"Am I?" Kellian leaned down, the blade pressing harder. Devon saw the Trolan flinch back, bleeding now from a shallow cut on his neck.

Godrin reached up to touch the wound, his hand coming away wet with blood. As he turned his gaze back on them,

Devon saw the familiar hate lurking behind his eyes. It seemed not everything had been an act. Stepping up beside his friend, Devon gently lowered Kellian's hand.

"What a world we live in, when it's the butcher who stays the innkeeper's hand," Godrin spat. Rising slowly to his feet, he glared at Kellian. "Well?"

Kellian didn't answer, leaving Devon to address the Trolan. Devon sucked in a breath, seeking to quell his own anger, even as Kellian circled the room, collecting a sword and several more knives from the fallen Stalkers.

"I'm…sorry for our anger," he said at last. "You were true to your word, I can't fault you that, sonny. Might be you could have found a…gentler subterfuge, but you have my gratitude for getting us this far."

Godrin smiled coldly. "If you don't mind, I require a little more than just gratitude." He walked across to the table and hefted *kanker*.

Devon narrowed his eyes, his heartbeat quickening at the sight of the Trolan holding his ancestor's weapon. "That's mine," he said.

"Yes, well, times change," Godrin replied. When Devon said nothing, he sighed and waved at the door. "You came here to save your friend. I understand that, though I can't bring myself to wish you luck. I only came here to kill the Tsar."

"You're welcome to him," Devon growled. "What does *kanker* have to do with it?"

Godrin grinned. "You didn't think I hadn't heard the rumours, did you, Devon?" he asked. "The whole Empire has been talking of it, how you defeated a demon, and fought off a hoard of Stalkers, even one with magic. It's simply not possible for a mortal to have accomplished such feats—not even for a warrior like you. Not unless…" he trailed off, his eyes drifting to the hammer, "not unless you had a magic hammer."

Devon swallowed, his words abandoning him, and Godrin nodded.

"I thought so."

"You can't have it," Devon hissed.

"Think of it as a loan," Godrin said.

"We don't even know if its powerful enough to defeat his magic," Devon argued.

"Yes, well, that's a risk I'm going to have to take," Godrin murmured. "If it's not...then at least I'll be making up for running away while your army overtook Kalgan." As he spoke, a haunted look came over his face, and Devon caught a glimpse of the pain within.

The fight went from Devon then, as he realised the crime lord shared Devon's own sense of shame over his decisions during the war. Yes, he had saved lives by fleeing the city with his cohort and a ship full of civilians. But in doing so, Godrin had abandoned his comrades, leaving them to their death.

He sighed. "Fine," he said, "just make sure you don't get any scratches on her."

Godrin chuckled. "I'll take good care of her." He paused as Kellian returned to stand alongside Devon. Silently, he handed over a short sword, then turned his gaze on the crime lord. Godrin coughed, only finding his voice after several seconds of strained silence. "As for your friend...I asked some of the Stalkers about her, told them you were looking for her..."

"Yes?" Devon pressed when the Trolan did not continue.

"They laughed," Godrin said, his eyes on the floor. "They said...they said she'd be the death of you, Devon. If you ever found her."

Devon frowned. "What are you talking about?"

"They didn't elaborate. But she's here, in the citadel. I got that much from them."

"In the dungeons?"

"No, the eastern wing. From what I managed to discern,"

Godrin said.

"Can you take us there?" Devon asked.

"You know I can't," Godrin replied. "I have my own mission. If I wait until you free the girl, the chance will be lost. No, we must part ways here. I can only send you in the right direction."

Swiftly he outlined the passageways they would need to take to reach the eastern wing of the citadel. They were close, fortunately, but once there Godrin's instructions ran dry. They would need to locate Alana's room themselves, and find a way to avoid any guards stationed in the hallways along the way.

"Good luck, to the both of you," Godrin said finally.

Devon swallowed, then stretched out his hand. Godrin took it after a moment's hesitation. "I expect you to live, sonny," Devon grunted. "Don't you go disappointing me. I like that hammer."

"I'll do my best." Godrin grinned.

"I can't say it's been a pleasure," Devon added as they broke apart.

Godrin laughed. "Oh, I don't know about that," he replied. "I got to beat the Butcher of Kalgan, after all. Something to tell the young ones about one day."

"You'll be telling them how you lost your teeth in a minute," Devon growled, but the Trolan was already disappearing through the door.

Alone now with Kellian, he glanced at his friend. "I have to say, he's starting to grow on me."

"He would," Kellian replied wryly. He rolled his shoulders, wincing in pain, before looking at Devon again. "Well, shall we get on with it? The night's already old, and we've got a princess to save."

Gripping the unfamiliar short sword in one hand, Devon nodded, and together the two of them passed through the door, and out into the passageways of the citadel.

"Sir, a moment?"

Quinn looked up from the reports he was reading, irritated at the interruption. Unable to sleep after his argument with Alana, he had headed for his office, intent on finalising his reports on the army's preparation. But his irritation faded as he recognised the Stalker standing in the doorway as one of Darnell's squad, the ones who'd been tasked with hunting down Devon. He rose to his feet and waved the woman inside.

"Has something happened?" he asked, his heart beating faster.

If Darnell had made a mistake and let Devon slip through her fingers, the hammerman might even now be close, in the city even, seeking a way into the citadel. A sliver of ice seeped into his stomach as he thought of facing the man again.

Gripping his desk, he lowered himself back into his chair and indicated for the Stalker to do the same. Unconsciously he reached for his magic and felt it surge within him. The fear subsided, replaced with a cold determination. If Devon came, he would be ready. Hammer or no, the man could not face all the forces at the Tsar's command and expect to survive.

"No, sir."

Quinn's head jerked up at the woman's words. The Stalker sat nervously across from him, her eyes flickering from Quinn to the doorway. His irritation returning, Quinn scowled. "No?" he growled. "Then why are you here, soldier?"

"I…Darnell sent me," she said quickly. "She wants you in her chambers."

"In her chambers?" Quinn said, momentarily confused. "She's here?"

"Yes, sir," the Stalker replied, "we arrived just after sunset."

Speechless, Quinn stared at the woman for a long moment, before finally finding his words. "She has given up the pursuit of Devon and Kellian already?"

The Stalker swallowed. "That's…not for me to say, sir," she said. "The captain only said for you to come as quickly as possible. She wishes to brief you herself."

Quinn glared at the Stalker, and watched with satisfaction as she shrank in her seat. "The captain thinks to command *me?*"

"I…no…she only requested…your presence, sir," the woman finished lamely, her eyes blinking rapidly in the fading light of a single candle.

"Tell me why you're here," Quinn growled, "instead of chasing down the renegades, as you were *commanded* by the Tsar."

The woman blanked. "We…we already have them…sir," she managed.

"What?"

"We caught them," the Stalker said. "They were taken unaware by the Trolans. All we had to do was march up and arrest them."

"Devon is *here?*" Quinn said, leaping to his feet.

"Yes, sir."

"Then take me to him," Quinn growled.

The Stalker snapped to attention, and sweeping up his sword, Quinn followed her out the door. In the corridor he strapped his sword belt to his waist as they started on their way. The Stalker constantly flicked glances back at Quinn as they walked, revealing her fear. She had betrayed her captain's command, and while Quinn had given her little choice, no doubt Darnell would make her life a living hell for it.

In that moment, Quinn didn't care. His hand drifted to the hilt of his sabre, gripping it tight. The hammerman was *here*. How had that happened?

He's in custody, Quinn reminded himself.

Yet something didn't seem right about the story. Devon and Kellian were wily men; it was unlikely they would be taken unawares by anyone, let alone some washed-up ex-soldiers from Trola. Jaw clenched, he picked up the pace, yelling at his companion to do the same.

They reached Darnell's quarters a few minutes later. A single door hung open and unguarded. Inside, they found the crumpled bodies of Darnell and one of her Stalkers, their life blood spreading slowly across the tiled floor.

The woman who had led Quinn there stood frozen in the doorway as Quinn strode past.

"I...I..." she stuttered.

Ignoring her, Quinn studied the room. Darnell lay face down, a dagger buried in her throat. The other Stalker had managed to crawl a few inches, before he too expired, succumbing to the terrible wound someone had torn in his belly. Of Kellian and Devon, there was no sign.

"Alert the guards. Devon is in the citadel. Send men to the princess's quarters—he'll be heading there," Devon said, swinging on the Stalker still standing in the doorway. When she didn't move, he roared: "*Now!*"

His command echoed loudly in the room and the Stalker

leapt to a salute. She made to turn, then paused. "Sir…" she said, her voice fading as he glared at her.

"What?" he snapped.

"There was someone else here: Godrin, the Trolan who betrayed the two renegades."

"Of course," Quinn growled. "Now go!"

So the Tsar's informant had double-crossed them. Darnell should have expected it—Trolans could only be trusted as far as their next bribe. No doubt the thought of being a thorn in the Tsar's side had been too tempting for the man to pass up.

He frowned. Turning back, he surveyed the room, searching for clues, but the Trolan's motive remained a mystery.

Why would the a Trolan help Devon?

His anxiety was growing. With every passing moment, Devon could be drawing closer to Alana's quarters. He fought the urge to go racing there immediately—now that the princess was herself, she was more than capable of taking care of Devon. A smile came to his lips as he thought of the shock Devon would receive if he found her.

The smile faded as his thoughts returned to the Trolan spy. Here was the real mystery—and danger. He knew of Godrin's reputation. He did not take unnecessary risks, certainly not ones that were sure to end in his death. And however impressive his deception was, he couldn't hope to escape the citadel with the Tsar's daughter. Not alive.

No, he had to be here for some other reason. The man had not come all this way to die for a hopeless cause.

Perhaps he wants to assassinate the Tsar.

Quinn smiled at the thought. By all accounts, Godrin had no magic. He wouldn't stand a chance against the wealth of power at the Tsar's command. The man would be destroyed with a whisper.

Yet still something nagged at Quinn, as though he had the

jigsaw puzzle before him, but a single piece was missing. He left the dead captain's quarters and started walking. Without thinking, he headed for the Tsar's private quarters. They made up the entire south wing of the citadel, and it wasn't long before he reached their outer limits.

Here he paused, surprised to find no guards standing on the doors. Cursing, he pushed on the double doors, but they were locked against him. His fear growing, Quinn raised a hand and summoned his magic. Outside, the wind swirled, then with a roar, it came racing into the corridor. It hissed around his arm, catching on his cloak. He sent it rushing at the doors with a gesture, caving them inwards.

Striding through, he stopped for a second to inspect the dead bodies of the guards. The head of one was crushed, while the other had been killed when a blunt instrument had caved in his armour. Quinn swore again. There was little doubt the wounds had been caused by *kanker*. Had Devon decided to come for the Tsar instead of rescuing Alana?

Everything he knew of his former comrade said no, and yet…silently, he cursed the reduction in guards around the citadel. If only someone had heard the commotion, the hammerman would have been surrounded the second he engaged with the guards. Instead, he was now inside the Tsar's quarters, with little more than a few patrols standing between his hammer and the ruler of the Three Nations.

Quinn's breath caught in his throat at the thought.

The hammer!

Now he was running, sabre already in hand, his boots slapping hard against the smooth stone. He took the corners without slowing as he mapped out the path to the Tsar's room in his mind. It was still some minutes away. Gritting his teeth, he picked up the pace.

As he turned the final corner, a shout echoed down the corridor. Breathless, Quinn raced towards the open door to the

Tsar's rooms, sword raised, magic gathering in his chest. He burst through the door, a roar on his lips, the wind already swirling around him.

Halfway across the room, a man turned and saw him. He held *kanker* in one hand and blood covered his jerkin. For a moment, shock registered on his face. Then, lifting the ancient hammer above his head, he screamed a battle cry and leapt at the poster bed in the middle of the room.

Quinn threw out his arm, and the wind raced from him. Above the intruder's head, *kanker* began to glow. Quinn cursed as he sensed his winds being sucked into the weapon, but he kept on. A strange whisper spread through the room as the gale vanished into the hammer. Yet not all of the gusts were consumed, and with a muffled *thud*, what remained struck the stranger hard in the back.

There was enough power in the blow to send the man toppling forward. Crying out, he flung out his arms, and *kanker* slipped from his fingers to fly across the room. Triumphant, Quinn sent another blast of wind at the man. He went flying backwards and struck the corner post of the Tsar's bed with a hard *thud*. As he slumped to the ground, Quinn lowered his arm.

Movement came from the bed as the Tsar, looking more mortal than Quinn had ever seen him, sat up. He frowned as he saw Quinn. His gaze transferred to the intruder, and his frown deepened.

"What is going on here, lieutenant?" he said calmly.

Quinn stepped into the room. "The citadel has been... compromised, your majesty."

A groan came from the intruder. His head shifted, his eyes flickering up to look at Quinn.

"You must be Godrin," Quinn said.

Grimacing, the man looked around, assessing the situation. Quinn smiled. *Kanker* lay on the ground at his feet, and idly he placed a foot on the weapon's haft, pinning it down. "Looking for this?" he asked.

But Godrin wasn't looking at him. His eyes were on the bedpost he had come to rest against. Quinn followed his gaze upwards, and saw with horror a sword looped over the corner of the poster bed, just within reach of the intruder.

"Don't–" he started, but the Tsar's voice cut him off.

"You came to kill me?" he whispered, pulling himself from the bed.

The Tsar looked undignified in his silken pyjamas, but Quinn could sense the power radiating from him. Smiling, he relaxed. Without the hammer, the assassin stood no chance now.

Godrin looked from the Tsar to the sword, obviously trying to judge whether he could reach it before being incinerated by the man's powers. Quinn frowned. Was it his imagination, or was there light seeping from its hilt?

"Go ahead," the Tsar said, gesturing at the weapon. "Perhaps you have what it takes."

The Trolan hesitated. The Tsar stood before him, his hands empty and wearing only his night clothes. Even knowing of his power, Quinn could see the temptation. If ever there was an opportunity to strike down the ruler of the Three Nations, this was it.

With a roar, Godrin surged to his feet and swept the blade from its sheath. Light flashed across the room as it slid clear, but to Quinn's surprise, it did not originate from the Tsar. A white glow shone from the blade, bathing the room, forcing Quinn to shield his eyes as he struggled to glimpse the Trolan.

The light died as quickly as it had appeared, revealing the two men still standing in place, unmoved. Quinn looked at the Tsar, noticing the grim smile on his unshaven face, before turning to the Trolan. The breath caught in his throat.

Godrin no longer breathed. The skin of his face had hardened to crystal, his eyes turned as black as coals. His hair had burnt away, leaving his head smooth, shining with the dim light still emanating from the sword. Quinn retched as a putrid stench hit him, of scorched hair and roasted flesh. Perhaps it was his imagination, but he swore a distant scream whispered to him on the breeze.

Then with a suddenness that made Quinn flinch, the Trolan shattered, his body disintegrating before their very eyes. Shards of crystal crashed to the ground and turned to dust. The sword rang as it struck the stone tiles, then lay still, a faint light still dancing in the blade. Silence fell over the room.

Quinn bit his tongue to keep from screaming. An awful voice was yelling at him to run from that place, to flee whatever magic was capable of dealing such an awful ending. Instead, he remained where he stood. Licking his lips, he looked at the Tsar, wondering if he would soon be following the Trolan for allowing an intruder so far inside the citadel.

The Tsar smiled. "My thanks, lieutenant," he said. "Though perhaps next time, you could stop the assassin before he reaches my quarters."

❦ 23 ❦

"**A**lana."

The voice whispered through the darkness, soft, rich with sadness. Alana shivered as she found Devon's amber eyes watching her.

"Alana," he called again, sending ripples racing through her spirit.

She went to him then, arms outstretched, soft sobs tearing from her. "Devon," she cried, "please, help me! She's destroying me—please!"

"It's okay," he said as his muscular arms encircled her, holding her tight. She sighed, his warmth filling her with a feeling of safety.

"Please help me," she whispered. "I don't know how to escape her."

"We will face her together," came his reply.

She nodded, pulling back and smiling up at him. Standing on her tiptoes, she made to kiss him. Before their lips could meet, an awful pain tore into her. She cried out and stumbled, her fingers fumbling for the wound and finding the hilt of a dagger piercing her stomach. The strength went from her legs, sending her crumpling to the ground. Green fire rose to encircle her. She tried to scream, but the burning green went pouring down her throat, choking off her cry.

Desperate, she stretched out a hand for Devon, but he was no longer looking at her. He still stood above her, but his eyes were fixed on the woman in front of him. Smiling, he opened his arms to embrace the other

Alana. Their lips locked, their spirits joining as they fell against each other. Anguish filled Alana as Devon began to kiss her neck. Cackling, the other woman glanced back, pure malevolence in her steely eyes.

And the darkness rose to claim her once more.

Back in her room, Alana gasped awake, the dream still clinging to her. Heart racing, she smiled as she recalled her other self's screams, the despair that had filled the girl as she took her precious Devon for herself.

"Alana?"

She jerked as a voice spoke from across the room. Sitting bolt upright, her hand fumbled for the sword she kept beside her bed. Her eyes swept the darkness, searching for the intruder, as her hand wrapped around the sword hilt. Beside her, the bed was empty, but the voice was not Quinn's. He wouldn't dare try to approach her yet, not until the light of day. Yet still, it sounded familiar.

"Who's there?" she hissed, rising naked from the bed, sword in hand.

A lantern was unshuttered, illuminating the faces of Devon and Kellian. Alana's mouth dropped open, words slipping unbidden from her mouth. "Devon, how are you here?"

"Nice to see you too, Alana," Kellian muttered as he moved forward, carrying the lantern. His eyes were drawn to the sword in her hand. "They gave you a weapon?"

Alana looked at the blade, then back at the two of them, lost for words. Slowly she closed her mouth. Despite herself, she felt a sudden sadness, a terrible regret for what would come next. "You should not have come here," she heard herself saying.

"Nonsense, princess," Devon replied. "We came to rescue you."

She shook her head, her sadness welling. "But I don't need rescuing, Devon."

The big man frowned, and Kellian shifted on his feet.

"What's going on here, Alana?" the innkeeper asked. "Why do you have a sword?"

Alana placed the blade back on her bedside table. As she did so, the realisation she was naked gave her pause. The men seemed to realise it at the same time, and averted their eyes. Her cheeks flushed and she quickly pulled a sheet around herself. Then her anger flared.

What did she care for modesty? She was Alana, Daughter of the Tsar, Princess of an Empire. She took what she wanted. She didn't care what anyone thought of her!

Yet when she glanced back at Devon, the warmth in her cheeks grew, and she kept the sheets wrapped around her.

"Is Braidon okay?" she whispered, seeking to distract herself from the heat in her stomach.

"He's safe," Devon replied, stepping closer. "We knew you'd never forgive us if we brought him along, so we left him with Enala—Tillie, I should say…there's a lot to catch you up on. Anyway, she will protect him. And teach him to use his magic."

Alana nodded, before the meaning of his words struck her. Her head snapped up, a sudden fear clenching at her chest. "No!" she hissed. She grabbed Devon's hand. "He can't…" she trailed off, unable to express where her terror had come from.

For a moment, a memory flickered to life, rising from the missing gaps in her past. She saw Braidon sitting on the lawns of the garden, his eyes wide with dread, but it faded again before she could grasp its meaning. She cursed beneath her breath.

"No?" Kellian asked, frowning. She noticed his hand had dropped to the short sword he wore on his waist. "What's wrong with you, Alana?"

Heart hammering in her chest, Alana clenched her eyes closed. Emotions whirled inside her mind, pulling her in every direction, threatening to tear her apart. The memories of her time with Devon and Kellian were strong, and though that part of herself remained locked away, she could not forget the kindness these men had shown her. Looking at them, she saw again how they'd protected her, how Kellian had argued on her behalf, how Devon had faced down a demon for her.

And she realised no one in her life had ever shown her such loyalty.

"You shouldn't be here, either of you," she said quietly.

"You shouldn't be here either, princess," Devon said. Tentatively, he reached out and patted her shoulder.

A sad smile touched Alana's lips. "You're wrong, Devon," she murmured. "This is exactly where I'm meant to be."

"What?" he whispered.

She looked up at him, her eyes misting despite herself. "I am the Tsar's daughter," she said. "This is my home, my life."

Devon frowned. He shifted on his feet, towering over her. "No, you're wrong," he said. He reached out again, but she flinched away. "He's placed some spell on you–"

"No, Devon," Alana said sharply, cutting him off. "It was me that placed a spell on *you.*"

"What are you talking about?"

She forced herself to laugh, to ignore the light in his eyes. The harsh sound echoed off the walls as she spoke. "That is my power, Devon. I manipulate the minds of men. *That* is why you helped me, why you have crossed the Three Nations to find me." The lie tasted foul on her lips, but she needed them gone, before someone discovered them here. She knew she should turn them in, and yet...

"Go!" she said quickly, even as part of her screamed for her to stop them. "Leave me!"

Devon stood in silence, his eyes sad, staring down at her, and for a second she thought he would obey. Her heart wrenched with the pain of loss. Then he shook his head.

"No," he said quietly, sitting on the bed. "I'm not leaving without you."

A sudden hope swelled in Alana's chest, but as he touched her, her mind shifted, her anger rising. She opened her mouth to warn them, but her jaw snapped closed before she could voice the words. Rage filled her, at her weakness, at her hesitation.

"Very well, Devon," she said.

Smiling, she faced them, letting the sheet fall away. Devon rose cautiously, his cheeks red as he kept his eyes averted from her nakedness. "Alana, what…"

"Get back, Devon!" Kellian said, stepping between them and forcing the hammerman back.

Before Kellian could retreat, Alana stepped forward and placed her hands on his chest. The magic rose within her, the Feline roaring, but she thrust it aside and drew the power to her, pouring it into the helpless innkeeper.

Kellian stiffened, his eyes widening as he tried to pull away, but it was already too late. Her magic rushed through him, overwhelming his thoughts, replacing them with her own. He sagged, and the light went from his eyes. A cold smile on her face, Alana stepped back.

"Kellian, my dear," she said quietly. "Be so good as to secure Devon for me."

"What–?" Devon began.

Before he could finish, Kellian twisted towards him. Moving with frightening speed, he leapt into the air and drove his boot into the side of Devon's head. The blow sent the hammerman staggering back. Losing his balance, he tripped over the sofa and went crashing to the floor.

Kellian followed after him, but Devon surged to his feet, and a meaty fist caught the innkeeper in the stomach. Kellian doubled over, but recovering quickly, he spun on his heel and lashed out with his other foot. The kick went low, sweeping

Devon's legs out from beneath him. As he crashed to the ground, Kellian surged forward, his boot slamming down into Devon's face before he could raise a hand to protect himself.

Groaning weakly, Devon slumped to the ground and lay still. Kellian stood over him, statue-like, his hawkish eyes watching intently for signs of movement.

Alana sighed as she strode across to them and looked down at Devon. "You should have left, Devon," she said, a smile twitching on her lips.

Behind her, the doors to her room burst open and guards rushed inside. Swords rasped from sheaths as they saw Kellian beside her, but he did not react. Blades extended, the guards advanced on him. Alana stepped between them, eyes flashing with rage.

"You're a little late, boys," she snapped.

The men paused, frozen by the sight of the naked princess standing before them. She glanced back at the two men, Devon unconscious on the ground, Kellian still trapped by her magic. Smirking, she waved at the guards.

"Get them out of my sight."

24

"Are you ready, Braidon?" Enala asked, her eyes shining in the moonlight.

Braidon sat across from the old woman, seeing the compassion in the softness of her face, the deepening of the wrinkles around her lips. Idly he wondered what had driven her to take him under her wing. There were other Magickers in the city, Magickers less important to the city than she was, who could have been spared to teach him. Yet Enala had never so much as suggested the idea. Perhaps it was their shared journey, their flight across the Three Nations that had bound them together.

Either way, he wasn't about to question it now.

Rubbing the exhaustion from his eyes, he forced his fear back into its cage. They were sitting out under the stars, the cold kept at bay by the flames burning in Enala's palms.

"Okay."

He nodded, and closing his eyes, Braidon sought out his calm centre. It was not an easy task—not after having his entire life turned upside down. Delving down into the darkness, he found himself questioning every memory, every thought. How did he know this was really the right course of action? Was this what he would have done before, in that other life he could not remember?

For a moment, confusion swamped him and he started to panic. His chest constricted, and he found himself hardly able to breathe. Gasping, he sucked in another lungful of air, his hands gripping hard to the rock beneath him.

"Focus, Braidon. I believe in you."

Her words sliced through the panic, though he still felt lost, alone amongst the chaos of his mind. Who was he? What was true, what was false?

His sister's face sprang into his thoughts, crisp and clear, a smile on her pale lips, her eyes shining.

I love you, little brother.

Braidon's shoulders swelled as the words swept through him. He clung to them like a lifeline, the one immovable fact in his unstable past. Instinctively, he sensed the truth behind the words, that their love for one another had in fact been real. Everything else might be false, but Alana was truly his sister.

Holding the image of her in his mind, he allowed all other thoughts to fall away. Slowly he found himself drifting, and a strange otherworldliness came over him, as though his spirit were no longer weighed down by the trappings of his body. Opening his eyes, he looked on the familiar darkness, his spirit a flickering light alone in the void.

Except he wasn't alone.

Turning his eyes outwards, he saw the distant white glowing in the distance, and felt the old fear return.

I need you, Braidon…

He could no longer tell whether his sister's words were real or imagined, but her voice gave him courage, and he shot towards the distant light. It swelled before him, as though it already sensed his approach, could taste its victory. He watched as it shifted, growing larger, changing, until the awful Feline stood, jaws wide, its roar sending ripples through his very soul.

The need to flee rose within him. He shook as the beast approached, the great claws reaching out. His fear was like a tangible force now, turning his strength to water, his courage evaporating like smoke before the breeze. As it had so many times before, it filled him, demanding he turn and run.

Please, Braidon...

Trembling, fists clenched, Braidon stood his ground as the Feline stalked forward. He could sense its hate, its raw hunger radiating out before it, surrounding him, threatening to tear him down. Yet still, he did not move.

Now it stood directly over him, its breath hot, the light quivering dangerously behind its monstrous eyes. Leaning down, it roared, the sound sending vibrations down to the very core of his being. Closing his eyes, Braidon waited for the end to come.

Nothing happened.

After a long moment, he opened his eyes again. He flinched as he found the creature's giant maw mere inches from his face, and for a second it seemed the Feline would lunge forward and tear into his flesh. He was gathering himself to bolt when he heard his sister's voice again, crisp and clear, rising from the vaults of some memory.

I believe in you, Braidon.

He froze. A snarl of hatred came from the Feline, but still it did not move. Slowly Braidon's fear seeped away, fleeing out into the void. His legs ceased to shake, and as he drew in a breath, his spirit swelled. He felt himself growing in size, fuelled by his courage, even as the substance leached away from the beast.

Reaching out, he touched a hand to the Feline's mane. As his hand met the creature, it burst asunder, collapsing in on itself, becoming a swirling pool of light that stretched out before him. Pure heat washed across him, gentle and reassuring. He thrust his hand deep into the pool, and felt a surge of power, the crackling of his magic's energy as it filled him...

Back on the mountainside, Braidon opened his eyes, and smiled.

"I did it," he whispered.

Enala sat across from him, her aged face stretched with worry. She straightened at his words and leaned forward, staring intently into his eyes.

"Is it truly you?" she asked.

"It's me, Enala," he replied.

Within, he could feel the magic swirling, its power spreading to fill every inch of his body. But he no longer sensed a threat from it. Amidst the darkness of the void, he and it had become one, their purpose joined as the beast finally recognised its master. Its power was his to command now.

Working by instinct, Braidon concentrated on the ground beside him, imagining a replica of himself sitting there. Light flickered, and an image sprang into life. Braidon jerked as he suddenly found himself staring into his own crisp blue eyes. It was like staring into his own reflection.

"Wow," he murmured, glancing down at his own hands. They were aglow, a bright white flickering out to dance alongside the fire in Enala's palms.

The flames died away, and Enala embraced him. "Well done, Braidon," she whispered. "I knew you could do it!"

Braidon smiled, and the image of himself vanished. "I'm glad someone did. I thought the beast had me for a moment!"

"But you faced it down!" Enala replied. "You stood your ground like a man. You should be proud."

"It was Alana that gave me the courage."

Enala reached out and gripped his shoulder. "Never forget the power of love, my child. There are some who believe the world should be governed by fear and pain, but in my life, I have found the bonds of love to last far longer. The Tsar's people may fight for him out of fear, but should his power abandon him, so will they. The Northlanders love their Queen —they will fight for her to the end."

"It may come to that, because of me," Braidon whispered.

"No, my child," Enala replied. "War was coming whatever we decided. But perhaps we can find a way to change that, when we reach your sister."

"So you'll come with me?"

"Ay," Enala whispered, her eyes turning to the dark slopes far below. "I should have returned to Ardath a long time ago, when my brother stood against the Tsar. As it is, I fear I will be too weak to make a difference now. Only time will tell."

"I don't know what I'll do when we get there…" Braidon murmured, his heart sinking. "I don't even know how to find Alana."

To his surprise, the old priest smiled at that. "Don't you worry about that, my child," she replied. "Leave the planning to me."

For the second time in as many days, Devon woke to a pounding in his head that made him wish he'd never left Northland. Opening his eyes, he watched as strange squiggles of light danced before his eyes, slowly fading to darkness. Blinking, he waited for his vision to clear, but the black remained. For an instant, he wondered if he was dead. Then a low groan came from his right, the rattle of chains from his left. The cold stones beneath him seeped through his leggings, and the stench of what smelt like an open sewer wafted in his nostrils. Retching, he rolled onto his side, and the world finally began to take shape through the gloom.

Concrete walls surrounded him on three sides, a row of bars on the fourth. Beyond the bars he could see candles flickering down the length of a corridor lined with a dozen more cells. Turning away, he ran his gaze over his own cell, and noted he had two companions in the darkness. The first was an old man, his ghostly white hair long and filthy, his skin hanging in bags from his face. The man was asleep, his soft snores whispering lightly from the stone walls.

The other occupant was Kellian. Devon's heart beat faster

as he remembered their confrontation with Alana, how Kellian had turned on him at the woman's command. A knife twisted in his chest at her betrayal. Taken by surprise, Devon had hardly been able to get in a blow before Kellian overwhelmed him. His friend was unconscious now, and Devon prayed to the Gods that whatever spell Alana had worked on him would wear off by the time he woke.

He shivered at the thought. Alana had magic! With a single touch, she had taken control of Kellian. His mind reeled at the implications, returning to her words in the darkness of her room.

I am the Tsar's daughter. This is my home, my life.

No, it couldn't be true. He knew her, knew her heart. It wasn't possible for her to have worked such a deception on them, not through all those long days of travel. And then there was Braidon—sweet, innocent, Braidon. He could not have pretended...

And yet, what else could explain her sudden power? Could the woman they'd met have been an imposter?

The thought gave him hope, yet he knew it wasn't true. Alana had recognised them—he had seen it in her eyes. And she had begged them to flee, to leave her behind, before it was too late. In his stubbornness he had refused to listen, to believe her, but the truth had been laid bare now.

I am the Daughter of the Tsar.

He shook his head. It couldn't be true. And yet...he turned the words over in his mind, reliving the events of the past few weeks through different eyes, seeing again how Quinn had seemed to recognise her back in the temple of Sitton, the lengths he and the Tsar had gone to capture Alana and her brother. Demons and dragons had been sent against them, yet none had attacked Alana or the boy Magicker directly.

An icy cold slid down his spine. The woman he'd encountered in the bedchamber above had been Alana—he couldn't deny it. Yet it had also *not* been her. There had been a hardness about her, a stony cold to her eyes that allowed no emotion.

"It doesn't make sense," he muttered to himself.

"In my long life, I've found little really does," an ancient voice replied from across the cell.

Looking up, Devon found the eyes of the old man on him. The man lifted himself from the floor and propped himself up against the wall, his emaciated limbs seeming to hardly have the strength to move him. His clothes were little more than dishevelled rags, and his skin was so pale that Devon could see the thin blue veins beneath. Weeping sores covered his arms and legs, while a long white beard reached almost down to his waist.

"How long have you been here?" Devon whispered.

To his surprise, the old man smiled. "Not so long," he murmured, his voice sounding weary. "Thirty years, forty?" His eyes flickered closed as he rested his head back against the wall. "What does it matter?"

Devon suppressed a shudder. "How have you survived?" The old man's laughter echoed through the cell, and Devon frowned. "Why do you laugh?"

"Because in my long life, I have faced death many times. It has stalked me through all these years, a constant companion, waiting for me to make a mistake, to take me. And yet here in this dungeon, far from sword and monsters and Magickers, you ask me how I have survived?"

"I only meant…"

"I know what you meant," his companion sighed. He shook his head, and for a second Devon saw the despair lurking behind his eyes. "In truth I never expected to see fifty. Yet here I sit, creeping slowly towards an unremarkable end. I never imagined this would be my fate."

"You were a warrior?" Devon now noticed the thin white

streaks of scars on the old man's arms, threading their way between the filth and sores.

His cellmate nodded. "A warrior. A Magicker. Once upon a time."

"A Magicker?" Hope stirred in Devon's chest, before cold hard reality returned to crush it. If the man could have used his powers to escape, he would have done so long ago… "Can you not use your powers to escape?" he asked anyway.

The old man smiled. Lifting his hands, he shook the bracelets he wore on either wrist, fashioned from silver and studded emeralds. "Not with the Tsar's gift," the man said.

"They block your magic?" Devon asked.

"That, and more." The man turned his eyes on Devon. "You must be a dangerous man, to end up in these dungeons. Once they were used to contain the vilest of creatures, though the old kings refashioned them after the fall of Archon. The Tsar only keeps his most dangerous of enemies here."

Devon shrugged, but before he could answer a groan came from across the cell. His heart skipped a beat as Kellian sat up, and he stared at his friend, searching for some sign of recognition. Kellian blinked in the dim light, his gaze finally settling on Devon. Frowning, he touched a hand to his head, and groaned again.

"You always bring me to the most interesting places, Devon…" he murmured.

Relief swept through Devon, and he swept his friend up into a hug. "You're back!"

"Ugh, Devon, get off! My head feels like you hit it with your damned hammer," Kellian said as he tried to disentangle himself from Devon.

Chuckling, Devon released him, though he gave his friend an extra thump on the back for good measure. Kellian winced and quickly retreated across the cell, only slumping back to the ground when he was well out of range. He winced, pain still etched across his face.

"What the hell happened? Where are we?" Blinking, he seemed to notice the old man for the first time. "Who the hell are you?"

The old man laughed. "I could ask the same of the two of you."

"Devon and Kellian," Devon replied quickly. "Former soldiers, current renegades."

"Names…" the old man sighed. "How little meaning they have now. Down here we are nothing, our lives extinguishable at a whim."

"I don't plan on staying long," Devon growled.

The old man did not reply, but his eyes said it all. In the corner, Kellian was still holding his head. "How did we get here, Devon?" he asked. "The last thing I remember was finding Alana…"

Devon swallowed. The words were slow to come, and when he spoke his voice was taut with pain. "Alana betrayed us."

Kellian looked up at that. "What? How?"

"She said she was the Tsar's daughter."

"I remember…" Kellian said after a moment. "But how is that possible?"

"The Tsar's daughter, you say?" The old man said. Devon shivered as he found the ancient eyes on him. "Not a pleasant woman, from what I've overhead from the guards."

"It's not true," Devon snapped.

"Perhaps," their cellmate replied carefully, "but I have heard of her power. An Earth Magicker, capable of manipulating human minds."

"I…" Kellian frowned, looking at Devon. "She touched me, and everything went black. What happened, Devon?"

Devon looked away, his hands curling into fists. "You attacked me, old friend."

The colour drained from Kellian's face. "I don't remember," he murmured. A strained silence stretched out before he added. "I guess we finally answered the question of who's stronger though…"

"I wasn't exactly fighting for keeps," Devon growled, but his heart wasn't in it. He turned back to the old man. "You were talking about her power?"

"Yes," he sighed. "She's able to manipulate people's minds —their thoughts, memories, actions."

"That explains how she was able to control me," Kellian said, "but…not why she was so different from the woman we knew. She was like a completely different person."

The old man looked thoughtful. "It is strange, but perhaps…perhaps she used her power on herself."

"Why would she do that?" Devon demanded.

"Who could say?" the old man shrugged. "There's only one person who can answer that—and by the sound of it, she's not interested in talking with you any longer."

"You're saying the Alana we first met…was a completely different person from the woman who attacked us?" Devon pressed.

"As I said, it's possible, but only the girl herself could tell you for sure."

Devon sucked in a breath, struggling to comprehend the old man's theory. "If that's true…how can we know which was the true Alana? The woman we helped…" he trailed off, his mind turning to the night he'd spent with Alana in the moonlit springs south of Fort Fall. The image faded, replaced by one of her sneering down at him. "Or the one who had us imprisoned as traitors?"

"I'm sorry, my friend," their cellmate replied, his eyes soft, "but from what you say, her old personality has reasserted itself. Perhaps some of the woman you knew remains, but her true self? That can only be the one able to manipulate her magic.

And from what you've told me…" Devon didn't need him to finish.

Tears burned in his eyes and he looked away, a lump catching in his throat. An awful weight settled on his chest. Alana was gone, her existence snuffed out as though she'd never been. In her place was a stranger, a hard and unforgiving woman who hadn't hesitated to set his friend on him. She may have spared their lives…yet what did that matter when they were imprisoned in the Tsar's dungeons? Sooner or later, the man would send for them, demanding retribution for stealing away his children.

"Devon…" said Kellian from across the cell.

Devon shook his head, raising a hand to fend off his friend's words. "Just…leave me, Kellian," he whispered, his voice breaking. "Just…leave me."

Hanging his head, Devon began to sob.

❧ 26 ❧

A lana's footsteps echoed loudly on the stone floor as she wandered across the andron, the large adjoining chamber set behind the throne room. Royal guards lined the room, their golden helmets gleaming in the morning sun, while in the centre stood a great table of gilded oak. Whispers carried across as she approached, though the men and women seated at the table had yet to notice her.

The Tsar sat at the head of the table, his hands clasped before him as he listened to his advisors. Alana dragged out an empty chair and sat. Silence fell around the table as the advisors turned to stare at her, but she ignored them. Leaning back in her chair, she lifted her legs and rested them on the table.

"Daughter, how nice of you to join us," the Tsar murmured. "How are you this morning? I heard your night was...disrupted."

Alana snorted. Her eyes flickered around to the gathered advisors, enjoying the sudden fear that had appeared behind their eyes. To the Tsar, she raised an eyebrow.

"Yes, and I trust our unexpected guests have been settled into appropriate accommodation?"

The Tsar scowled. "They have been seen to. I will question them later, when more urgent matters have been dealt with. Perhaps we can then ascertain how they were able to get so far inside the citadel."

"You should look to your guards, father," Alana replied with a smirk. She sat up suddenly, her boots slamming back down on the hard floor. The others at the table flinched as she stood, but she barely spared them a glance. She strode across the andron to where the ring of guards stood. "I fear some of your men have grown fat and lazy."

Striding down the line, she studied the face of each man, finally coming to a stop before one she recognised. She stepped in close, and smiled as he looked nervously from her to her father.

"You, what is your name?"

The guard swallowed. "An...Anthony, princess."

"Anthony..." she said. "Tell me, do you remember me?"

He stared blankly at her. "Remember you from where, princess?"

"The Firestone Pub, I believe it was called," she murmured. "I suppose you don't, considering you were lying unconscious in a pile of garbage by the time I arrived."

The guard blinked, uncomprehending. "What?"

Alana stepped in close, so that their faces were only an inch apart. "I was there, *fool*. The night Devon knocked you unconscious, I saw you. If only you weren't such an incompetent warrior, you might have seen me too, might have recognised me. Alas, you allowed a drunken coward to knock you on your ass."

"I...I...I'm sorry, princess," he stammered.

"Don't be," she hissed.

Quick as lightning, her hand flashed down, dragging the dagger from his belt. The guard cried out, scrambling uselessly for his sword hilt, but she buried the blade in his throat before he could draw it. Gasping, he staggered back, his hands clutching uselessly at his throat. A dull gurgling noise came from his chest as she tore the dagger loose. Blood gushed from his neck as he staggered back two steps, then sagged to the floor.

Alana tossed the bloody dagger on his dying body, her gaze turning to the other guards and councillors. Every man and woman in the room stared back at her, open terror on their faces. She laughed.

"Relax, boys and girls!" she shouted. "You look like you've seen a ghost."

Smiling, she wandered back to the council table and resumed her seat. The Tsar's advisors continued to stare at her as she lifted her feet back to the table. Folding her hands in her lap, she let out a long sigh.

"I feel so much better," she said. Seeing the blood on her hands and let out an exasperated snort. She tugged a handkerchief from the breast-pocket of a stunned looking councillor and used it to clean them. "I needed to calm my nerves," she explained to the terrified man as she returned the ruined cloth.

Beside her, the Tsar chuckled. "You truly are yourself again."

"Did you doubt it?" she asked.

"Quinn mentioned you'd been having…trouble with your former self."

"She's under control," Alana snapped, her irritation with Quinn redoubling. Since taking him to her bed, he always seemed to be around, meddling in her affairs. Their argument the night before had only been the latest in a series of growing nuisances. And now he was informing on her for her father…

The Tsar stared at her for a long moment before nodding. "Good. Devon and Kellian's capture will be a blow against Enala. She will have to surrender your brother now, or her beloved Northland will face annihilation."

At the mention of her brother's return, Alana shivered, the hackles rising on her neck. Something tugged at her memory, a fleeting fear that shouted for her to denounce her father. She clenched her teeth, fighting back against the emotion, knowing it was only that other part of her. After a moment it faded, and she brushed a lock of golden hair from her face.

"You think so?" When the Tsar nodded, she smiled. "It will be good to see him again."

"Yes." Her father's voice was distant. "This…delay to his training is unseemly. He should have been ready for his final examination by now."

Unconsciously, Alana's hands balled into fists. A faint anxiety tugged at her, and she stared into space, waiting for the sensation to fade once more…

"Alana?"

She blinked, and found her father staring at her. There was a pause before she realised he'd asked her a question. "Apologies, father, my mind was elsewhere. What did you say?"

He frowned, and for a moment she thought he would press her. But he only waved a hand and said. "Quinn tells me Braidon's power concerns illusions. What else do you know of it?"

Alana shrugged. "Yes, I…*she* didn't know until the end. It was as much our surprise as Quinn's when we realised at Fort Fall. I cannot remember his power awakening though—my memory of his sixteenth birthday is still lost."

"That is the night you both vanished."

"Interesting," Alana mused, turning the fact over in her mind. Magic could only arise on the anniversary of one's birth. It was curious, that her magic had scoured their minds on the same day her brother's magic had appeared. Surely that could not be a coincidence?

Straining, she sought again to lift the fog from her lost memories, but still they would not come. Finally she shook her head. "It might be there is more to his power than illusions," she said, "but not from what I saw of his wild magic."

The Tsar nodded. His brow creased as he looked at her. "You look tired, my daughter."

"Yes, well, my strength still has not recovered from my...*her* loss of control. My midnight guests did not help."

"Then you should rest, allow your powers to return. You were lucky you had the strength to stop Devon and his friend. Especially after your little...incident with the woman, Krista."

"She was weak." Alana snorted. "It did not take much of my power to remove her. I am surprised you elected such a poor choice of guardian for the children in my absence."

"There were other matters on my mind," the Tsar rumbled, "but...you are right, I should have dealt with her. Still, your students will not miss you for one morning. I will see that Quinn takes over for the day...unless you would rather he attend to you?"

Alana forced a smile to her lips, even as the dream from the night before rose in her mind. In the dream, she had taken Devon to spite her other self, to crush her hopes, to show her everything she'd ever loved was hers now. Yet as she'd imagined herself with him, she'd felt the girl's emotions rising from the void, entangling with her own...

"No," she said sharply, her mouth dry. "And I do not want him near my students...But, it shall be as you say. I will rest, and see to the children in the afternoon."

Rising, she left her father and his advisors to their boring discussions of governance and war, and found her way back to her quarters. There she threw herself down on the bed, sighing as she burrowed into the soft silk sheets. A memory rose from the depths of her mind, of the mud and dirt and cold she had endured on the streets of Ardath.

Alana shivered. How could she have sunk so low, convinced

herself she was nothing but a pauper, a street rat to be crushed by better people?

Yet as she recalled the abject poverty she'd condemned herself to, the image shifted, and she saw her brother alongside her. As the days had grown shorter and the temperature had dropped, the two of them had taken to sleeping beneath one blanket, sharing warmth to fend off the winter's chill.

Watching herself embrace the young boy, tears came to Alana's eyes, and for a second she wished she were back in the abandoned hovel with her brother. At least they'd been together then.

She cursed, flinging the thought away and turning her mind to the future. Her brother would return soon, they would be together again. She would no longer be alone.

Yet imaging him back in the citadel, running through the gardens, she felt only fear. There was something strange about the thought, a wrongness that tickled in the back of her mind. The warmth she'd felt when picturing the hovel was missing.

Quinn's words from the night returned to haunt her.

"And what about your brother? Is that what you wish for him, when he returns?"

Rolling over, she punched the pillow, cursing herself for a fool. It was the girl! It had to be, working her feeble emotions, her weakness into her every thought. She was like a parasite, eating at Alana from within, no matter how many times the magic burned her.

Alana sucked in a breath, forcing herself to recall the joy she'd experienced as the guard's hot blood spouted over her hands. Within, she felt a part of her recoil, and laughed to herself. "This is you," she whispered to the empty room. "This is who you are, girl. Accept it!"

There was no voice inside to reply. Finally at peace, Alana closed her eyes, and allowed her weariness to take her…

In her dreams, Alana awoke, and found herself amongst a great forest.

Tree trunks rose around her, so high she could not see their canopies. Craning her neck, she sought out the sky, but in place of blue horizons and light, there was only…nothing.

Mist clung to the ground, creeping across the forest floor, though there was no cold, no wind, no movement. Alana spun, looking around and around, trying to recall how she had come to be there, but the memory was lost.

A cold fear gripped her then. Her father's enemies must have come for her, stealing her from the citadel. But they had made a mistake, left her alive. She would make sure they lived to regret it.

Alana set off through the trees, though without any sense of direction, she had no way of knowing where she was headed. The mist seemed to follow her, billowing across her feet, obscuring the ground below. Though there must have been branches and leaves on the ground, there was no sound as she moved. Crouching down, she tried to sweep the fog away. The movement did nothing to pierce the white, and she changed tact, thrusting her arm deep into the fog. It was stopped abruptly by what she presumed was the ground, though it was cold and smooth as glass.

"What is this place?" she whispered, fear gnawing at her stomach.

"My domain," came a girl's voice from the trees.

Her heart racing, Alana sprang back to her feet and reached for her sword. Only then did she realise she was unarmed. Weakened as it was, she turned instead to her magic, and felt it come to life inside her. To her surprise, a green glow lit the forest, seeming to come from her chest itself.

"You would use my own power against me?"

Movement came from the trees, a young girl appearing between the endless trunks. She walked forward, her soft brown curls bouncing with each footstep. A strange light lit her face, revealing a tiny button nose, a smattering of freckles, and dimpled cheeks. She wandered through the trees, no more than a child, a smile on her youthful face.

Alana lowered her arm, as the girl looked up at her, revealing violet eyes. Looking into them, it seemed as though the universe were staring back at her, infinite and terrifying. The strength went from Alana then, and she stumbled, a cry on her lips.

"Who are you?" she gasped.

"The Goddess of the Earth," the girl replied. "Antonia."

Alana shook her head. "No, that isn't possible!" she said. "The Gods are dead!"

"Only our bodies," the girl replied, her eyes aglow. "Our spirits remain, as they always have, and always will. We are a part of the land, a part of the magic within you."

Alana's hand drifted unconsciously to her breast. "My magic?"

"Yes, child. Your power comes from the Earth—but then, you knew that." Alana shivered as the Goddess's eyes hardened. "You have been a great disappointment to me, child."

Alana's anger flared. "I didn't realise you had expectations. I thought you left."

The Goddess looked up, her eyes catching Alana's and holding them. She found her heart suddenly beating hard against her chest, and she sensed in that moment the vast power in the girl before her. Not just that, but an anger, a yearning to reach out and tear Alana's heart from her chest.

Then Antonia blinked, and the moment passed.

Alana swayed on her feet, then sank to her knees.

"I am sorry," Antonia said gently.

She waved a hand, and the towering trees seemed to retreat. Rocks cracked and a boulder lifted through the mist. Moving to it, Antonia seated herself cross-legged atop it, and gestured for Alana to join her.

Still on her knees, Alana sucked in a breath. Unable to summon the will to speak, she shook her head.

"You are not beyond redemption, Alana," the Goddess said, looking down at her from the boulder.

"Who says I need to be redeemed?" Alana hissed, rage giving her courage.

Anger returned to Antonia's face. "I do," she growled, and Alana reeled back before the force of her words.

For a moment the child seemed a giant, with the power to reach out and crush her beneath one thumb. Alana gasped, her will crumbling, and she threw herself flat against the ground.

"Please, don't hurt me!" she begged, and hated herself for it.

Laughter came from the Goddess. Looking up, Alana saw she had returned to normal, though the dark gleam remained in her eyes. "I thought you were strong, Alana. Is that not what your father taught you, to show strength before mercy? Could it be, your strength comes from the part of yourself you seek to crush?"

"No!" Alana yelled, standing now. *"She is the weak one!"*

"She is only the girl you wished yourself to be—one free of your father's manipulations."

"You lie," Alana snapped. *"I would remember."* Comprehension came to her and she stumbled back. *"I know why you are here!"* she gasped. *"You seek to be reborn, to usurp my father and rule Plorsea in his place."*

The Goddess looked sad. *"My siblings and I have no wish to return to your mortal world. We never wanted a part of it in the first place. But you are right—it is your father who has drawn us back, forced me to interfere once more in the lives of mortals."*

"What are you talking about?"

Antonia sighed. *"Matters beyond your understanding, my dear Alana."* There was a sadness in her face that made Alana shudder. With an inexplicable feeling of shame, she looked away.

"Tell me, girl. Do you wish to know the truth?" Antonia asked.

"The truth?" Alana asked suddenly.

"The truth about what has happened to you. The truth about how you lost your memory."

The breath caught in Alana's throat. She stared at the youthful Goddess, sensing the trap. If she allowed this creature into her mind, who knew what damage she might do, what would happen to her? Would she feed strength to her other self, allowing the girl to bury her back in the darkness?

"I will not harm you," Antonia said, as though already reading her thoughts.

Alana shivered. Despite her suspicions, she believed the girl's words. Still she hesitated, an unknown fear lodging in her throat. What was so important about the month she'd lost, between her brother's birthday and the moment she'd woken in the stepwell? What had changed?

Yet Alana could not allow the fear to rule her. She had learned that lesson once, long ago when she'd first mastered her power. Her father had trained her well, breaking her spirit, crushing her soul, only to reshape it, allowing the Daughter of the Tsar to be born. It was that woman who had first faced her magic, who'd overcome her terror and conquered the force within.

Her decision made, she looked at the Goddess.

"Show me."

❧ 27 ❧

"**E**nala!"

Braidon spun as the Queen's voice echoed down the tunnel, his eyes widening to find her standing on the path behind them, her chest heaving, hand clutched at her breast. Without her guards and crown, she no longer looked like the intimidating woman who'd ordered his capture, but vulnerable and human, her eyes shining with emotion.

"Merydith, what are you doing here?" Enala asked.

"Please, Enala, you can't leave us. Not now, when we need you most," the Queen gasped, the words rushing from her in a torrent.

A lump lodged in Braidon's throat. Around the corner ahead, the light of a new dawn beckoned. There, the dragon Dahniul waited to fly them south, deep into the Tsar's territory. Enala had thought to leave in secret without causing upheaval, but apparently the Queen had heard of their plan.

Yet she had come alone, without guards or advisors, to beseech the ancient Magicker to stay, when she could have brought an army to stop them.

"Merydith," Enala murmured, stepping forward and

placing a hand on the woman's shoulder. "You do not need me. You are a brave, intelligent woman. I believe in you. If anyone can lead Northland through this turmoil, it's you."

The Queen swallowed, a tear streaking her cheek. "Through all our short history, you have stood beside us, Enala." She broke off, swallowing hard. "You served my father, and his mother before him. You are the only thing that stands between Northland and chaos."

"That's not true!" Enala said, both hands on the Queen's shoulders now. "For decades I have watched you grow, Merydith, and barely needed to lift a finger to aid you. Northland has its own spirit, its own soul, and *you* are the heart of that. I am but a remnant, a shadow that holds you back. That is why I left the first time, all those years ago, to return to my homeland." She smiled, reaching up to stroke the woman's cheek. "You have outgrown me, girl."

"What if I make a mistake?"

"You won't," Enala insisted.

The Queen took a great, shuddering breath and nodded. Braidon watched as her shoulders straightened, her face settling back into the familiar mask. For a moment, he'd glimpsed the woman behind the crown, seen her humanity, her vulnerability. But now it was the Queen who stood before them once more, regal, untouchable. She sighed, gesturing to the way ahead.

"You would take our most powerful weapon as well?" she asked.

Enala sighed. "You know Dahniul is not ours to command. She has chosen this path—it is not our place to question her."

"Very well." She looked at Braidon, and he shivered as she approached him. To his surprise, she knelt to meet him at eye-level. "I wish you would stay, young Braidon," she said, her voice soft, "but I respect your decision to search for your sister. I pray it does not prove the end of you."

"It won't," Braidon replied. "I know her."

"We can only hope," the Queen replied, drawing him into an embrace. "Good luck."

Braidon nodded, surprised at the warmth in the Queen's voice. "Thank you," he said. Then, as the Queen drew back and stood, he added: "Good luck to you as well. I hope your decision to refuse the Tsar's emissaries does not prove too costly."

The Queen's face hardened at his words. "I am sorry, Braidon, for how I acted. It was wrong, I see that now. Do not concern yourself with us. If the Tsar comes, at least we will meet him as a free people."

"He will come, Merydith," Enala said, moving alongside them, "with all the forces at his command. You must prepare yourselves."

"We have already begun," the Queen replied, a sudden weariness coming over her. "After a century of peace, North-land rises once more. Did you think you'd live to see it, Enala?"

The old woman chuckled. "It is the way of things. The wheel turns, comes full circle. Only now it is your people who fight for freedom, the Three Nations the conquerors. Oh, how my brother would laugh to see it."

With her words, Braidon sensed an awful sadness in his mentor, and for a moment it seemed the weight of all her years had caught up to Enala. Her shoulders sagged, the folds of her aged face deepening. He swallowed, unable to imagine what it must be like for her—over a century old, all her friends and family gone, the last of a golden age of heroes. Reaching out, he squeezed her arm, and the old woman seemed to shake herself free of her melancholy.

"I'm sorry, Merydith, but we must be on our way. Time is short," Enala said.

"Very well," the Queen replied, "but please, be careful,

Enala. You have been like a mother to me all my life. I couldn't bear to lose you."

"Of course you could, child," Enala chided, "and if it comes to it, I will die with pride, knowing you will carry on the fight."

The Queen smiled wryly. "Fine, just, do your best to avoid it, okay? The Tsar knows you're alive. He will be waiting for you this time."

Enala waved a hand. "The man isn't half as smart as he thinks. Braidon and I have his number."

"I hope so," the Queen replied with gusto. "If not, I fear we will not be able to stand against him."

"We will never be able to stand against him," Enala replied sadly. "Not unless the Three Nations rise as one against him. We can only pray that the Gods have a plan."

"The Gods are gone."

"No, Merydith. They never left." Enala tapped her chest. "When she was within me, I saw things, felt things…an eon's worth of knowledge. I remember but a fraction of it now, but they were watching over us long before our priests made them flesh. They will continue to do so long after I'm gone. They may be spirits, but their power flows through all of us now."

The Queen looked unconvinced, but she nodded anyway. "I pray you are right."

Enala smiled. "I usually am."

❧ 28 ❧

"**Y**our friend is dead, Devon," Quinn announced as he stopped outside the squalid cell.

He smiled as he looked through the bars and saw the three men sitting within. Only a few hours had passed, but already their clothes were stained by the grime within, their skin filthy with it. Lifting the lantern higher, he watched the rats go scuffling into their holes. Devon sat on one side of the cell, Kellian on the other, alongside an old man who looked like he'd been in the dungeon for decades.

Blinking in the harsh light, Devon looked up at him. "Quinn," he said, "I might have guessed you'd come."

Grinning, Quinn hefted the bundle he held in his other hand. Pulling back the cloth, he lifted *kanker* into the light. He watched the pain flicker across the hammerman's face, savouring the sight.

"I thought you might be missing this," he said.

Devon glared back at him. "So you killed the Trolan?"

Quinn shrugged. "Didn't need to."

"Tsar did the dirty work for you, did he?"

Chuckling, Quinn leaned against the bar. "Still playing the

hero, I see. You think your little act fools me? Look at where you are, man! Food for the rats, while I stand free, a hero in the eyes of the Tsar...and his grateful daughter."

"Bastard!" Devon surged to his feet and threw himself at the bars. "If you touch her...!"

Quinn stepped back quickly and laughed in the man's face. "Me, touch her?" he said, though he hadn't talked to her since their fight. "I can barely keep her hands off *me!*"

"Liar!" Devon roared, straining uselessly against the steel bars.

Shaking his head, Quinn sneered. "You're pathetic, Devon. To think I once considered you a rival. You were a hero, a warrior, and what did you do with it? You threw it all away! How a man descended from Alan could be so weak, I don't understand. Your ancestor would be ashamed, to know his progeny betrayed the nation he gave his life to defend."

Devon fell back, his shoulders heaving, teeth bared. For a moment, his eyes seemed to glow, and despite himself Quinn shivered as he met the fiery gaze. He swallowed, suddenly glad for the bars between them.

"Alan stood to protect the weak from evil," Devon murmured.

"*You* are the weak one," Quinn hissed. "You could have had it all!"

"Is that why I'm here, then?" Devon asked. "Because I refused to use my strength against those who could not defend themselves?" He let out a long breath. "If that's the case, so be it. I'd rather be in here, standing on the side of good, than out there with you, allied with evil."

His anger flaring, Quinn stepped back up to the bars. "Who are you to accuse me of evil?" he snapped. "Was it not you who led the charge against the Trolans, who cracked open their defences, slaughtered their people?"

"Ay, and I'll hold that guilt in my heart to my dying day. But what of yours, Quinn? Does your guilt burn you?"

"There is no guilt!" he yelled. He pointed a finger at Devon's chest. "And you'd best close that mouth of yours, lest I decide to shatter every bone in your body."

Devon did not move, but a soft laughter came from behind him. Inside the cell, the old man lifted himself from the ground and wandered across to join them. Blue eyes glittered as the prisoner stopped and leaned against the bars.

"Quinn, is it?" he asked, his voice rasping with untold age.

Jaw clenched, Quinn nodded before he could stop himself, and the laughter came again.

"I've heard of you," the old man continued. "The guards talk. Nothing much else to do while on duty down here, I suppose. I hear you're a great man: lieutenant of the Stalkers, renown warrior...a Magicker with powers over the wind."

"What of it, old man?" Quinn growled.

The old eyes flickered to the stone ceiling. "Not much of the Sky element this far underground, I think you'll find, lieutenant..."

Quinn bared his teeth. "Let's find out shall we, old man?"

Within, his magic stirred, its blue light seeping out to fill him. There was a moment of resistance, as it sought to break free, but he was no apprentice and quenched it in an instant. Then he was reaching out, extending his consciousness beyond himself, searching for the wind, and finding...nothing.

The ancient prisoner's laughter came again. Quinn's stomach lurched and he felt his cheeks grow hot.

"Guess you're not so great after all, lieutenant!" the old man taunted him. "Next time why don't you bring some wind with you. I could use the fresh air."

Still cackling to himself, the prisoner retreated back into the cell, leaving Quinn staring impotently after him.

Grinding his teeth, Quinn gripped *kanker* tighter in one

hand and reached for the door to the cell, ready to crush the insolence from the feeble man. But as he touched the bars, he froze, sensing Devon's eyes on him. The hammerman was watching him, his hands clenched into fists. Beyond, Kellian was crouched on the ground, poised to spring.

His hands trembling, Quinn slowly let out his breath. He turned to Devon and forced a smile. "Enjoy your stay, old friend. I suspect you'll be here a long time."

With that, Quinn turned on his heel and fled up the corridor, his blood still boiling at his embarrassment by the old man. Silently he raced up the winding stairs, repeating the conversation over and over in his mind, seeking where it had gone so wrong.

The stairs opened out into a small room that served as the entrance to the dungeons. Here, two guards quickly stood to attention and saluted on Quinn's approach. He slowed his stride to speak with them.

"Ensure they have no visitors," he ordered.

He strode past them, then paused, the weight in his hand reminding him he still carried the ancient hammer. His stomach twisted in disgust. He had thought to make it a trophy, a prize that could sit on his mantle as a reminder of his conquest over his rival. But looking at it now, he felt only a deep sense of disgust.

Contemptuously, he tossed the hammer on the table alongside the wall of the guardroom. "Add it to the other confiscated weapons."

Then he was striding through the open door, down a narrow corridor, and out into the hallways of the citadel. Yet even with the hammer discarded, his thoughts kept returning to Devon. The confrontation had not gone as he'd imagined. He'd wanted to see the hammerman on his knees, broken— and he had been so close. Taunting him with Alana had almost pushed the giant over the edge—until the old man had intervened.

"Dammit!" Quinn cursed.

He shook his head, forcing a smile to his lips. Despite the loss of face, Devon was still the one behind bars. And despite her wilfulness, Alana was truly herself once more—her betrayal of her former friends proved it. They might disagree with how to train the new Magickers brought to the citadel, but that was nothing new.

His humour returning, Quinn straightened his shoulders and took the next corridor on his left. After his confrontation with Devon, he felt a need to see Alana again. It was past time they made up. Striding quickly through the citadel, he made his way towards her bedchambers.

He was just nearing the princess's rooms when a scream echoed down the hallways from ahead of him. His heart lurched painfully in his chest and drawing his sword, he sprinted towards the sound. His mind raced, trying to determine who or what could be attacking Alana now. For a second he wondered if there'd been another traitor working with Devon, if their capture had been some ruse...

Turning the last corner, the door to Alana's bedchamber came into sight. The guards that Devon and Kellian had immobilised last night had not been replaced, but the heavy wooden door remained closed. Sabre in hand, Quinn charged forward, bursting into the room with a shout. His eyes swept the gilded interior, taking in the empty sofa, the open curtains, the shining sun, the bed...

He froze as he found Alana staring back at him, her eyes wide with shock. She was sitting up in the bed, the sheets tangled around her naked body, her breasts uncovered. Quinn lowered his sword, swallowing hard as he felt the beginnings of desire.

"Alana," he said quickly, his heart still hammering. "Are you okay?"

She stared at him a moment, her lips parted, face pale. Then she blinked, a frown creasing her forehead. "I'm fine," she answered shortly. For a moment it seemed that was all she would say, and he was about to jump into an apology for the night before, when she shook her head. "No, nothing is okay, Quinn. Everything is wrong. So wrong."

Quinn sheathed his sword and crossed to her. Seating himself on the bed, he drank in her naked body, savouring the sleek curve of her neck, the hollow of her throat, the pale mounds of her breasts. He smiled and reached out a hand to stroke her hair.

"Everything is fine, Alana," he said. Her eyes fluttered closed at his touch, and he went on. "You're safe. Devon and his friend are locked—"

At the mention of Devon's name, Alana flinched away from him. Her eyes snapped open, rage appearing in their stony depths. She pushed him, catching him in the chest and sending him toppling from the bed.

"I didn't say you could touch me," she snarled, climbing from the bed to stand over him.

"Alana…" Quinn murmured, staring at her.

A shudder went through her, and her eyes softened. "I'm sorry…Quinn," she whispered. She shook her head and turned to the trunk at the foot of her bed.

She rummaged around inside, dragging out a pair of underwear and trousers. Quinn approached cautiously as she began to dress herself.

"Alana, what is going on?" he asked.

"Nothing," she answered, pulling on a pair of breeches.

But her breath was racing, and Quinn could see her hands trembling as she struggled into the clothes. Pulling on a shirt, she turned and tried to get past him, but he stepped into her path.

"What is going on, Alana?" he asked again, his voice hardening.

She tried to sidestep him, but he blocked her way once more. She raised her hand to strike him, but Quinn retreated, and the blow never fell. Letting out a long breath, the anger seemed to flow from her. She lowered her hand to her side.

"I'm sorry, Quinn," she said suddenly, a smile appearing. "I can't right now. Later, I promise."

Stepping forward, she stroked his arm, pulling him to her. Desire rushed through Quinn as he pressed his lips to hers. He shuddered, pulling her tightly against him, and ran his hands through her hair, tangling his fingers in her blonde locks, drawing her deeper into the kiss...

Then a bright light burst across his vision, and somewhere in his mind a voice cried out. Opening his eyes, he found himself on his knees, the strength gone from his legs. Letting out a groan, he swayed and looked around, finding Alana now standing in the doorway. For a moment their eyes met, and he realised with horror she'd used her power against him.

"Alana..." he managed, his voice barely more than a whisper.

"I'm sorry, Quinn," she said sadly. "Truly I am. But I need to talk to my father."

With that, she was gone, and the darkness rose up to claim him.

❧ 29 ❧

"So, Alan was your ancestor, ay?"

It was a while before Devon registered the old man's question. They had been sitting in silence for hours now, and the cold of the cell seemed to have seeped into his soul. The brief pleasure he'd gotten from Quinn's humiliation had already faded away, replaced by a growing despair. Inside this cell, his physical strength meant nothing, and Quinn's words went round and around in his head, taunting him. He shivered at the thought of spending his remaining years down here in the darkness, while above Quinn breathed fresh air, free to...

"What was that?" he asked, snapping his thoughts free of the images that were circling his mind.

The old man grinned. With an audible click of bones, he stretched his neck. "The boy said Alan would be ashamed of you—I take it that means you are his descendant."

Devon nodded. "Ay, he was my great-grandfather."

"An interesting family. Alan was a legend—even in his own time. But it was his father-in-law who always had my respect."

"The Magicker?"

"You've heard of him?" The old man seemed surprised. "It is good to hear he has not entirely been forgotten."

"A priest told me of him, though she did not mention his name. Apparently he placed a spell on *kanker*, Alan's hammer."

"Interesting. Does it protect its wielder from magic?" the old man questioned.

Devon blinked. "How did you know that?"

His cellmate scratched his long white beard. "He had a sword with the same power, though it was destroyed during the final war against Archon. It seems reasonable he would create a similar protection for his son-in-law."

"Do you know his name?" Devon asked.

"Alastair." The old man spoke the name with a sigh, almost like a prayer. "A greater man even than Alan, though few know his name now. It was he who thwarted Archon's first invasion. While he enjoyed an extended life span, Alastair was still ancient by the time the Dark Magicker returned. Even so, he answered the call, and gave his life to train a new generation of Magickers to stand against the darkness."

"Like Enala?"

The old man's head whipped up at the mention of the old woman's name. "Enala still lives?"

Devon nodded. "She was the priest I speak of, though she went by Tillie when I met her."

For the first time since he'd woken in the dank cell, Devon saw the light of hope on the old man's face. He sat up straighter, and it seemed some of the wrinkles had fallen from his cheeks.

"Truly? That…" he shook his head, tears appearing in his eyes. "Perhaps…perhaps there may be hope after all."

"I'm not so sure." Seeing his cellmate's confusion, Devon swallowed and went on. "She has the boy, Braidon with her. If…if Alana is truly the Tsar's daughter, then Braidon must be his son. What if it was all a trap, to trick Enala into trusting the boy, or to lure her out of hiding?"

The old man smiled. "Enala will not be fooled so easily. Perhaps she already knew their identity when you met—it would not surprise me. Either way, she won't easily be taken."

Devon sighed. "The two are in Northland. I doubt they'll be venturing south anytime soon."

"No…" Some of the energy went from the man then, and he slumped back against the wall. "No, I suppose not."

A groan came from the corner of the cell as Kellian sat up. "You two are great company, you know?" he muttered, rubbing his eyes. "If you're not going to let me sleep, you could at least find a more pleasant topic!"

Devon felt a sick sense of responsibility settle around him. "I'm sorry, old friend. This is my fault, I should never have dragged you into this business."

Kellian snorted and moved across to join them. "That's hardly fair, I chose to come, didn't I? Alana was my friend as much as yours."

"Some friend," Devon murmured. "Seems she never needed our help to begin with."

"Perhaps, perhaps not," the old man replied. "But it does not lessen your sacrifice."

"Yes, well, if I'm honest I would have preferred avoiding the sacrifice altogether," Kellian added. "As it is, I'd rather not spend the rest of my life here." He coughed. "Err, how long exactly did you say you'd been here?"

"I'm afraid I lost track after the first decade."

"Great," Kellian muttered. "Guess we'll count you out for escape plans. What about you, Devon, any ideas?"

"No," Devon replied, trying to keep the despair from his voice.

"What about your magic then?" Kellian turned back to the

old man. "You said the bracelets keep you from using it. Is there any way to remove them? They look fragile enough."

The old man laughed bitterly. "You think I have not tried?"

Kellian sighed. "True. Suppose it's up to me then!" Seemingly nonplussed, he stood looking out through the bars. "What about the other cells? I...what's wrong with them?" His voice rose several octaves as he finished.

Devon frowned at the fear behind Kellian's words. Rising, he joined him at the bars and looked into the opposite cell, watching as shapes formed in the gloom. There were three people sitting on the floor opposite them—two women, and a man. If their cellmate had seemed in poor health, these three looked like the life itself had been drained from them, leaving only empty husks of their former selves. Little more than skin and bone, their flesh was raw and cracked, their eyes lifeless white globes, their hair hanging in tufts from their skulls.

Then he saw the soft rise and fall of their chests. Staggering back, his stomach swirled, and he struggled to keep from throwing up. With one hand he fumbled for the wall, using its solidity to right himself. Taking a great, shuddering breath, he faced the old man.

"What's wrong with them?" he said, repeating Kellian's question.

The old man lifted an emaciated wrist, and the dim light of the lantern in the corridor caught on the emerald bracelet. "The Tsar's gifts are like a parasite," he said. "To keep our power locked away, they infect us with their dark magic. It harries the spirit, devouring the soul bit by bit. Eventually, there is nothing left but a tiny spark, and the Magicker becomes a shell, a remnant that lives only to serve the Tsar's purpose."

"Then how have you survived so long?"

"Hate," the old man whispered, his eyes shimmering. "Everything else has been lost to me—hope, love, joy. Only the hate remains, burning like a candle within, holding the darkness at bay."

"What did he do to you?" Devon whispered.

"He took someone dear from me," their cellmate replied, looking away. He gazed out at the corridor, an infinite sorrow etched across his ancient face.

Devon swallowed, unable to find the courage to ask who. Instead, he turned the conversation back to the Tsar. "Why is he keeping all of you alive though?" he asked. "I thought the Magickers who defied him were all executed."

"Would that we were," the old man replied bitterly. "No, he can't kill us. He *needs* us. Every Magicker brought before him is offered a choice—serve him, or spend the rest of their lives rotting in these cells. Most choose a life of service, rather than this stinking pit. All but his most trusted Magickers wear the bracelets."

Devon's skin crawled. "What do the cuffs do then, if those above still wear them? Surely there is no need, if they're wielding their magic in service to the Tsar."

There was a haunted look on the old man's face now. "A long time ago, the Tsar discovered a way of robbing Magickers of their power. But there was a flaw in the spell: it required the Magicker's death. He did not realise it in those early days, but with the original Magicker's lifeforce extinguished, the magic he stole could not be renewed. Once used, it was gone. So he devised a new way of taking our magic, one that would allow him unlimited power."

"The bracelets," Kellian hissed.

"Yes," said the old man. "They siphon off our magic one drop at a time, providing the Tsar with a constant source of power. By now, he must have hundreds of Magickers to feed off of, both down here and in his service across the Three Nations. So long as we all live, the Tsar's power is unassailable."

"But if the bracelets are broken, his power would vanish?" Devon asked.

The old prisoner's laughter whispered through the cell. "Mortal strength will not touch them. Only with death will we be released—and even that is denied to us. The other prisoners would have perished long ago, but the bracelets feed their life-force, holding them to this world."

Shivering, Devon shook his head. "There must be a way."

"Even if there were, do not forget the countless Magickers who serve the Tsar willingly. Each also lends their power to the Tsar. I see your Stalker friend no longer wears the bracelets... but he would be one of the few."

"We could weaken him at least," Kellian murmured, still standing at the bars to the cell, "if we freed you and the others."

"That is true." The old man shrugged. "But how do you plan on doing that while sitting in this cell?"

"A good point," Kellian replied with a grin. "I guess we'd better set about getting out then."

At his words, the *bang* of the outer doors echoed down the corridor. Footsteps followed, drawing nearer, though there was no sign of light. Devon frowned—usually the guards carried lanterns when they went about their rounds. As he watched, a shadow appeared in the corridor beyond their cell. The shadow approached Kellian, who smiled and leaned towards it. Soft whispers passed between them. Then it was gone.

Smiling, Kellian turned to face them. A jingling sound carried across the cell as he held up a loop of keys.

"Always have a backup plan, old friend," he said.

✦ 30 ✦

Wind hissed in Braidon's ears as the dragon drifted lower, catching in his hair and sending shivers down his back through a rip in his clothing. Squinting in the bright sunlight, he gasped as they dropped towards the clouds, his stomach lurching uncomfortably. In front of him, Enala let out a whoop of joy as though she were still a ten-year-old girl, and the dragon roared in response.

Despite the cold, Braidon found himself grinning at the old priest's youthful exuberance. Since he'd met her, he had rarely seen beyond the woman's calm, reserved exterior. Only up here, far above the worries of the world, did she seem free. Her eyes flashed as she glanced back at him, a smile of her own on her lips.

"We're close!" she cried out, the rushing air whipping away her words almost before Braidon could comprehend them.

Are you ready, young Braidon? Dahniul's voice spoke in his mind.

"I think so!" he shouted back, his heart beating faster at the thought of the coming challenges.

They had flown all night and day, racing across oceans and

desert, mountains and forests, to reach the distant Plorsean capital. Enala had filled him in on her plan while they flew, but now that the time had come, he found himself suddenly doubting her words.

After all, her entire plan rested on his magic.

"I believe in you, Braidon!" Enala said, as though reading his mind.

She stood suddenly. Balancing precariously on Dahniul's back, she turned and lowered herself back down so she was facing him. She reached out and took his hands in hers, her aged face alight with the sun's warmth.

"Have faith, the Gods are with you," she said.

Braidon shivered. "Easy for you to say, you've seen them," he muttered.

Enala laughed. "I've *been* them, but the point is well taken. Have faith in yourself then. You have conquered your magic once already. When you reach for it now, hold to that memory. You *know* you can do this."

He smiled. "Let us see, shall we?"

And closing his eyes, he reached for his power. White light flickered in the void of his mind, rising up, the Feline taking shape. Only now, to Braidon's surprise, he found himself able to face the creature without fear. Bemused, he watched it roar, the great jaw opening wide. Chuckling to himself, he strode towards it, and the beast's power faded away. His hand stretched out, thrusting deep into its core, and the magic collapsed in on itself.

Braidon gasped as white-hot heat filled him, rushing to every pore of his body. Opening his eyes, he saw a world awash with colour. Enala still sat before him, only now it was not the old woman who watched him, but a figure of brilliant, shining red. Braidon gasped as he saw the amber swirling within the dragon, shining out to fill the sky. Further afield, he sensed other spirits, other powers all around, and felt a sudden yearning to go to them.

A strange motion followed, and then Braidon was soaring through the sky, beyond Enala and the dragon, outside his own body. Colours whirled around him, a stream of blue and white and red dancing across the sky. He watched the dragon and its tiny passengers, mystified by their brilliant light.

Only then did his purpose return to him. Enala believed he could use his power to shield them from the Tsar's view, allow them to infiltrate the citadel and find his sister without being detected. His spirit flickered as he considered the problem. The magic of the priest and dragon shone across the sky, his own power small alongside them. If he wanted to shield them from the Tsar, he would need to do more than just hide them from sight.

Drifting closer to Dahniul, he reached out with his spirit to touch the aura surrounding her, and it rippled away from him, changing. He frowned, concentrating on it, willing it to alter, to become one with the sky. To his surprise, the amber colour faded, becoming the same multicoloured light that he had drifted through earlier. Slowly, the dragon faded from the sight of his spirit eyes.

Braidon smiled then, pleased with his success, and quickly turned his attention to Enala and his own flickering power.

When he finally opened his eyes, Braidon let out a long groan as the weight of his body returned. He swayed on the dragon's back, but a firm hand settled on his shoulder, holding him in place. Blinking, he found Enala smiling at him.

"You did it, Braidon!" she exclaimed.

There was a strangeness to Enala's face as he looked at her, and it was a moment before Braidon realised he could see straight through her. His mouth dropped open. "What the...?"

Enala laughed. "A side-effect of your spell," she said, answering his unfinished question. "I *believe* we should now be invisible to anyone outside the spell, while to those within we merely appear…less substantial."

"Are you sure?" Braidon asked. They were still above the clouds, but once they dropped below them…

"Only one way to find out!" Enala replied with a youthful grin. "Dahniul, take us down!"

Before Braidon could reply, his stomach lurched up into his chest as the dragon folded its wings and dived. Screaming, they plunged into the clouds. For a moment, everything vanished, and all Braidon could see was a thick white mist. Only the solidness of the dragon beneath him convinced Braidon he was not plummeting to his death.

Then the clouds were gone, and Braidon was left looking out over the lands of his home. Shining water stretched out below, the waters raging with the afternoon winds sweeping in off the plateau. A sprinkling of ships were racing across the lake, and Braidon's chest tightened at the sight of their pitch-black sails.

Ahead, he saw the towering cliffs of his island home rising from the lake. Here, even more ships bobbed at the docks, their black sails like a stain on the lake around them. Their colour could only mean one thing—the Tsar was preparing for war.

His heart beating faster, he shouted at Enala. "The emissaries couldn't have reached the city already," he breathed.

"No," Enala replied, voice grim, "the Tsar never intended to honour his offer of peace. Look over there." She nodded to the far side of the lake. Beyond the rolling hills bordering the waters, an army spread across the land as far as the eye could see.

Braidon clenched his jaw. "We have to stop him."

"Yes," Enala replied. "But first, we must find your sister."

At that, Dahniul swept down, and the tall white walls of Ardath's citadel came racing up to greet them.

❧ 31 ❧

"Where...?" Devon started, then trailed off, too stunned to finish the question.

Laughing, Kellian moved to the iron door. A solid *thunk* followed as the lock disengaged, then a loud squeal of rusty hinges as the door swung open. Kellian gestured them forward.

"Well, don't just stand there! I don't know how much time we have before the real guards return!"

The old man rose with a chuckle. "You know, I think I like you, innkeeper." He wandered past Devon and out into the corridor. Stretching his arms, he groaned. "Ahh, but it's good to be out of that hole. You coming, youngster?" he said to Devon.

Shaking his head, Devon strode after them. "What about the guards?" he asked gruffly, glaring at Kellian. Just moments before, he'd been on the brink of despair. Now it seemed Kellian had had a way out all along.

"Don't look so glum, old friend," Kellian laughed, thumping him on the back. "The guards are taken care of...or at least, I hope they are. Hard to know how much of my message Betran managed to deliver."

"Betran?" Devon repeated dumbly.

"I left him with some papers to give my contacts in Kalgan, in case anything happened to us. I don't know about you, but I didn't like the idea of spending my remaining days locked in a dungeon when your brilliant plans inevitably unravelled."

"I wouldn't advise it personally," the old man offered.

"Such faith you have in me," Devon grunted, but Kellian only grinned.

"Lighten up, Devon! We're free, aren't we?" he said. "Or we are for now. I think we'd best be leaving. Who knows how much time my patrons have managed to buy us? Old drinking buddies can only get you so far. What's say we see about those bracelets of yours, my friend?" He rattled the keys at the old man.

Their companion sighed. "I'm afraid there's no key for these, innkeeper. Powerful magic locked them in place, and it will take magic equally as powerful to remove them. We'll have to rely on our wits alone to take us the rest of the way."

"Figures," Kellian grunted, lowering the keys. He shared a glance with Devon, then turned to the neighbouring cells. Now that they were in the corridor, they could see down the length of the dungeons—or at least as far as the light reached. There were at least a hundred cells, all full of people. "What about them?"

"There's little we can do for them now," the old man replied. "Not unless you have it in you to kill them?"

Devon's head jerked up. "*What?*"

The old man's eyes shone. "They are the source of the Tsar's power," he replied. "Them, myself, his Magickers upstairs. So long as we live, so long as we wear the bracelets, his power remains."

"We'll wake them…" Kellian began, but the old man was already shaking his head.

"They're past that now," he shot back. "And we cannot

carry them." Moving to the front of a cell, he looked in at the occupants and let out a long breath. "But you are right. I don't have the stomach for it either—though no doubt they would thank us for the mercy."

"Well, if we can't help them, let's at least help ourselves," Kellian said briskly, starting towards the stairwell.

Devon offered the old man his shoulder, but now that they were free, their cellmate seemed to have regained his vigour. He sprang after Kellian, leaving Devon to bring up the rear. Ahead, Kellian lifted the single lantern from its bracket and started up the stairwell. The others came close behind, ears straining for sounds of movement from above. The stone steps wound upwards, spiralling past more levels of dungeons. Silently, Devon wondered how many cells there were, how many Magickers the Tsar had imprisoned over the decades.

Shivering, he recalled the Trolan Magickers who'd been captured during the civil war. There had been hundreds—and the Tsar's power had been insurmountable even then. What new feats might he be capable of now?

Finally, the stairwell came to an end, the stone steps giving way to a wide guard chamber. They paused in the doorway, scanning the room for signs of danger. A desk was pushed up against the far wall, two chairs behind it. Two men were seated there, but both were slumped unconscious across the wooden surface. A crevasse of wine stood on the table between them, along with two empty mugs.

Devon looked at Kellian and raised an eyebrow. His friend only shrugged and entered the room. The guards were armed with knives and swords, and he quickly helped himself to them. The old man found himself a short sword, while Kellian secreted several daggers about his person. Hefting a spare short sword, he offered it to Devon.

Scanning the room, Devon's heart leapt as he glimpsed a black haft poking out from beneath the desk. Crouching down, he reached out and gripped the familiar weapon. A weight lifted from his shoulders as he straightened, *kanker* settling easily into his hands.

"I'm beginning to think we might make it out of this alive after all," he said, grinning.

"*Kanker*," their cellmate whispered. He moved slowly across the room, staring at the hammer. "Gods, I never thought I would see it again."

Devon narrowed his eyes. "I told you he was my ancestor."

Their companion smiled. "Yes, but then, I never thought I'd leave that cell either." He paused, swallowing. "It's magic... I wonder...?"

Devon gripped the weapon tighter. "You think it could free you?"

"I'm not sure Alastair's spell will be strong enough."

"Can't hurt to try."

"Oh, it can," the old man replied, "but it's worth the risk."

He held out his hands. Devon extended *kanker* and tapped it lightly to the bracelets around the man's wrists. As it connected, a hiss like a boiling kettle whistled through the room. The old man's face tightened, his jaw clenching as though to muffle a scream. Still, he did not back away.

An instant later, a brilliant flash lit the room, followed by a sharp *crack*. The light faded away with the soft tinkling of metal striking stone. Looking down, Devon saw the old man's wrists were now unadorned.

"It worked!"

Grimacing, the old man rubbed his hands. "Ah, but that hurt," he said. Then he smiled and clenched his fists. To Devon, it seemed the temperature in the room dropped several degrees.

"What now?" Devon asked.

"My friends have done what they can," Kellian answered.

"I say we get out of this citadel and this city as quickly as possible, before anyone discovers we're gone."

"We'd best move quickly," the old man added, "before the next shift arrives…" He trailed off as a distant *thud* carried to them from the doorway leading out of the dungeons.

Devon advanced on the exit. The heavy wooden door was closed, but from beyond he could hear footsteps approaching. The scraping of a key in the lock followed, and the door shifted slightly. Then a voice called out.

"Hey, lads, give us a hand will ya? You know it sticks!"

Kanker gripped in one hand, Devon waited on the other side of the door for his moment. The others closed in behind him, but he waved them back. The doorway was narrow, and there wouldn't be room in the corridor beyond for more than one man to fight.

He eyed the door, and seeing it shift, he surged forwards, his boot lashing out to crash against the wood. The door flew backwards with the power of the blow, and beyond, a voice cried out. Then Devon was charging through, *kanker* in hand, and he was amongst them. There was no time to count his foes, only to attack. Taken by surprise, they fell back before his fury, their swords still sheathed at their sides. Scarlet guardcloaks became tangled around boots, and the first man was still clutching his head where the door had struck him when *kanker* caught him in the chest, hurling him back.

Leaping the fallen body, Devon swung again, slamming his weapon into the face of the following guard. The man was still scrambling for the hilt of his sword, but as the hammer struck, his body stiffened, and the half-drawn blade clattered to the ground.

Beyond, a third guard cried out and turned to flee. Hefting *kanker*, Devon hurled it at the man. The weapon hissed through the air and caught him in the small of his back. He cried out and crashed face-first into the ground, his legs twitching uselessly as he tried to crawl away.

Striding down the corridor, Devon retrieved *kanker*. Looking down at the injured man, his anger flared. These men had sought to cage him, to lock him in the darkness, while blood suckers like Quinn and the Tsar enjoyed the light as heroes. Teeth bared, he lifted *kanker*, ready to bring it down on the man's skull.

"Devon!" Kellian's voice carried down the corridor, halting his blow.

He looked back. "What?"

Kellian walked towards him. "They're done," his friend said softly. "You beat them. Leave him, there's more where they came from."

Devon sucked in a breath, seeing the concern in his friend's eyes. At his feet, the fallen guard was trembling with terror. Still, the anger clutched at Devon, demanding retribution.

"You remind me of him a lot, you know." said the old man, his voice carrying down the corridor.

Devon frowned. "Who?"

The old man joined Kellian. At his feet, the guard groaned. "Your ancestor."

A sharp pain lanced through Devon's chest at the reference. "Alan?" he growled. "How could you possibly have known him?"

"No, not Alan, though he was even larger than you." The old man smiled. "I was talking of Alastair. In his day, there were few Magickers more powerful than him. No mortal foe could hope to stand against him—yet he rarely used his power on those without magic. You are strong, Devon, powerful like him. But are you merciful?"

Devon sighed, his anger dying like flames before the water. "Fine," he agreed. "Let's get out of here, then."

Without waiting for a reply, he turned and started down

the corridor, leaving the others to race after him. Pushing through another set of wooden doors, they found themselves in a broad corridor. Devon searched for some point of reference that would tell him where they were in the citadel as the old man strode to a window in the opposite wall. Light was streaming through the glass, and their companion's eyes flickered closed as it bathed his face. He stood still as a statue, the years seeming to fall from him, while in the courtyard beyond, birds chirped.

"I never thought I would see the sky again." The old man's words shook. "I thought I would never leave that place."

Devon reached out and placed a hand on the man's shoulder. "You're free now," he said softly.

To his surprise, the old man shook his head. Reaching up, he wiped the tears from his cheeks, then looked at Devon. "I can never be free," he said. "I did not lie before, my friend. There is nothing left of the man the Tsar sent into the darkness. Only the hate remains. It binds me to him still. I cannot join you."

"You must," Kellian replied. "Even with your powers restored, you cannot hope to match him alone."

The old man smiled. Clenching his fists, he let out a long breath. Devon's ears popped as the windows shattered inwards, and a swirling wind went rushing into the corridor. A dull *boom* echoed around them, and looking down, he saw lightning dancing along the old man's arms.

"Perhaps not," the man said quietly, "but even so, I will try. At the very least, it will give you a distraction."

"You don't need to do this," Devon argued, but the blue eyes turned to stare at him, and the words left him.

"I have lived long past my time, Devon. But my death can still have meaning. I can still leave this world a better place than when I entered it. Now go. Run. Don't turn back."

He started down the corridor, but Kellian's voice called him back.

"Who *are* you?"

The old man paused, his eyes shining as he smiled. "My name is Eric."

Then he was gone.

❧ 32 ❧

Alana stood before the throne, fists clenched, her whole body trembling as she faced the man who dared to call himself her father. Several of his councillors stood around him. He still hadn't noticed her presence, but the ring of guards were watching her from the dais, their eyes alert. No doubt they were still weary after her earlier display with their comrade. In that moment, Alana hardly cared.

In her mind, she saw again the memories her father had kept from her, the ones Antonia had unlocked. She remembered it *all* now—the reason she had fled the citadel with her brother, why she had wiped their memories.

For years she had marched children off to their examinations, many never to be seen again. Those who survived became Battle Magickers for her father, while the ones who failed were consumed by their magic, becoming the demons her father sent to destroy his enemies. Either way, Alana had never really cared—so long as the Tsar's power grew. At least, not until her brother's time had come...

Braidon.

The name was like a bell tolling within her, filling her with fear, with terror. The Magickers she'd tutored through the years had been beneath her, commoners who lived only at her father's mercy. But her brother...she couldn't face the thought of losing him, of watching him fail. And he would, she knew. Perhaps it was her own love that had made him weak, her mercy that had blighted him...but it mattered little now.

She had known he would fail, long before his magic surfaced. Even after a year of tutoring, of meditation and training, he had still been too soft to face his magic. It would have overwhelmed him, swept away the boy she loved and replaced him with one of the black-eyed creatures who served the Tsar.

And her father hadn't cared.

Alana reached down and drew her sabre from its sheath. The guards tensed as the rasp of steel on leather whispered through the throne room, but she ignored them and advanced up the stone steps towards her father. One of the guards moved towards her, his spear bristling, steel plate mail rattling loudly. His weapon swept down, the point pressing lightly against her chest.

She glanced at the spear, then into the eyes of the man holding it.

"Get out of my way," she commanded.

Magic surged from her, catching on the tip of the spear and racing up the weapon into the man. He shuddered, a battle taking place behind his eyes, but it was one he could not win. With another rattle of metal, he stepped aside, and Alana marched past. The other guards stayed out of reach, but quickly moved to position themselves on either side of her father.

He was watching her now, his eyes following her as she topped the stairs and came to a stop before the throne. The other councillors fell silent as he stood to meet her.

"Alana, I thought you were resting–"

"I know everything, father," she interrupted, her voice like stone. "I remember."

For half a second, she thought he would deny it. A flicker passed across his face, but then the mask settled back into place, the emotion fading away. He turned to his councillors. "Leave me."

He swung back to Alana without allowing them a chance to argue. They hesitated a moment, before striding past Alana and down the stairs to the exit. The guards remained, spears still bristling, but at a wave from her father, they lowered the weapons and retreated.

"And what is it you remember, my daughter?" the Tsar said finally.

Alana advanced, her skin still crawling at the thought of what he'd wrought on her memories, the hole he'd left when he'd helped restore her past. She felt a sick sense of betrayal rise in her chest.

"*Everything*," she snapped, lifting her sabre to point it at his chest. "You *dared* to interfere with my memories?"

To her surprise, the Tsar chuckled. "Me, daughter? I only did what you asked. It was *you* who made such a mess of them in the first place!"

"To hide from *you!*" Alana shrieked.

The guards started forward again, but she was faster still. She closed in on the Tsar, her sabre lancing forward. He made no move to stop her, and she felt a moment's thrill as the blade plunged towards him. But as the point touched his chest her sword shrieked and grated to a stop, as though she'd struck solid stone. Her hands jarred at the impact, the vibrations almost tearing the hilt from her grasp. Instead of fading, the shrieking sound grew until it reached a fever pitch, and with a sudden *boom*, her blade shattered.

A wave of energy struck Alana, throwing her on her back. Shards of steel rattled on the marble floors as the remnants of her blade scattered across the dais. On the ground, Alana groaned as she struggled to regain her breath. She lay staring up at her father, hate curdling in her stomach.

The Tsar pursed his lips, face impassive. "It was smart, I'll admit," he said pleasantly, as though she had not just tried to stab him. "Altering your own mind, and your brother's, to conceal yourselves from my powers." He shook his head. "I trained you well."

Alana shivered, seeing again the memories Antonia had unlocked, of her brother coming to her before his birthday, his eyes alive with fear.

I can't do it, Alana, he had told her.

Looking into his eyes, she had wanted to tell him it would be alright, that he would discover the strength he needed to master his magic. Yet the words had died in her throat, and all she could see was the bright child she had helped raise after her mother's death; the one good, pure thing in her otherwise joyless existence.

And Alana had seen the truth then—that one way or another, she would lose him. Either he would become the hard, unyielding man their father wanted him to be, or he would perish, consumed by his own magic.

That life of darkness was all Alana had ever known. Long ago, she had come to terms with her place in the world, sacrificing her freedom and embracing her role as the Tsar's daughter. She had hoped she might spare her brother the same fate, but she had only delayed the inevitable.

The day Braidon had come to her, she'd known what she needed to do. That very night, she had smuggled them both out of the citadel, to what she hoped was freedom. As the midnight bell chimed, Braidon's fear had taken hold, unleashing his magic, but she'd used her own power to render him unconscious before his power could be detected. She'd managed to carry him deep into the city, but slowed down by his dead-weight, they hadn't reached the gates in time. The city guard were already on alert for their disappearance.

So they had taken refuge in the city, concealing themselves from their father's magic in the mass of humanity that was the slums of Ardath. For weeks, they'd fled from abandoned buildings to crumbling shacks, waiting for the hunt to die down. Through all the long days and nights, she had sensed her father's power, humming in the skies overhead as he searched for them. It was only then that she'd realised they could never escape him. The moment they left the crowds of Ardath, their minds would be exposed, and his magic would find them.

Only when the boy's wild magic had set fire to the stepwell, had Alana seen her opportunity. Using his power to mask her own, she had turned her magic on herself and Braidon. Wrapping their minds in bands of green fire, she'd buried their memories deep, allowing their subconscious to form new lives for themselves. They had become new people—people her father would not have recognised, even had he touched their minds with his magic.

Alana was still surprised by the girl who had emerged to replace her. Perhaps she had only unlocked a part of herself she'd never known existed, one buried deep by her father's teachings, consumed by the harsh reality of life as the Daughter of the Tsar.

Thinking of her other self now, Alana's animosity faded, replaced by a cautious respect. Whatever her faults, the girl had escaped the Tsar's Stalkers, had succeeded in rescuing her brother, where Alana herself had failed. With the release of her final memories, she felt almost at peace with her other self.

Their hatred for the Tsar had united them.

Glaring at her father, Alana climbed slowly to her feet.

"I won't let you bring him back," she said.

"You cannot stop me, my daughter," the Tsar replied. "He must face his examination."

"He will fail!"

"Such little faith, my daughter," her father replied. "He is of the blood of kings. He will prevail—as you once did."

"Ay, I remember how you prepared me," Alana replied bitterly.

"Did you not impart on your students the same preparations?" The Tsar responded. "Did your teachings not prepare them for the challenge, and a life in my service?"

Shame filled Alana as she recalled her charges, their terror as she faced them. She knew the emotion came from her other self, but with memories of her brother's terror fresh in her mind, she embraced it, finally seeing the mindless cruelty of her actions. Her methods had been pointless—only necessary because the young Magickers were given just a month to prepare for their examinations.

In all the time Alana had served as teacher, she had never regretted her students' suffering. After all, their torments were nothing to what her father had subjected her to. She clenched her fists, recalling the agony of losing a limb, only for the Tsar to touch her with his power, restoring it. A shudder swept through her as she looked up into his eyes.

"You are a monster. You will destroy your own son."

"If that is his fate, then so be it," her father replied sadly. "If he does not have the strength to master his magic, he is no son of mine."

"*No!*" Alana shrieked, throwing herself forward. An invisible barrier brought her up short. She slammed her fists against it. "You will not turn him!"

Against her will, she saw again the demon that had come for her on the ship back in Lon, its youthful face and jet-black eyes. She knew now that had not been the first time she'd seen that face, the first time she'd looked into those eyes—though before they had been sky green. With her memories restored, she knew now who he was.

His name was Anish, and he had been her student.

Before his magic took him.

The thought of her brother facing the same fate set her stomach heaving, and she slid down the invisible barrier to the floor. Looking up at her father, she shook her head, sobbing now, powerless before his magic.

"Please," she whispered.

He shrugged. "His fate is in his own hands, daughter," he replied. "When our emissaries return with him, he will face the examination like any other Magicker. I will release the bonds of his magic. He will face the beast, and either defeat it, or succumb to its power. I have no wish to see my son a demon, but I will not save him should it take him."

"But you could!" Alana shrieked. "You saved me!"

"You were not yourself."

"I...I don't want to be myself!" Alana said, her voice fading as she realised it was true. Her eyes burned as she thought of Devon and Kellian, locked away because of her. Pain wrenched at her heart. "I want to be free."

The Tsar moved towards her. "Free?" he sighed. "What is freedom? I have given you *everything*, child! Life, magic, an empire! I have endured your wilfulness for years, yet still you demand more."

"I don't want anything from you."

Her father sighed, his eyes shining. "Then I will take it all. You *will* serve me, daughter. You think your magic can protect you? I have a dozen Magickers in my thrall with the same power."

Ice spread though Alana's stomach as her heart started to palpitate. Her father's eyes had hardened, all traces of kindness draining from them. Taken by a sudden fear, she rose and backed away on trembling legs. Another invisible barrier brought her up short. Her father started towards her.

Alana spun, slamming her hands against the barrier,

desperate to escape. But there was nowhere to run, and she froze as a hand clutched her by the shoulder, forcing her to look back. Her mouth parted as she looked up at her father, her vision shimmering.

"No…" she said.

The Tsar shook his head. "Why do you hate me, daughter?" he asked. "Everything I have ever done was to build a better world for you. Yet still you spurn me."

Hot tears ran down Alana's cheeks. "Go ahead and do it," she said. "You have already taken everything from me. My childhood, my joy, my soul. You made me into your executioner, had me drive scores of children into the darkness. And you have the gall to ask me why I hate you?"

"I am sorry," he murmured, still holding to her shoulder. "This is my fault. I thought I could fix you by holding back your memories. But the weakness is rooted too deep."

"And weakness must be destroyed," Alana whispered.

"I will start afresh," her father agreed. His face tightened. "But you will feel nothing."

Before Alana could react, she felt the burning touch of his magic wash through her. She gasped, her own power rising to defend her, but it was nothing to the forces in the Tsar's command. The burning green of her magic was engulfed, swept away like a sandcastle before the incoming tide. Her body shook as she fought him, but it was no use. She opened her mouth to scream…

And the roar of thunder filled her ears.

❧ 33 ❧

Devon stumbled to a halt as a crash echoed through the corridors of the citadel. Kellian drew up alongside him. Together they looked back. Flashes of light burst through the open windows, and it seemed as though the very air was alive with energy. They shared a glance, then returned their eyes to the lightning flickering in the sky.

Somewhere in the citadel, the old man had engaged with the enemy.

Eric.

The name sent a shiver down Devon's spine. It couldn't be true…and yet, surely it could not be a coincidence? Eric was the last Magicker to have seen the Gods alive, the last to have wielded the Sword of Light, one of the few to stand to the end against the Dark Magicker, Archon.

And he was Enala's brother.

"You think he can win?" Devon heard himself asking.

"No," Kellian replied shortly.

Devon nodded, though he wasn't so sure. Somehow Eric had survived the Tsar's corrupting magic, had lived for decades in the darkness below the citadel, where so many others had succumbed. And when he'd looked into the man's eyes, there had been an indomitable will there, a determination to finally have his revenge.

Yet now Eric stood against the most powerful Magicker in the Empire, a man who could draw on the magic of hundreds, who commanded demons and dragons with a wave of his sword.

In the distance, the rumble of thunder died away, and outside the clouds parted. A ray of sunshine burst over the citadel. Seeing it, the hope withered in Devon's chest as he realised Eric's storm magic had been defeated. He turned back to Kellian.

"Let's go," he said.

They started down the corridor, but they'd only made it a few more feet when they heard the soft patter of running boots ahead of them. Before they could react, a squadron of black-garbed Stalkers raced into view. Quinn stood at their head, his eyes widening as he saw them standing in the middle of the corridor.

"What—?" he started.

Hefting his hammer, Devon charged at Quinn, but the man already had his sword drawn, and the blade leapt to meet his attack. Steel clashed as Kellian joined him. Devon ducked as Quinn's sabre slashed for his face, then he dropped his shoulder and drove it into Quinn's chest. The blow hurled his foe back into his comrades, creating a hole. Devon rushed through it, *kanker* sweeping out, catching a Stalker in the head with a sickening crunch.

Then they were clear, the scattered Stalkers turning to follow. Angry shouts chased them down the corridor as Devon glanced back, his heart pounding hard. Kellian was just behind him, a blade in either hand. They shared a grin as a voice chased after them.

"*Devon!*" Quinn roared.

A shriek came from the windows alongside Devon, and he looked up in time to see the glass shatter. Spinning, he lifted *kanker* in time to meet the gale Quinn had summoned with his power. It came rushing into the corridor, but with a hiss it was absorbed by his hammer, though its force still pushed Devon back several steps.

Alongside him, Kellian was not so lucky. Without the protection of *kanker*, Quinn's winds caught him midstride, and hurled him backwards. He struck the marble wall of the corridor with an awful *thud*, his blades skittering loudly on the stone floor, and he slumped to the ground, unconscious.

Devon cried out and started towards him, but Quinn's voice brought him up short.

"Don't move, hammerman," he hissed, "or I'll crush his skull against the bloody wall."

The lieutenant came striding towards him. The Stalkers followed, though Devon noted several lay on the ground behind them, unmoving. He smirked.

"Can't say it's good to see you, sonny," he said.

Fury etched across his face, Quinn stepped up and touched his sabre to Devon's neck. "Drop the hammer."

Devon hesitated, and the wind whistled louder. The *thunk* as *kanker* hit the ground echoed loudly in the corridor.

A dark smile spread across Quinn's face as he withdrew his sabre, then slammed a fist into Devon's stomach. Unprepared, Devon doubled over, the breath whistling between his teeth. He looked up in time to see Quinn's knee rising to catch him in the face, before stars exploded across his vision as he toppled back.

When his vision cleared, he found Quinn looking down at him. "So, the rats escaped their cell."

Devon struggled to find a reply, but Quinn's boot slammed into his ribs. Something went *crack* as pain tore through

Devon's chest. Rolling onto his side, he coughed, the agony redoubling as he found himself suddenly breathless.

"Get them up," Quinn said. "I'd like to continue on our way to the throne room. Something is going on with Alana and the Tsar."

Despite himself, Devon's chest clenched at the mention of Alana's name. He groaned as rough hands gripped him beneath the arms and hauled him up. Head swimming, he saw Quinn already moving away. Two more Stalkers had hefted Kellian between them, though his friend still appeared unconscious.

As Devon was dragged down the corridor, he tried to get the lieutenant's attention. "I hope Eric killed him."

Quinn paused. "The old man?" he raised an eyebrow. "*That* was the legendary Eric?" Laughter echoed in the corridor. "I guess age makes fools of everyone, in the end! Now stop delaying, Devon. Or Kellian will suffer for it."

Devon knew he wasn't bluffing. The last of the fight went from him as he slumped in the arms of the men carrying him. His stomach twisted as he realised one held *kanker*.

Quinn chuckled as the Stalkers dragged Devon alongside him. "I must say I'm impressed, Devon," he said conversationally. "You'll have to tell me how you escaped, one day. It's a shame your weakness betrayed you in the end. I mean, you must know you're both going to die now? You could have saved yourself, but instead you chose…what? A pointless death?"

"A man like you wouldn't understand," Devon whispered.

One of the men carrying him paused long enough to slam his fist into Devon's stomach. He cried out as the broken rib sliced deeper into his chest. His vision swirled, red closing in on all sides, but he fought to stay conscious.

"It's no wonder Alana spurned you," Quinn was saying now.

"Where is she?" he gasped, barely able to breathe.

"She's mine now," Quinn snapped, though Devon sensed there was more behind his words.

"Is that so?" he rasped.

Quinn hesitated. His face was dark, his eyes shining with suppressed rage, but he made no move to attack Devon again. After a moment, he shook his head and swung away.

"She'll never be yours, Devon."

Devon was about to reply when a cry came from the Stalkers carrying Kellian. Somehow, he had slipped from their arms, tripping one of them as he tumbled to the ground. The other was bending over them, trying to get them up, but as Devon watched, the man jerked, stiffening suddenly.

"What's going on?" Quinn growled, running towards the men.

In that instant, Kellian rolled, leaving the second Stalker to topple dead to the floor. He held a bloody dagger clutched in one hand, and with a flick of his wrist, sent it hurtling at Quinn.

Quinn saw it just in time. He lurched back, and the blade hissed past, just a hair's breadth from his throat. With a scream, he threw out an arm. The wind roared, rushing down the corridor to catch Kellian where he still crouched on the ground. He flew through the air, his legs slamming awkwardly into the wall, and an awful *crack* echoed down the corridor. Screaming, Kellian crumpled to the ground clutching his leg.

Devon tried to summon the strength to go to his friend, but the two Stalkers only held him tighter as Quinn advanced on Kellian.

"Bastard innkeeper, I'll see you bleed for that," he shouted, drawing his sabre with his left hand.

Kellian tried to scramble back, but Quinn's boot crashed down on his injured leg, forcing a scream from him. Surging forward, Devon fought to reach the man, but a third Stalker stepped in and slammed a fist into his face. He sagged in the men's grip, the red flaring again, filling his vision. Blood pounded in his ears, but over it he heard another scream. Fear for his friend rose within him, but it was too late now. His strength had already fled, and with a cry, Devon felt himself falling away.

34

When the light finally died away, Alana found herself lying sprawled alongside the throne. Groaning, she forced herself to sit up, but a thousand flashing lights danced across her vision, and she slumped back to the ground. A harsh ringing in her ears drowned out all other noise—then with a sharp *pop*, sound returned.

Screams echoed through the throne room. Her vision cleared, revealing men scattered across the marble floors, their bodies blackened, their plated armour now twisted and misshapen. The sight of their scorched skin and torn bodies made Alana's stomach swirl, and rolling onto her side, she vomited. Silence settled like a blanket around her as the last screams died away.

Looking at herself, Alana was surprised to find her own body free of marks. She guessed her lack of armour or sword had saved her from…whatever it was that had struck them. Even so, she ached with the force of being picked up and hurled across the room. Across from her, black smoke still clung to the dais, but it was beginning to clear now, revealing the twisted remains of the golden throne.

And the Tsar still standing atop the stairs, staring down at the open doors.

Her head pounding, Alana followed her father's gaze and saw an old man striding towards the dais. His blue eyes shone with power, though his face was wrinkled and bleached white hair hung down around his shoulders. In his hands, lightning crackled.

"Eric," the Tsar's voice whispered across the room. "So good to see you again. I'm sorry to see the years have not been kind."

Silently, the old man continued his advance, the lightning growing in his hands. Her father laughed, and with a roar, Eric threw out an arm. A bolt of lightning flashed across the throne room, crackling as it went.

Her father lifted a hand, and the lightning froze mid-air, the sound of its thunder still booming off the walls. With a flick of his finger, the Tsar sent it careening up into the ceiling. White light flashed as it struck, almost blinding Alana.

"So you removed the bracelets," the Tsar said conversationally as he started down the steps of the dais. "Fortunately, you are not the only Sky Magicker in my…service."

Baring his teeth, the newcomer spread his arms. A roar came from the windows high above as they shattered inwards. Alana threw herself face first on the ground as glass crashed down around her.

In the middle of the room, her father laughed as the howling wind encircled him. "Have we not had this fight before, old man?" he shouted.

Alana watched in astonishment as ice grew around her father, stretching up from the marble floors. The harsh *crack* of splitting stone rang out, while amidst the ice, her father continued to smile, even as his breath misted before him. He lifted his hand, and fire appeared in his palm, growing and swelling, then rushing out to consume the ice. With a flick of his fingers, he sent the flames rushing towards his foe.

Moving with an agility that belayed his age, the old man hurled himself aside. Behind him, a column of marble was engulfed by the fire, its heat washing across the room to even where Alana lay. Surging back to his feet, the old man drew a sword and rushed at the Tsar.

Her father laughed again. She watched with a sinking heart as the Tsar allowed the intruder to close in on him. Then with a sudden decisiveness, he pointed a finger. Nothing appeared to happen, but the old man came to an abrupt halt, as though held by some invisible force. Sword raised above his head, he glared at the Tsar.

The Tsar gently lifted his hand, and still frozen in place, the old man rose slowly into the air.

"Ah, Eric, why in the Three Nations did you come here?" he asked of the prone Magicker. "You could not defeat me in your prime, what hope do you have now?"

Electricity crackled in the old man's hands. With a *boom*, it shot towards the Tsar. Cursing, her father thrust out a fist, and the bolt shattered into a thousand sparks. But the distraction had freed the old man from his power, and dropping lightly to the ground, the intruder hurled his blade at the Tsar.

Alana gasped as it flew for her father's face, her soul divided between hope and horror, but at the last second it halted mid-air. The Tsar stared at the blade a moment, his face darkening, then sent it spinning off into the corner with a flick of his finger.

Only a few feet separated the Magickers now, and they stood facing each other, their twin blue eyes shimmering with unrestrained power. Neither was willing to give ground.

"You know I couldn't walk away," the old man said suddenly. "That I couldn't let you live, not after what you did."

Her father sighed. As he spread his hands, the power in his eyes faded. "What would you have me say, Eric? I cannot change the past. I am sorry your son had to die, but he had something I needed."

There was pain in the old man's eyes as he looked at Alana's father. "He was your *friend*," he said. "How could you do it?"

"My friend?" Her father seemed puzzled. "Yes, I suppose it might have looked that way. But no, Calybe was never my friend, no more than you or your sister were. You were *Gods*, Eric, compared to the rest of us mere mortals.

"You were *family*, Theo," the old man whispered.

"Family?" There was anger in the Tsar's voice now. "Maybe in name, but I was never *family* to you, never a part of your plans. Not like Calybe. No, I was just Theo, the magicless, the mortal, forever despised for my weakness."

"We loved you, Theo, Enala loved you," Eric replied. "How could you have betrayed her, betrayed us?"

"Betrayed you?" Her father shook his head. "All I have ever done is try to live up to your examples. I have sacrificed *every-thing* for the greater good. And I am so close now."

"If your idea of the greater good is locking away hundreds of innocent Magickers, I pity you," Eric replied.

The Tsar spread his hands. "Are you so blinded by hate, Eric, that you cannot see it? Surely even in your black cell, you have heard. For the first time in a thousand years, the Three Nations are truly at peace. There is no war, no great destruction between nations or Gods. Even the scourge of magic will soon be consigned to the pages of history."

"Except for your own," Eric said.

"No," the Tsar responded, "when I am done, not even my own power will remain. I will draw the magic from the land, so there will never again be Gods or Magickers to bring bloody slaughter to the Three Nations. Surely, you of all people understand the pain magic has brought to this world."

Eric laughed. "You must have truly lost your mind, Theo, if you think the genocide of Magickers will be the end of magic."

"Of course not." The Tsar smiled. "I have found another way, one that requires no more to die." His voice dropped a notch. "I am close, Eric, so close now. Your son's sacrifice will not be in vain—if only you could set aside your hatred, you would see it. With your help, we could finally rid this world of magic's curse."

"I will never help you, Theo. And I am done talking!"

With the words, Eric sent a lightning bolt arcing for her father. But the Tsar was ready, and his hands swept out to freeze the blue fire in place. The crackling of lightning hissed through the throne room as he sent it ricocheting backwards. Thunder crashed as it struck the old man in the chest and hurled him across the room.

"Very well, Eric." The Tsar's words boomed over the thunder as he advanced on the fallen man. "Then death it shall be."

He raised a hand, but before he could summon his magic, the sharp squeal of hinges carried across the room. The Tsar swung around, and Alana watched in shock as Quinn and a troop of Stalkers led Kellian and Devon inside.

Quinn paused in the entranceway as he saw the destruction the two Magickers had wrought on the throne room. The bodies of the guards still lay in scattered piles, and fire and lightning had left blackened scorch marks on the walls. In several places, the carpets and curtains were smouldering. Swallowing visibly, Quinn led his men between the bodies to where the Tsar stood.

"I found them trying to run, your majesty," he said.

"Someone must have helped them and the old man escape their cell.

"Obviously," the Tsar answered. Turning, he smiled at the old man. "So after all this time, that was to be your final achievement, Eric? Your life thrown away as a distraction, so two mortals could escape me." He shook his head. "How low you have fallen, that you could not even do that."

$\mathcal{H}$ 35 $\mathcal{H}$

Devon staggered to a stop in the entrance to the throne room and stared at the chaos within. He had seen battle Magickers in action during the civil war, but never before had he seen so much carnage in one setting. The men lying scattered across the marble floors had never known what hit them, and stomach surging, he forced himself to look away.

His heart sank as he saw the old man on his knees, the towering figure of the Tsar standing over him. He quickly averted his gaze, sensing that even to look into the ruler's eyes was to risk annihilation, and found Alana standing nearby. The breath caught in his throat, and he saw an awful sadness cross her face. Her lips parted, and for a moment it seemed she would speak.

"I had intended to interrogate you later, Devon, Kellian."

Devon swung around as the Tsar spoke from nearby, and froze as he found the man's face just a few inches from his own. Despite standing almost a foot taller, Devon took an involuntary step back. Fear flared in his chest and he longed for the feel of *kanker* in his hand. The hammer had broken the Tsar's enchantment on the bracelets—did that mean Enala was wrong, that the ancient weapon *could* defeat the man himself?

Seeing his fear, the Tsar laughed. "It is good to finally meet you, Devon," he said, advancing on him. Devon tried to retreat, but the Tsar's hand rose, and suddenly it felt as though a vice had closed around his neck. Choking, Devon clawed at his throat, but there was nothing there to dislodge.

"Thrice you have defied me," the Tsar continued, his eyes hardening. "But no longer."

Devon gasped as the invisible force hauled him into the air, the vice tightening. His legs kicked out, finding only empty space. Darkness swirled at the edges of his vision as he watched a cold smile spread across the ruler's face.

"I forgave you the first deviance, when you spurned my service. But the kidnapping of my son and daughter, the attempted escape, the freeing of a dangerous Magicker, these transgressions I cannot ignore."

The Tsar gave a contemptuous flick of his hand. A force like a stampeding horse struck Devon in the chest, driving the last breath from his lungs and sending him sprawling across the ground. He came to rest near the old man.

Beside him, Eric was struggling to his feet. Blue lightning crackled in his fingers, but the Tsar swung on him before it could be released.

"*Enough!*"

With the Tsar's roar, the lightning died in Eric's fingers. Now it was the old man's turn to rise ponderously from the ground. He hung, suspended there, as the Tsar turned his attention back to Devon.

"Before I kill you, hammerman, I would like to know where my son is. I had thought the Northland Queen an intelligent woman, but now I learn she is sending assassins behind my back. Who knows what she might do with my dear Braidon."

Looking into the man's icy eyes, Devon's courage withered. A shudder swept through him, and he tried to look away, but he was trapped now. He was about to blurt out everything he knew about Enala and the Queen and Braidon, when the young boy's face flickered into his mind. He saw again the innocent smile, the sparkling intelligence behind his blue eyes, so like his father's. Yet that was all the two shared. In that moment, Devon knew he would do everything in his power to keep the boy from the Tsar.

Devon climbed to his feet. "He is safe from you, monster. I will not betray him."

"Devon…" Alana's voice came from behind him.

"You will tell me, hammerman," the Tsar interrupted.

With his words, he opened his hands, and a trickle of flame seeped from his fingers. Before Devon could throw himself back, they wrapped around his legs, burning through his leather leggings, searing his flesh. Pain unlike anything Devon had experienced rippled through his body, and he screamed. He tried to flee, to move, but the invisible force had him again, holding him to the fire.

As suddenly as the flames had begun, they died away. Cold spread down his legs, almost as painful, and Devon watched as his melted flesh knitted itself back together again. Sobbing despite himself, he slumped to his knees, tears streaming down his face. Soft footsteps approached.

"I will give you one last chance," the Tsar whispered. "Next time, I'll leave you a cripple."

His vision blurring, Devon looked up into the frigid eyes. "Go to hell!"

"I don't think that I will," the Tsar replied, smiling, "but you may go in my place."

He drew the sword at his waist. For half an instant, Devon thought he saw light flickering in the steel blade, but when he blinked, it had vanished. In its place, he saw his own haggard face reflected there, his unkempt beard and bloodshot eyes, the bruises and cuts. Still on his knees, he looked like a broken man. Looking up at the most powerful man in the Three Nations, he tried to find the strength to stand.

"I have always preferred the sword, you know," the Tsar said. He twirled the blade in his hand before pointing it down at Devon. "After all, that was all I had, in the beginning. The strength of my sword arm, the speed and quickness of my mind. I was like you, hammerman, a warrior born in a Magicker's world. It pleased me to see the magicless advance ahead of those like Quinn. I am afraid you will not live to see it, but one day soon, men like yourself will rule this world."

"You and I are nothing alike," Devon croaked, "I never wished to rule anyone."

The Tsar chuckled. "Yes, perhaps you are right. Watching you during the war, I thought you were a strong man. But you didn't have what it took. There was a weakness in you."

"How is it weakness to refuse to kill the innocent?"

"Innocent?" The Tsar seemed genuinely puzzled. "Were the Trolans innocent when they sent their soldiers into our lands, breaking the peace I had built so carefully? Were they innocent when they attacked our border towns, slaughtering hundreds?"

"You slaughtered *thousands!*" Devon spat.

"And saved tens of thousands," the Tsar said.

Anger fed strength to Devon's limbs. Despite the pain of his burns, he climbed slowly to his feet. "You're a coward," he snapped. "Men like you will always take the easy path, justify anything if it means you can hold onto power. But you're just like the Magickers you so despise, hiding behind your magic. If you truly wish to be mortal again, put *kanker* in my hands, and I'll show you what death feels like."

To his surprise, the Tsar laughed. "Ah, you do not disappoint, Devon!" he said. "And another time, I might have granted you your wish. But there is much to do now, and I have no time to play your games. Still though, I must thank you for your part in the excitement. It has been a long time since anyone put up such a fight."

Devon watched, unable to move, as the Tsar's sword rose, then arced towards his face.

"*No!*"

Suddenly Alana was between them, sword in hand. Steel rang out as the blades met, echoing loudly in the cavernous room.

❧ 36 ❧

Alana stared up at her father, the sword she'd taken from a fallen guard still vibrating from the deflected blow. Standing there, she could scarcely believe what she'd just done. She saw the same shock reflected in her father's eyes, but it quickly retreated, giving way to rage. His lips tightened.

"Daughter," he hissed. "Get out of my way."

"Alana, what are you doing?" Quinn's voice carried from across the hall.

Ignoring him, she turned the full force of her glare on the Tsar. She knew all it would take was an instant, a second's hesitation, and he would overwhelm her as he had before.

"I won't let you hurt him," she heard herself saying.

The Tsar shook his head. "It seems I underestimated your newfound weakness, daughter," he murmured. "Could it be you *care* for this fool?"

"It is not *weakness* to care for others," she replied, though her voice was wavering now.

"Is it not?" the Tsar asked. "Is that why these new-found friends of yours lie defeated around me? Why you find yourself standing alone?"

"It is a different kind of strength."

Her father laughed. "I see. Well, it will matter naught. I will burn it all from you, and start anew. Perhaps then I will finally have a daughter worthy of my empire."

Alana shivered, the sabre wavering in her hand. With his words, it felt as though a cold hand had reached into her chest and torn out her heart. Looking into his eyes, she could see the truth there, that he would not hesitate to obliterate her, to remake her in a fresh image.

As she had with the teacher, Krista.

"You have no right," she whispered.

"I have every right!" the Tsar boomed, his eyes shining with power. "I am your father, I am the Tsar. No soul lives within my realm except by my consent."

"I would rather die than live beneath your yoke."

"Alana, no!" Quinn called. She heard his footsteps approaching, but didn't dare look at him.

You should listen to your lover, Alana, the Tsar's voice spoke in her mind. *You think this one will want you, when he learns the truth?"*

"Stay out of my head!" Alana shrieked, staggering back from the words shrieking in her skull. But they only rose in volume.

You are mine, Alana! her father thundered. *You think you have the power to defy me?*

She felt a foreign presence enter her then, a darkness slithering into her body, wrapping around her thoughts, seeking out the most intimate corners of her mind. She stumbled back, dropping the sabre and clawing at her skull. And still the voice persisted.

You will not escape me this time.

"*Get out!*" she screamed again.

Somewhere within, her power responded. Surging up from the void, the green flames rushed to meet the Tsar's darkness. A dull *boom* sounded in the confines of her skull, and for a second her spirit soared, her soul swelling with the sudden retreat of her father's power.

But within an instant it pressed back, the darkness growing to dwarf her tiny flame, until it seemed she stood alone amidst the cosmos, with only a lantern to light the way. Even so, Alana clung on, holding to the green, as waves of black fought to sweep her away.

Then with a sudden popping sensation, the darkness vanished, the pressure relenting. Opening her eyes, Alana realised she had fallen to her knees. Her blade lay discarded alongside her, but she made no move to reach it. Looking up, she found her father towering over her.

"You are stronger than I thought, my daughter," the Tsar sighed. "But it will avail you nothing. I shall deal with you later."

He turned away then, exposing his back. Rage swept through Alana at his show of contempt, and clutching the blade, she launched herself at him. But again the blade struck empty air and ground to a halt. She sobbed in frustration as the invisible force held her back.

The Tsar looked back at her, a frown on his lips.

"Stay, daughter."

At his words, the sword in Alana's hand came alive. Tearing itself from her grip, the metal twisted back on itself and lifted into the air. Before she could react, it shot towards her, wrapping itself around her neck. She gasped as the cold steel enclosed her throat, the sharp edges biting into her flesh. Blood trickled across her skin as she staggered back, screaming her fury.

"And be silent," the Tsar added calmly.

Alana gasped as the sword contracted further, stealing away her voice and leaving her barely able to breath. She clawed at the metal, but it had hardened once more, becoming unmovable. Struggling to inhale, the strength slowly fled her legs, and she slumped to the ground, her vision spinning.

Above her, the Tsar turned to Devon. "Any last words, hero?"

Devon's eyes flashed as he stared at the man, jaw clenched, defiant. With a shrug, the Tsar raised his sword once more. Her vision fading, Alana watched in silent horror as her father prepared to strike down her friend.

Then, with a flash of silver, a blade came whirring through the air to bury itself in the Tsar's forearm.

Screaming, he stumbled back, his sword clattering uselessly to the marble floor. For a second, he stood staring down at the blood pumping from his arm, and the blade embedded in his wrist. Pain flashed across his face as he bared his teeth, his eyes sweeping the room in search of his assailant.

Alana stared in disbelief as a pale-faced Kellian surged to his feet and hurled another dagger. Forgotten by his captors, he had been left unconscious in the middle of the throne room while the Stalkers and Quinn encircled those still standing.

Blood was dripping from his forehead, and as the second blade left his hand, Kellian staggered, almost collapsing back to the ground. But his aim was true, and the blade hissed across the room at the Tsar. Only now the Tsar was expecting it, and with a cry of rage, the dagger froze a hair's breadth from his face. He grimaced, and the blade reversed its flight, rushing back to slam into Kellian's shoulder. The blow knocked the last strength from the innkeeper, and groaning he collapsed back to the ground.

Breath whistled between the Tsar's teeth as he tore the dagger from his wrist. He paused for a moment, staring at the wound. In an instant it had healed over, the flesh knitting itself back together as though it had never been torn.

Bloody dagger still in hand, the Tsar advanced on the innkeeper. "Kellian," he spat, unbridled rage in his eyes now.

"Another soldier with such potential, another disappointment. Perhaps it was Devon's influence on you, but it no longer matters—you will join one another in death now."

Beside Alana, Devon had managed to regain his footing, but as he tried to follow the Tsar, he was brought up short by an invisible barrier. Crying out, he slammed his fists into it, but could go no further.

Kellian had managed to haul himself back to his knees. He looked up at the Tsar with open scorn. "Go ahead. You cannot change the truth. You are evil, and so long as good men stand against you, you'll never succeed."

"Then I had best kill all the good men, hadn't I?" the Tsar replied.

He surged forward, his dagger plunging into Kellian's stomach. Kellian reared back, a scream on his lips, but the Tsar caught him by the neck and dragged him forward, driving the dagger deeper.

"Happily, I'll start with you," he whispered, the words carrying to every corner of the throne room.

🕊 37 🕊

All was chaos as Braidon and Enala crept amidst the drifting smoke. Looking around, Braidon felt a sudden sense of déjà vu as a mirror image seemed to super-impose itself over the room. He saw himself, kneeling before the throne, the dark eyed Tsar towering over him, sword in hand. Then he blinked, and the image vanished, leaving only the awful sight of the Tsar plunging his dagger into Kellian's stomach.

In that moment, time seemed to stand still. Braidon stood frozen in place, still concealed by the magic pulsing around him, yet unable to act, unable to do anything but stare in open-mouthed horror as his friend collapsed to his knees. Rooted to the spot, he did nothing as the Tsar released the innkeeper and reached down to retrieve his sword, could do nothing but stare as the blade flashed down.

"*No!*" Braidon cried out as Kellian's body hit the ground, his scream muffled by the spell.

Tears streaked his cheeks as Braidon sank to his knees. In the corner, he glimpsed his sister on the ground, her fingers clawing weakly at what looked like a steel collar around her neck. Beyond her, Devon stood pounding at empty air, as though unable to take another step towards his friends. His impotent cries echoed around the room.

"We're too late, he whispered.

"No."

Enala strode past him, but she did not move against the Tsar. Her eyes were fixed on an old man who lay near the dais. He was on his side, eyes closed and face a paled grey, his breath coming in ragged gasps. Enala knelt beside him. His eyes flickered open as she gripped his hand.

"Eric…" she breathed, tears streaking her cheeks.

Concentrating, Braidon forced his magic to expand, engulfing the old man in his spell.

"Enala," the man whispered. The lines on his face deepened and his eyes took on a haunted look. "You should not have come here…"

"You were here all along…" Enala croaked, ignoring the old man's words. She shook her head, quickly wiping the tears from her cheeks. "I would have come long ago, if only I'd known…"

"Then you would have met the same end as me," he said.

Enala shook her head. "Why did you face him alone, Eric?" she whispered. "We could have taken him, together."

Eric seemed to have regained some of his strength now. He pushed himself up onto one arm, and reached out to grip her shoulder. "When I discovered the truth, I knew…I knew I couldn't do that to you. I thought I could spare you…"

"He was my responsibility," she said.

"He was all of our responsibility," Eric replied.

Enala swallowed. Her lips trembled for a moment, then a fresh resolve came over her face. "Ours then," she said, tightening her grip on his shoulder. "It's time we ended this. Together?"

Eric sighed. "I'm afraid I have nothing left to give, sis."

Leaning forward, Enala embraced him. "Oh, Eric, what has he done to you?"

"He granted me a fate worse than death, ensuring I lived on long after my son passed from this world," he croaked. "You have no idea how many times I wished for death…"

"I would have come for you…" Enala repeated.

"I know." Eric forced a smile. "I'm glad you didn't. I'm glad you were free."

"Free and helpless," she sighed. "You have no idea the horrors he has wrought through the decades. I wish I knew where we went so wrong."

"You did nothing wrong, Enala," Eric replied sadly. "Somewhere along the path, he lost his way."

"Ay, but is it not a mother's job to lead her son back to the light?"

A chill spread down Braidon's back at her words. He stared at the two siblings in disbelief, but they only had eyes for each other. Silently, he tried to comprehend Enala's words. Could it possibly be true?

But that would mean…

"I need you, Eric," Enala said softly. "I cannot fight him alone."

"I have nothing left…" Eric began, but Enala silenced him by gripping him by the wrist. His eyes widened and he shook his head. "Don't, it's too dangerous. Not even Alastair–"

Eric's words were cut off as his head snapped back, his body suddenly going taut. Red light flashed between Enala's fingers, flowing into Eric's wrists, setting his veins aglow. An unholy fire seemed to light the air around them, and Braidon had to redouble his concentration on his own magic to keep them concealed from view.

Across the room, the Tsar was advancing on Devon. But a low keening from Eric drew Braidon's attention back to the siblings. For a second, Eric's eyes seemed to turn red—then

Enala snatched back her hand, and the light died as quickly as it had begun. She slumped beside him, her breath coming in ragged wheezes. It seemed to Braidon the lines on her face had deepened, but after a moment she sat up and climbed back to her feet.

"Are you ready?" she asked her brother.

Nodding, Eric rose slowly. Braidon stared at the old man, shocked to see the wrinkles had faded from his face, his colour returning. He gave a sad smile as he looked at Enala.

"Thank you," he murmured. "Though you could have killed us both."

Enala chuckled. "I'm not still some green apprentice, Eric. I have spent two lifetimes mastering my power. I know what I'm doing. Now come, we have a job to do."

Together, the two Magickers turned to face the Tsar.

❧ 38 ❦

"**N**o!" The cry tore from Devon's lips as his friend collapsed, the Tsar's dagger embedded in his stomach. Jumping to his feet, he leapt towards his friend, but the invisible barrier brought him up short. Desperate, he pounded the empty air with his fists, yet even his immense strength could do nothing to pierce it. His eyes met Kellian's. His friend opened his mouth, as though to say something, but he never got to speak the words.

With a flash of silver, the sword in the Tsar's hand swept down. Devon screamed again, a wordless, toneless cry of grief and loss. Across the room, the *thud* of Kellian's lifeless body striking the ground seemed impossibly loud. Blood streamed from Devon's knuckles as he fought to reach the man who'd saved his life so many times before.

Standing over Kellian with bloody sword in hand, the Tsar smiled. Suddenly the barrier vanished, and almost losing his balance, Devon staggered forward. Fists clenched, he rushed to Kellian and dropped to his knees beside him.

But it was already far, far too late. Not even the Northern

Earth Magickers could bring him back now. Choking, Devon clutched at Kellian's shirt, hauling him into his arms, overwhelmed. For half a decade they'd had each other's backs, from the very first battle in Brunei Pass. It would be difficult to find two more unlikely friends, yet the war had bound them together, blood brothers forever.

Except now Kellian was gone, his life expunged by the very man whose name they'd fought beneath all those years ago.

A shudder swept through Devon as he saw the Tsar watching him. "Bastard," he hissed.

The Tsar only shrugged, gesturing at the broken body with his sword. "Did you think this could end any other way, Devon?" he asked. "I am the Tsar. The power of five hundred Magickers courses through my veins. I will not be defeated, not by anyone."

Devon slowly climbed to his feet. "I'll kill you."

"You won't," The Tsar shook his head, as though the fact saddened him. "I cannot allow it. My work is not done yet."

"I'll tear you apart with my bare hands," he growled, stepping towards the ruler.

"Very well," the Tsar replied, and tossed his sword aside.

Before Devon could react, the man stepped in close, and a fist hammered into his forehead. Reeling back, Devon shifted his feet, widening his stance to ride with the blow. Then he straightened, surging forward. Blood pounded in his head, washing away the agony of his injuries, leaving only a single, cold-minded determination.

To destroy the man who had killed his friend.

As he charged, the Tsar side-stepped, moving far too quickly for a man three times Devon's age. A blow slammed into Devon's stomach, then another struck him in the jaw, lifting him from his feet.

Growling, he twisted, his own fist careening into the Tsar's forehead. Pain lashed his knuckles as the blow landed—it was as though he'd struck a stone wall. Even so, he followed with two more, smashing a right hook into the ruler's chest, then jaw.

In the past, such blows had shattered bones and left opponents unconscious on the floor. The Tsar only laughed. Stepping back, he wiped a streak of blood from his lip.

"Not bad," he said, "but I'm done playing now."

The Tsar surged forward. Raising his fists to defend himself, Devon managed to deflect the first blow, but agony flared down his arm as something in his wrist went *snap*. Casually, the Tsar battered aside the last of his defences, and slammed a blow into Devon's chest that hurled him backwards off his feet.

Striking the stone floor, Devon gasped, unable to breathe, his strength lost to him. The Tsar approached, the sword in his hand once more.

"It's been fun, Devon," he said, raising the blade, "but now it's time to die—"

A terrible *boom* interrupted his words, and the ground beneath Devon started to shake. A flash of light lit the throne room, followed by a *whoosh* of air and a sharp *pop*, as though the pressure in the chamber had just dropped several points.

Then blue and red fire rushed across the room to engulf the Tsar, and he vanished into the conflagration.

Eric came striding into sight, his sister Enala at his side. Arms outstretched, faces set, they unleashed their combined power against the Tsar. Lightning boomed and flames roared, causing Devon to scramble back, heat searing at his face.

Within the flickering red and blue, a dark shadow writhed, and it seemed to Devon that a soundless voice cried out. Watching the figure, hope surged through Devon. Surely, *surely*, not even the Tsar could survive such an attack? In the old tales, it had been Enala and Eric together who'd thrown back the might of Archon. What was a mortal such as the Tsar to the ancient Dark Magicker?

And still, the two siblings did not relent. Energy poured from them in an endless river, filling the throne room with the stench of burning. Devon saw Eric glance back, and glimpsed the sorrow in his cellmate's face. A sick sense of certainty struck him as he realised the Tsar was not defeated, only delayed. The look in Eric's eyes was a farewell, a plea for Devon to run and save himself.

Because Eric and Enala would not run. Neither would retreat from the Tsar, not this time.

Tears forming, Devon nodded back at the old man and clambered to his feet. Many of the Stalkers were down, caught in the initial explosion of magic. The rest had fallen back, giving Devon a chance to escape.

But as he turned, he saw there was still one left standing.

Quinn.

Anger rushed through Devon's chest. Silently, he started towards the man.

Quinn was staring at the spot where the Tsar had vanished, and did not see Devon's approach. He held *kanker* loosely at his side, and Devon's eyes settled on the weapon. He needed it back. With it, the foul Stalker would not stand a chance.

Slipping behind him, Devon strode forward, readying himself to tackle the Magicker. At the last second, however, his foot scraped against a fallen blade, sending it clattering across the floor. Quinn spun, but Devon was already hurling himself forward, and a straight left caught the lieutenant in the jaw, sending him reeling.

Devon followed after him, hammering a punch into his stomach, and then dragging him forward into a headbutt. The last blow dropped Quinn to his knees. *Kanker* slipped from his fingers, and Devon swept it up. Strength rushed back to his tired limbs as his hand closed around the black shaft.

Taking a breath, he looked down at Quinn. The man's eyes eyelids flickered and he groaned, but he made no attempt to rise. An awful desire rose in Devon, to slam his hammer into the man's face, to crush his skull and end the man forever. Every fibre of his being wanted it…but to do so would be a betrayal of Kellian's final wish: that Devon hold to the path of good. Murdering a defenceless man…as much as Quinn deserved it, Devon could not do it.

Devon quickly surveyed the ongoing battle. The conflagration had lessened, the last sparks of magic dying away from the hands of Eric and Enala. Both were pale now, their eyes suddenly weary, the lines on their faces deepening. It was clear they had given everything they had.

But it had not been enough. Where the Tsar had stood, a great bubble hung in the air, its surface opaque, swirling with the last remnants of the combined attack. Now it grew clearer, until it seemed a sphere of glass hung in the centre of the throne room. Within, the Tsar stood unmoved, his face tight and jaw clenched hard, but unharmed.

The last of Devon's hope fell away then. Looking at Eric and Enala, he considered joining them. Perhaps with *kanker* in hand, he might prove the difference…

He shook his head. If the power he'd just witnessed could not kill the man, the spell imbued inside *kanker* would be overwhelmed in an instant. No, he needed to escape, to carry the fight on for another day. He could make no difference here.

Silently, he headed for the exit, but a voice, weak and in pain, brought him up short.

"Devon, help me, please."

Devon saw Alana on the floor then, the steel sword the Tsar had brought to life still wrapped tightly around her neck. She lay helpless amongst the chaos, her fingers gripped around the blade, blood streaming down her neck where the sharp edge had bit her.

His heart pounding hard in his chest, Devon watched her. Their eyes met, and he heard her silent beseechment, her pleas for his help. In a rush, he saw the night they'd spent in the spring south of Fort Fall, felt again the quiet companionship, the beginnings of...something, that had begun in his heart.

He stepped towards her, but another image came rushing forward before he could reach her. He saw again Alana in the bedroom of the citadel, her dark eyes filled with scorn, her laughter as she set Kellian against him with her magic. He heard again her words, her confession that everything he'd felt for her had been from some spell she'd cast over him.

And he saw Kellian falling, the dagger in his stomach, the Tsar's sword descending.

Hate rose to drown the warmth in his chest. An icy cold replaced it as he studied the helpless woman.

"No," he said, his voice trembling. "Help yourself."

❧ 39 ❧

Alana found herself sobbing as Devon strode from the throne room. She tried to summon the strength to call him back, to beg, to use her magic even, but her will had abandoned her. Gasping, she fumbled at the blade around her neck, seeking to bend it back, to allow herself a complete breath. It felt as though the life was slowly being strangled from her, each inhalation barely enough to keep her from blacking out.

Darkness swirled at the edges of her vision, threatening to engulf her. She fought it, knowing if it won she might never wake again. And that if she did, it would not be as herself. Her father had unlimited power now—even her own magic could be his if he wished. He would have no trouble tearing her fractured consciousness from her skull, and remaking her in his own twisted image.

It was why she had wiped her own memory in the first place, to keep him from seeking her out, from tracking her thoughts across the endless miles of the Empire.

Her mouth went dry at the thought of losing herself again. Seeing the disgust in Devon's eyes, the full weight of her actions had come crashing down on her. With the Goddess's vision, her two personalities had merged, and while there was still a disjointedness about them, she knew now how wrong she'd been. She should never have used her power against Devon and Kellian, against her friends.

Krista's face swelled in her thoughts, and her guilt redoubled. The woman had been innocent, only wanting to defend her students from the brutal teachings of the Tsar's daughter. And Alana had washed her away for it, banishing her to a life with no memory, left her alone to wander the streets of Ardath in squalor.

Alana's hands fell from the blade. Her fingers were sticky with blood where the edge had cut them. She struggled for another breath, knowing that with one wrong movement, the blade would slice through the arteries in her neck. It would be over in moments. Swallowing, she closed her eyes.

You don't deserve to live.

A sob tore from Alana, but she couldn't bring herself to end it all. Screams came from all around, but there was no telling now who they belonged too. Smoke billowed across the throne room, lit by eerie flashes of lights. She sensed movement from somewhere, and rolling onto her side, she saw a figure emerge through the smoke. Quinn appeared, limping now, with a lump on his forehead already turning purple. His eyes had a slightly distracted look, as though he wasn't quite sure where he was, but they cleared when he saw her. Stumbling forward, he crouched beside her.

"Alana…are you okay?"

Alana saw the concern in his eyes, but also the suspicion. He knew now she had used her power against him. And he had seen her earlier, defying the Tsar, defending his rival. Yet even so, they had known each other for decades, had been the closest of friends long before she'd taken him as a lover…

"Get me out of this, Quinn," she gasped, thinking quickly of a lie that would convince him she was on the Tsar's side again. "Please, the old Magicker, he helped free the girl, the *other* Alana, but I have her under control. My father needs my help!"

Seeing him dither, she drew on the memories of her crueller self.

"*Now!*" she snapped, with all the force she could muster.

He rocked back on his heels. "I'm not sure how…"

"Figure it out," she snapped. With the last of her strength, Alana pushed herself to a sitting position.

The hesitation left him and he closed his eyes. An electric tingling shot down Alana's spine as she sensed his magic building, though it was like a candle to the inferno of magic already bubbling around them. She shivered as a cold breath passed across her neck. Staring into his face, she saw his eyelids flickering, and prayed to the Goddess he knew what he was doing.

The temperature around her plummeted as a freezing wind whirled around her. Slowly it contracted, focusing in on her neck. Within seconds, her teeth were chattering, the metal burning where it touched her flesh. Her breath misted in the air as she wrapped her arms around herself, trying and failing to keep the heat from being sucked from her.

She began to sway where she sat, her skull aching with the change in temperature. Even the small breaths she took now no longer seemed enough, as though the air itself had been drained of oxygen. Her vision faded and all feeling had left her throat now. Pain flared in her chest, a desperate need to lurch upright, to gasp and cough and tear at the sword until she could breathe; but seeing the concentration etched across Quinn's face, she fought the instinct. She had no idea what he was doing, but she had to trust him, had to believe he knew what he was doing.

And if he failed, well, at least she would not become the monster her father wanted her to be.

Her final thought as the darkness rose to claim her was of her brother, running across the gardens, free.

————

QUINN COULD FEEL HIS MAGIC FADING QUICKLY, ITS ENERGIES burning low. He should have held back against Kellian and Devon earlier, but the two men had a habit of testing him. A habit he was glad had at least been halfway dealt with. If only he hadn't allowed Devon to take him by surprise, he might have finished the job.

His head still ached where the giant had struck him, and in truth he had been surprised to find himself alive a few minutes later, when the darkness had faded. After everything they'd been through that day, he would have killed the hammerman at the slightest opportunity. And with the loss of his friend, Devon had no reason to be offering mercy.

But then, Quinn supposed, the man was weak.

He forced his attention back to his magic, redoubling his efforts to draw the icy winds down from far above the citadel. The task required immense concentration to reach so far outside himself, almost to the bounds of his ability. Where Eric had found the howling winds that were now filling the throne room, Quinn didn't know, but apparently the ancient Magicker's abilities far exceeded his own. It was galling—though ultimately it would mean nothing.

The Tsar would kill him all the same.

Drawing the cold air miles down through the sky, and concentrating it on the sword around Alana's neck, was proving far harder than he had anticipated. The plan had come to him from nowhere, and without time to think, he had set it into motion. He still had no idea if it would work, and if he succeeded, whether Alana would survive the attempt.

Ice had begun to form on the steel blade. Before him,

Alana swayed on her knees and started to fall. He caught her and hugged her to his chest, though the winds still flowed around her. She was cold to the touch, the skin around her face blue, her lips quickly turning grey. Her eyes flickered closed, and he knew she didn't have long.

Despite the confusing torment of the last few days, Quinn's heart clenched at the thought of losing her. His only consolation was that he would not be long in following her if he failed —the Tsar would not be pleased if he killed his daughter.

Remembering her rescue of Devon, Quinn felt a pang of jealousy. What was it about the man that inspired such devotion from those around him? And while the glint in Alana's eyes and anger in her voice earlier had been that of the girl he knew, Quinn still found himself wondering what was going on inside her mind...

But it was too late to turn back now. Alana's breathing had all but ceased, and with the sword still clenched around her throat, she was mere moments from death. She needed to breathe, fully and unconstrained. He gritted his teeth as the last drops of magic left him, the wind dying, leaving the ice-covered blade before him.

Lying Alana down, Quinn drew his dagger and held it up before her. He took a breath, readying himself, then brought its hilt down on the ice-encrusted blade with all his strength.

A sharp, shrieking *crack* followed as the frigid steel shattered. Quinn dropped the knife and pulled the broken shards from Alana's neck, cursing as the freezing metal bit his flesh. Throwing it aside, he placed his fingers to Alana's neck, searching for a pulse.

"Come on, Alana!" he whispered, but there was no movement beneath his fingers. Her skin was like ice.

Cursing, he placed his palm against her chest, the other over the top. Shifting so he was crouched over her, he pushed down with all his weight. Again and again he pounded her chest, settling into the rapid rhythm of a drumbeat. Alana's lifeless body jerked like a ragdoll with each compression, but still there were no signs of life.

"Come on!" he screamed.

Leaving the compressions, Quinn leaned over her, holding her nose and pressing his mouth to hers. He exhaled hard, watching her chest rise as his breath filled her lungs. Withdrawing, he waited half an instant to see if she would respond, then leaned in to start the whole manoeuvre again.

Alana jerked beneath him. Her eyes flickered open and she gasped in a fresh breath. Immediately, she started to cough. Quinn helped her onto her side as she groaned. Her tiny body shook beneath his hands as she sucked in great, life-restoring breaths.

When he was sure she was stable, Quinn sat back, his own heart pounding. Relieved of his task, exhaustion swept through him. For a moment, he felt overwhelmed, the terror and relief crashing together inside him. Without thinking, he rubbed Alana's back, feeling the warmth coming back into her body.

"Thank you."

He opened his eyes as she spoke, hearing the raw, unbridled emotion behind her words.

Nodding, he offered a smile. "It's good to have you back, Alana."

She lowered her eyes. Her lips were still blue, but the colour was rapidly returning to her face. An awful bruise and shallow cuts ringed her neck, but she was alive, and that was all that mattered. He reached out a hand and lifted her chin to look at him. Leaning in, he pressed his lips to hers.

For a moment she did nothing, and a trace of doubt entered him. He started to pull away, when suddenly she was kissing him back, hard and fast, her tongue darting out to meet his. Despite his exhaustion and his worry for her condition, he moaned, drawing her to him, feeling the icy touch of her skin against his. Her fingers were in his hair, but then she was pulling away, shaking her head. She looked up at him, her eyes filled with tears.

"I'm sorry, Quinn," she whispered.

"What–?"

Before Quinn could finish his sentence, her fingers tightened in his hair. He tried to jerk away, but a fiery heat rushed into his mind, a green light filling his inner-eye—then all was darkness.

❧ 40 ❧

Lightning streamed from Eric's fingers and rushed across the room, joining with his sister's flames to strike at the Tsar, only to shatter uselessly a few feet from their foe. Through the flickering blue and red, Eric watched him laughing, the protective barrier flashing with each impact. The Tsar's familiar blue eyes, so like his own, watched them, waiting for the attack to cease. The man knew they could not outlast him.

Already Eric could feel his strength fading, the energy Enala had poured into him consumed by the relentless assault. He fought on anyway, pushing himself beyond all limits, knowing he would soon be consuming his own lifeforce. He no longer hoped to defeat the man, only to stall him as long as they could, so that the others might escape and fight on another day. The future of the Three Nations no longer rested in their hands, but in those of Enala's grandchildren.

His heart warmed at the thought of them, and at the sight of his sister fighting alongside him. He'd given up hope long ago of ever seeing her again. It had been so long now, decades since Eric had set out upon learning of his son's murder. He hadn't known the truth then, that it was his nephew, Theo, who'd been behind it. In fact, it had been his nephew, the newly crowned king of Plorsea, who he'd turned to for help. The man had sent Eric on a wild goose chase. It had taken a long time for Eric to realise his mistake—and by then, it had already been too late.

Maybe Enala was right, maybe they could have defeated him together, even then. But knowing the agony it would have caused her, Eric had kept his sister in the dark. He hadn't realized how much magic Theo had consumed, how much he had learned and studied, readying himself for the moment Eric came for him.

His heart filled with rage, Eric had returned to Ardath to confront his son's killer. But in his arrogance, he had underestimated the man. After all, this was no Archon, with dark magic to rival the Gods. This was his magicless nephew Theo, who had grown up alongside his only son, who he and his wife Inken had helped to raise.

But when he'd reached the shores of Ardath, Theo had been waiting. And he was no longer the boy Eric had once known, but a master of a dozen magics. Eric had been humbled, his body broken, his magic shackled.

And the endless days of darkness had begun.

He would have preferred death. At least death would have been a release. While he had long outlived her, he knew Inken and their son waited for him somewhere out in the void. Through the long years, he had yearned to join them. Instead, time had crept by, marked only by the slow dwindling of his soul, the corruption of his magic, the withering of his body.

Now, he was far too weak to challenge the man.

But he would not be shackled again.

He glanced at Enala, seeing the strain on her face as she continued the fight. But her power was finite, and the little she'd given Eric had drained her as well. She would not last much longer.

She couldn't be here when the end came. Eric didn't want her to see what he would become, when he unleashed the darkness.

Slim though it was, there was still one possibility of defeating the Tsar now, one chance of striking through his shield and tearing the magic from the man.

If Eric unleashed the demon within.

"Enala!" he called over the raging magic.

She flicked him a look. The fire in her eyes was fading, the red giving way again to blue, and he saw the desperation there. He smiled, attempting to convey all his love and warmth in that one gesture, a final farewell. Surprise registered on her face, but he was already moving, not giving her a chance to respond.

"I'm sorry, sis," he whispered.

Lightning still streaming from one hand, he raised the other, and sent a blast of wind rushing across the room to catch Enala. It picked her up, almost gently, and carried her backwards to where her grandson waited. Collecting him as well, the wind threw them both from the throne room. The door slammed closed behind them, a breath of wind settling in to hold it shut.

Turning back to the Tsar, Eric saw they were alone but for the fallen. Devon and Alana were gone, the Tsar's soldiers and Stalkers lying in piles around the room. Silently, he sent a prayer up to Antonia that Devon would make it out of the citadel alive. In the chaos, there was a chance he could pass unnoticed out into the city.

Eric let out a long breath and lowered his arm, drawing the winds and lightning back to himself. Clenching his fists, he watched the flickering light dance across his skin, then begin to fade into his flesh itself. It was a trick he'd learned a long time ago, one few Magickers could replicate. When he was done, the winds and lightning had vanished, but he could sense them still, lurking within, in the void alongside his magic.

The Tsar moved forward, his leather boots carrying him lightly across the scorched marble.

"You don't think you've saved them, do you?" he asked.

Eric shrugged. "I can only hope."

The Tsar chuckled. "I would have thought you'd learned your lesson by now."

Smiling sadly, Eric shook his head. "It doesn't matter that I cannot defeat you, Theo," he replied. "I don't matter at all, not here, not now." Eric gestured around him. "A mortal has rebelled against you, and lived. Your own children have turned on you. How long do you think it will be before your people follow? Before they learn you are no true God?"

The Tsar sneered. "Then they will die."

"Ay, many will. But you stand alone. You cannot kill them all."

"Time will tell the truth of that, but you will not be around to see it, Eric," he snapped. "I am tired of your company. Goodbye."

The Tsar lifted a hand. Light, brilliant and blinding, shone through his clenched fingers. Eric could feel the magic building, the sheer scale of his power, collected from hundreds of Magickers around the building. It would burn him to ashes.

Eric summoned his own power in response. Its blue light reared to life within him, the familiar wolf towering over his mind's eye. Eric stared up at it, recalling the terror he'd felt when it had first appeared. It seemed a thousand years ago now. These days the magic was almost like an old friend, the conflict between wolf and man a long played out game, more ritual than actual battle.

Until today.

As the wolf reared above him, Eric opened his arms, and offered his soul up to the beast.

And cried out as razor-sharp fangs tore into him, sinking deep into the dying light of his soul. In the darkness, Eric screamed as the magic encircled him, wrapping his soul in chains of fire. His terror swelled, granting new strength to the beast. Triumphant, it hurled him screaming into the depths of his consciousness.

Back in the throne room, Eric's eyes slid open. Only it was no longer Eric who looked out, but the magic.

"Freedom," the demon whispered, its voice distorted, metallic.

A dark smile twisted its lips as black eyes swept the room, settling on the man standing across from it. Sensing the unbridled power radiating from the clenched fist, the demon hesitated.

"You fool," the man whispered.

Energy crackled in the demon's fists as it faced the man. The magic within it was weak, exhausted by the foolish human. Yet there were other energies to draw on, it knew. The human's lifeforce was still a burning beacon within, a brilliant white against the void. And its former master no longer had any use for such a power.

Cackling, it drew the blue flames of its magic around the white. An awful scream sounded from somewhere deep inside its mind. The blue flames swelled, then roared back to life, the white igniting like wood on a bonfire.

In the throne room, lightning boomed. Gathering in the demon's hands, it doubled, then redoubled in size, the heat of its power washing across the marble surroundings. Bolts shot off around the room, wind swirling inwards to join it, converging on the demon.

Across the room, the man who stood against it cursed and threw out his hand. The power in his fist responded, forming a glowing beam of white. But as the white energies lanced towards it, the demon leapt into the air, and the power slashed harmlessly past. Lightning, more powerful than any its human master could summon, rippled out to hammer into its foe.

The demon grinned as the man staggered back, but to its surprise, he did not go down. Light swirled again in his hands, and the demon hissed as another flash of power slashed at it. Too slow this time, it cried out as the gathered energies of the Light struck its human body, hurling it through the air.

Hissing, the demon recovered. Around it, a maelstrom of wind and rain and lightning gathered as it swung around, searching for its foe. But the man had vanished.

The very air bursting with the gathered energies of the Sky, the demon scanned its surroundings, cursing the Light Magicker for concealing himself from sight. But it would avail the man little. Standing still, the demon threw out its arms, sending a blast of air rushing outward. Stones and tiles and bodies were lifted from the ground, filling the air with a million projectiles.

A cry came from its left, and spinning, the demon sent a flash of lightning at the man who had just appeared behind it. The bolt lanced towards him, but, impossibly, the earth shifted suddenly, a patch of marble rushing up to deflect the blow.

A rumbling began beneath the demon's feet, seconds before the marble stone split open, tearing the floor asunder. The demon leapt into the air, summoning the wind to carry it clear, but before it could escape, another force struck it like an invisible hammer from above. It dropped back towards the gaping fissure.

Rage surged in the demon's chest as it fought against the inexorable force. The human's power was awesome, but unbridled by human fears and limits, the demon would not be defied. Throwing out its arms, the demon sent lightning rushing outwards, filling the room with crackling blue fire.

This time the demon's attack found its mark. Crying out, the human staggered away, and the ground snapped closed once more. The invisible force surrounding the demon dissipated. Floating free, it drifted towards where the man had fallen. He had vanished again now, but the human could not have gone far.

With a roar, the man reappeared to the demon's left. Face mottled red, blue eyes defiant, he threw his arms together. Around the room, the swirling debris halted mid-air as a new force took possession of it. With a hiss, it reversed its track, and rushed inwards at the demon.

Moving with impossible speed, the demon ducked and twisted between the projectiles, but it could not avoid them all. A chunk of marble struck it in the face, shattering bone and splitting flesh, but there was no pain. The magic ruled now— the body was nothing but armour to host its spirit.

The demon regathered its spent lightning, forming a flaming wall of blue around itself to consume any projectile that came near. Then its consciousness soared skywards, seeking out the frozen air currents far above and drawing them down. The temperature plummeted as the icy winds filled the throne room. It might be immune to mortal frailties, but its foe was not.

But in the centre of the room, the man seemed to have given up all interest in fleeing. Flames lit his hands, sweeping outwards to cast aside the cold. Then, to the demon's shock, the wind was torn from its control. Raising his hands, the man sent the winds rushing through the flames, drawing them high to the ceiling before sending them swirling at the demon.

The demon fell back before the flaming vortex. The flames roared and gave chase, even the marble weeping before their heat. Fear touched the demon then, as it sought to understand the man's mastery of all Three Elements. Such a feat was not possible, not even for the Gods. What manner of man was this?

And while mere injuries did not concern it, if the flames consumed its mortal body, the demon too would perish.

Crying out in frustration, the demon sought to reassert its power over the winds, but its energies were burning low now, the last of its host's lifeforce flickering out. All these years the demon had waited for its chance, seeking the moment when it could seize control, to cast aside its master. So many years imprisoned, its power wasted by the cruel human who ruled it, unable to fly free.

Now, in its moment of triumph, it was about to be destroyed.

Rage flickered in the demon's chest as it drew on the last reserves of its strength. A single ball of lightning coalesced before it. Power crackled as the firestorm approached, its heat washing over the demon. Still, it stood its ground. Screaming, it pointed a finger at its foe. The burning ball of lightning rushed forward, tearing through the flames.

Across the room, a voice cried out, and with a sudden *whoosh*, the flames died, the winds dissipating instantly. The demon stared in shock as the smoke cleared, revealing its foe down on one knee, gasping for breath. A black scorch marked his tunic, and his face had paled, but it was clear the man still lived.

Without any magic left to spend, the demon started towards the human. Its eyes caught the glint of a sword lying nearby, and it quickly diverted towards it. Unlike the other weapons in the room, the sword remained intact, its blade somehow untouched by the energies that had melted marble and warped lesser metals. The demon collected the blade and approached the kneeling man.

The man looked up as the demon approached, his mouth wide. "Foul creature," he gasped. "That Eric would stoop to this." He shook his head and stumbled to his feet. "Well, you won't defeat me."

The demon laughed. "You have nothing left to give, mortal," it whispered. Closing on the man, it raised the sword.

A smile twitched on the man's lips. "Ay, but you picked the wrong sword, demon."

Before the demon could strike, the man flicked his fingers. A sudden light burst from the blade in the demon's hand, more brilliant than any it had seen before. The energies burned at it, scorching its already beaten body, lashing out at the spirit within. Hissing, it tossed the weapon aside.

Quick as lightning, the man darted forward and snatched the weapon from the air. Energy crackled as the man grinned, his eyes ablaze with renewed power.

The demon stood in shock, staring at the terrible blade in the man's hand. With his touch, the sword had swelled with light, filling the room, so that it seemed the very air itself were aflame. Sensing the power radiating from it, an awful fear lit in the demon's chest, as somewhere deep within a voice cried out, a memory of its past rising to the surface.

The Sword of Light.

As the realisation came to it, the man pointed the sword. And with a flash of light, the demon died.

❧ 41 ❧

"**N**o!"
Enala's screams echoed down the corridor as she threw herself at the door, pounding her fists against the polished wood. But the wind still howled on the other side, barring their passage back, sealing Eric within.

"Enala," Braidon said gently.

Stepping forward, he caught the old woman by the hand. She froze at his touch, but he could still feel the tension in her wiry limb, her desperation to save her brother. "Enala, you have to let him go. It's what he wants."

Trembling, Enala turned to look at him. He flinched from the despair in her eyes, the terrible grief. Tears streamed down her withered cheeks. "I only just got him back," she whispered.

He gave her shoulder a squeeze and pulled her into a hug. "He knows what he's doing," he said. "Let's not make his sacrifice in vain. Come on, Dahniul is this way."

She stared at him a moment longer, then sighed. "You heard what was said in there, about the Tsar?"

Braidon hesitated, then nodded. Enala smiled, pulling him into a hug of her own. "Whatever happens with your father and sister, I am proud of you, Braidon. I know Gabriel, your grandfather, would be as well. You have his spirit, his courage."

Braidon's eyes stung at her words and he blinked back tears. "We don't have much time," he said quickly, starting away so she wouldn't see the tears on his cheeks. "I can feel my power fading. Dahniul won't stay hidden forever."

Enala said nothing, but after a moment he heard her footsteps following. Taking the lead, he led them through the winding corridors, taking each turn by instinct, drawing on memories that still lingered just beyond reach.

He shivered as he realised he was leaving Alana behind again. He had glimpsed her only briefly in the throne room. Amidst the chaos, he hadn't noticed her lying in the corner, not until she had staggered to her feet, blood streaming down her neck. He had wanted to go to her, but the swirling vortex of magic had cut them off. She had fled through a set of double doors on the other side of the room without ever knowing he was there.

Silently, he prayed she had escaped. In the brief moments he'd seen her, it had been impossible to tell whether she was still the sister he remembered, or...someone else. Yet something in his soul told Braidon his sibling still lived. He couldn't for a moment believe that woman had been sponged, lost to him forever.

Shivering, Braidon forced his thoughts back to the present. Somewhere in the citadel, Devon and Alana were both at large, but it would be him the Tsar came for first. And Eric's interference had left them only one path to take—up.

In his mind, he called out to Dahniul, hoping the giant dragon would hear him, that his magic was still casting a protective net over the beast, concealing it from the eyes of the soldiers. It would only take a single flaw in his spell, one glimpse from the guards to send Magickers and Red Dragons after their only ally left standing. And powerful as Dahniul was, even she could not survive against such odds.

Hurry, Braidon!

The dragon's voice was barely audible in his mind, but he felt a thrill of triumph. He glanced at Enala, but her eyes were distant, her movements automatic as she followed Braidon. She wore her grief like a lead blanket, but there was no more time left to comfort her. Within, the last trickles of his magic were fading. They only had minutes before the dragon was discovered.

Footsteps pounded ahead of them. Grabbing Enala, Braidon pressed them up against the wall of the corridor. He held his breath as a troop of guards rushed past, their weapons drawn, eyes fixed straight ahead. Thankfully, not a single one noticed the blurring of air beside them, the slight flicker of movement.

When the men had passed, Braidon led Enala around the next corner and up a twisting stone staircase. Enala was struggling now, her face ashen, her hair hanging in scorched clumps across her face. The battle with the Tsar had cost her dearly, and Braidon wished there was something he could do for her. She had given some of her energy to Eric before the battle... but Braidon didn't even know where he would begin with such a feat. And besides, he had little left to give as it was.

Braidon slowed as they approached the top of the stairwell. Ahead, daylight beckoned, but as Braidon listened he heard the soft whisper of voices from above. It only took one look at Enala's face to know she wasn't up for a fight. He considered taking the sword from her and tackling whoever it was, but he would be no match for even one trained soldier.

There was no choice for it. They would have to risk his weakening magic in the daylight atop the walls. Silently, Braidon checked the concealment with his mind, sensing the holes appearing but knowing he no longer had the power to fill them. Then he took Enala by the hand, and led her up the last of the stairs.

Emerging into the sunlight, Braidon swallowed when he saw a troop of soldiers lurking nearby, their eyes watchful, hands clenched around their weapons. They stood atop the stairwell, scanning the ramparts and skies around them. Clearly, the explosions from the citadel had them on high alert.

Braidon shivered as Dahniul reared up behind the guards, giant jaws spread wide. The spell still clung to the creature, but like their own it was fading, causing the air to shimmer where the dragon sat crouched atop the walls.

Shall I kill them? Dahniul's voice echoed in their minds.

Braidon looked at the gathered men, remembering the horror that had unfolded in the throne room below, and quickly shook his head. These men were only serving their country, doing their duty. It was not their fault the Tsar had become a monster. He would not kill them if he could help it.

Moving quickly across the ramparts, Braidon breathed a sigh of relief as the men's eyes slid over them, unseeing. Reaching Dahniul's side, Braidon started to climb on to her back. A low rumble came from her chest as he settled into place, and the head of one of the men jerked up.

Braidon shivered as the man looked directly at them. A frown creased the man's forehead as he took a hesitant step towards the hidden dragon.

Dahniul shifted beneath him, manoeuvring herself to strike the man.

Not yet!

Braidon sent out a desperate plea, and she stilled. Perching himself on her back, Braidon reached down, offering Enala a hand. Silently she sat behind him, too tired to even take her usual position as rider. Braidon's spirits fell as he sensed her despair.

He glanced back at the guard. His stomach clenched as he

saw that the man was still approaching. It was obvious he had noticed something, but with the magic still clinging to Dahniul, he still couldn't figure out what it was. They had to be out of range of bow or magic before that realisation came.

Go! Braidon screamed in his mind.

Dahniul shifted towards the edge, her claws scraping loudly against the stone blocks. The hackles on Braidon's neck rose as someone shouted behind them. He risked a look back, and saw the man drawing his sword, the other guards rushing to join him. Crossbows bristled, pointing in their general direction. Then, Braidon's stomach lifted into his chest as Dahniul dove from the edge of the wall.

Letting out a wild scream, he watched the ground rush towards them, the three-pronged spire of a nearby temple seeming to point directly for his heart. Then with a great flap of Dahniul's wings, their descent halted. Another *thump*, and they went rushing upwards.

Crossbows *twanged* behind them as they rose above the ramparts, and Braidon turned in time to see steel arrows slash the sky. Roaring, Dahniul twisted, almost dislodging Braidon from his seat, but the bolts hissed harmlessly past. Below the men were already reloading, and Braidon realised his magic had abandoned him.

Rising higher, Dahniul swung towards the lake surrounding the island. The men of the citadel were behind them now, but ahead, the outer walls of the city were approaching rapidly. Maybe they could make it after all...

Then Braidon cursed as he realised they weren't yet high enough to avoid the great longbows being hefted by the guards. As he watched, one drew back his string and sent an arrow arcing towards them.

Dahniul turned again, and it flew harmlessly past, but already others were taking aim. Soon, the air would be thick with arrows. Dahniul couldn't avoid them all, and while she was protected by thick scales, her riders were not.

Braidon glanced back, and was shocked to see Enala slumped against the dragon's back. Her skin was so pale he could see the thin blue lines of her veins on her hands, and she was barely holding on. He swallowed and turned his attention back towards their escape.

Turn back, he said silently to the dragon. They needed to gain more height before passing the outer walls. It would bring them over the citadel again, but with the guards there armed with only crossbows, Braidon prayed the dragon would be beyond their range. So long as there were no Magickers waiting now…

Dahniul's wings swept down as she circled back, each wing-beat carrying them ever higher. He could see men gathering on the walls below, pointing in silent frustration, like ants below them. Braidon smiled; then felt the air shifting around them, heard the dragon's wings creak as a blast of wind struck them. Sensing the magic in the wind, Braidon clung to the dragon's scales as the gale tried to tear them from the dragon's back. Fear for Enala filled him, but in that moment there was nothing he could do for her.

Time to try for the walls, I think, came Dahniul's voice.

Braidon nodded, his eyes watering with the cold. All he could do was cling on as the dragon fought to break through the Magicker's winds. He prayed to the Gods that Enala was doing the same.

Then with a roar, Dahniul shot for the outer walls. The move caught the soldiers below by surprise, and they were on them before the first arrow rose to greet them. It made a sharp *crack* as it struck Dahniul's breast, but bounced harmlessly away. Braidon ducked low, knowing there was little else he could do. The hiss of arrows filled the air, and he heard the dragon snarl as one sliced through the soft skin of her wings, but she flew on.

Then the air was silent once more. Sitting up, Braidon saw they had made it past the city, past the walls. The cliffs of the island were already falling away, the glistening waters of Lake Ardath spreading out all around. Braidon shivered as the island shrank into the distance.

Beneath him, Dahniul powered onwards, her great wings carrying them rapidly across the lake. Soon, the water below turned to open fields, a single river winding its way through their expanse. Ahead, the dark trees of a forest approached. Behind, Ardath became a speck of black amidst the silent blue.

Yet as he watched the distant city, it seemed to Braidon that it shimmered, and a light appeared on the walls atop the citadel. He squinted, trying to make out what it was, what was happening. The light grew stronger, its intensity swelling until it blotted out the city.

No… he realised, icy fear turning his limbs to lead. *No…it's coming closer!*

"Dahniul!" he screamed, but it was already too late.

With a *boom* that seemed to come from all around them, the light came boiling up to meet them. Braidon cried out as it struck, an awful *shriek* filling his ears, a searing heat, a swirl of colours blinding him. He screamed as the dragon lurched beneath him, losing his grip on the golden scales.

Then he was falling, plummeting down, and an ocean of green was rising up to greet him…

EPILOGUE

Quinn's legs trembled as he approached the ruined throne, his mind whirring, struggling to come up with some excuse, some justification that would save him. But in the awful silence that had swallowed the throne room, his thoughts had gone blank, and with a growing sense of despair, he sank to his knees before the dais. Hours had passed since the confrontation with Eric, but there was still no sign of the fugitives.

The Tsar towered over Quinn, his once magnificent doublet and leggings now scorched and torn. His eyes were dark as he looked on the lieutenant, giving away nothing of his inner thoughts. A slight twitch to his lips was the only sign of his displeasure.

"Well?"

The sudden break in the silence made Quinn jump, though the Tsar had barely spoken louder than a whisper. A vice clamped around his chest as he struggled to find the words to reply. With painstaking slowness, he unclenched his jaw and swallowed the lump in his throat.

"She was dying." Once the words were out of his mouth,

Quinn realised they were the only argument that might work. "She was choking, bleeding to death. I feared she would die before you finished dealing with the intruders…"

His voice trailed off beneath the withering stare of the Tsar.

"Is that all?"

Quinn gulped. "I…I…" He clenched his eyes shut, and bowed his head. "I'm sorry, sir. I failed you. I let your daughter escape. I am prepared to accept my fate."

Despite his words, Quinn flinched as the soft rasp of steel against leather announced the unsheathing of the Tsar's sword. A cold draught slithered down his spine as footsteps padded down the half-melted steps, finally coming to a halt beside him.

"It is I who failed, Quinn," the Tsar's voice came from overhead, touched now with unmistakable sadness. Quinn looked up in surprise, his heart palpitating as the monarch continued. "I should have dealt with Eric long ago, should have known Enala still lived, that she would come for them when she realised what I'd done."

"What did you do?" Quinn whispered, hardly daring to breathe.

The Tsar lifted his sword into the air, and a brilliant white lit the blade. "I did what every Magicker since the fall of Archon has failed to do. I recreated the spell that brought the Gods into the physical realm."

"*How?*"

A smile crossed the Tsar's lips. "It cost me greatly, but we managed it, Eric's son and I. Fool that he was, Calybe volunteered to be the host. We both came from the right lineage, but I guess he took after his father. Eric always was the type for self-sacrifice. Even at the end…" He shook his head, as though to dismiss the memory of the old man, before going on: "We cast the spell, and let the spirit of Darius enter Calybe. Together, we brought the God of Light back to life."

Quinn looked around quickly, as though the reincarnation of Darius might suddenly appear before them. Then his eyes were drawn inexorably back to the sword in the Tsar's hand. It was the same blade the intruder, Godrin, had tried to wield. Merely touching it had crystallised the man. It couldn't be, and yet…

"But the God of Light…where?"

"Here." The Tsar smirked, gesturing to the sword. "That was Calybe's mistake. He thought we could only find peace by bringing back the Gods. But it was quite the opposite."

"But the Gods—" Quinn began.

"Were parasites," the Tsar interrupted, "using their powers to manipulate us, to rule us. They were no different from any other Magicker who has sought to rule us throughout the centuries. No, there is only one way to buy peace—by wiping every last trace of magic from our world. I *knew* I could do it, if only I could recreate the Sword of Light. So when the God of Light possessed Calybe, I was ready. Darius barely had a chance to breathe fresh air, before I plunged my sword between his shoulders, and used the spells I had perfected through the years to send his foul spirit screaming into the blade."

"Then…that truly is…the Sword of Light?"

"Yes." The Tsar smiled faintly. "But though I have spent decades studying its power, still I have failed to achieve my goal."

His shoulders slumped, and he sank to the bottom step with a soft *thud*. In that moment, Quinn had never seen the Tsar look so mortal. His knees beginning to ache, he sat up slowly, sensing there was more behind the man's words. When he spoke, he picked his words carefully, still half-afraid of incurring his ruler's wrath.

"But…?"

The Tsar did not respond. Then he started to laugh, softly

at first but quickly growing louder, until it seemed the walls themselves were trembling. Quinn shrank back as the Tsar stood.

"My children have abandoned me, betrayed everything I stand for. I can no longer ignore their transgressions. For years I searched for another way. With Eric, perhaps it would have been possible. But now I am left with no choice." He looked at Quinn, his eyes aglow. "Bring me my children, Stalker. They are the key to all this. Willingly or not, they *will* serve me in my final purpose."

For a second, Quinn hesitated, thinking of the girl he'd helped raise, who he'd taught and trained and spent long nights entwined with. Then he remembered how she'd used her magic against him, how she had betrayed him again and again. And he knew that he too could no longer ignore the truth. The Alana he yearned for was lost to him.

He bowed his head. "It shall be as you command, sir."

HERE ENDS BOOK TWO OF
THE LEGEND OF THE GODS

Continue the adventure in…
Dawn of War

NOTE FROM THE AUTHOR

Wow, okay, that was...the hardest story I've written yet. Between the demon possession and Alana's split personality, I always knew it was going to be a challenge, but I've really poured far more time into this book than I was expecting. Still, I hope the result was worth it, and you managed to understand everything that was going on! If you did have any questions, remember you can always email me at author@aaronhodges.co.nz. But hopefully you understood everything!

Oh, and if you were interested in some of the influences that went into this book, during its construction I travelled through much of Eastern Europe – including Prague and Budapest – all the way to the amazing land that is today known as Turkey (but which was once the Ottoman and Persian Empires!). If you look hard enough, you're bound to see inspirations from many of these wonderful places 😌

FOLLOW AARON HODGES...
And receive TWO FREE novels and a short story!
www.aaronhodges.co.nz/newsletter-signup/

THE SWORD OF LIGHT TRILOGY

If you've enjoyed this book, you might want to check out my very first fantasy series!

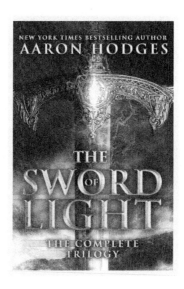

A town burns and flames light the night sky. Hunted and alone, seventeen year old Eric flees through the wreckage. The mob grows closer, baying for the blood of their tormentor. Guilt weighs on his soul, but he cannot stop, cannot turn back. **If he stops, they die.**

ALSO BY AARON HODGES